TWO OF A KIND

ALEXA RIVERS

To Kate
for making my stories the best they can be
and being a truly amazing cheerleader.

PROLOGUE

Jack Farrelly wished, not for the first time, that he wasn't such great friends with Logan Pride. If not for his loyalty to Logan, he'd have packed a tent and headed into the wilderness for a bit of R and R. Instead, the cherry on top of his shit-cake of a day was attending the annual New Year's Eve costume party Logan hosted at his pub, The Den.

"What are you supposed to be?" his friend demanded as he arrived, sauntering over in a pair of red swimming trunks and nothing else. The theme this year was, 'dress as your favorite fictional character', but Jack hadn't had the energy after running into his ex earlier—which had thrown him out of whack—so he'd rocked up in his usual.

"Bear Grylls."

Logan rolled his eyes, and swept his tousled blond hair off his forehead. "Not a fictional character. Come on, man. Make an effort."

Jack looked pointedly at him. "You're a fine one to talk. You look like you just rolled in off the beach." Logan had been a professional surfer in a previous life, and now taught classes when he wasn't busy at The Den. "Who are you supposed to be?"

He gestured down at himself. "Isn't it obvious? I'm Mitch Buchannon from *Baywatch*."

"Is that the show with Pamela Anderson in her golden days?"

Logan grinned, the edges of his eyes crinkling. "Now you're getting it." He jostled Jack with his elbow. "Come on. Grab a beer. First one's on me." As they made their way through the throng, navigating between the bar leaners that ran from the door to the classic old-school counter, where the drinks menu was scrawled across a surfboard—Logan's personal touch—he asked, "So, what's up with you?"

Jack grunted. "Claudia is in town."

Logan pulled a face like he'd tasted something bad. "She staying long?"

"God, I hope not." He hadn't asked, had just gotten away from her as quickly as possible. Since they'd broken up two years ago, he had seen neither hide nor hair of her, and that was the way he preferred it.

Logan rounded the bar, filled a pint glass, and pushed it over. Jack took a healthy swig then set it down to scan the room and pick out familiar faces. Logan's brother, Kyle, sat in the corner with their mutual friend, Tione, but Shane—the other man in their circle—was notably absent, most likely because he hadn't been able to find a babysitter.

A customer called Logan's name, and he shuffled along the bar to serve them. Beer in hand, Jack headed for the corner table to join his friends. He was halfway there when the door opened and a woman appeared, silhouetted against the dim evening.

His heart stuttered. The woman—she must have been a tourist because there was no way he'd have forgotten a face like hers—surveyed the room, her chin raised, very much the queen she'd come dressed as. He took a moment to appreciate her outfit, as did every other heterosexual man present. Khaleesi Daenerys Targaryen, the mother of dragons. Her eyes, a glorious blue, passed over him, then flicked back, resting on his face. He met her gaze and held it. Of their own accord, his feet carried him to her side.

Khaleesi's blonde hair fell over her shoulders in pale waves, and she wore her iconic battle costume, a fitted black leather dress with a cape attached. Her lips were baby pink and glossy. Jack wanted to capture that mouth with his own and devour her. He'd never been a big *Game of Thrones* fan, but Khaleesi was the woman of his dreams. Gorgeous, strong, take-no-prisoners. This woman, with her shoulders thrown back and her face tilted up, gave every impression of having walked directly out of his fantasies.

"Khaleesi," he rumbled, his voice gravelly and rough. "Do you have a date?"

She raised an imperious eyebrow. "Why is that any of your business?"

He put his hand to his heart. "Because if you don't, I'd like to rectify a terrible wrong by buying you a drink."

The corners of her glossy lips lifted, and a bolt of arousal shot straight to his groin. He shifted, and remembered Kyle and Tione, who were no doubt watching him from the corner. He couldn't get an awkward boner in front of his mates.

"As it happens," she said, "I don't."

"Excellent." He cupped her elbow and escorted her past the partygoers, many of whom turned to stare, into a private room out the back. Logan wouldn't mind him using it. Not under these circumstances. When Khaleesi gave him a questioning look, he said, "I have an in with the owner."

They sank onto the couch, and she gave him a cheeky little smile that sent a pulse of heat due south. "So, handsome man with an 'in'," she said, the tip of her finger tracing a line down his chest. "Who are you playing today?"

He willed his eager dick to play it cool. "Bear Grylls." His voice emerged even raspier than before. Being turned on tended to do that to him.

She nodded thoughtfully. "I see that. Manly, outdoorsy, hot as hell."

Her caress drifted lower, and his abdominals quivered in response. He clenched his jaw, trying to figure out how she'd managed to get him raring to go with no more than a gentle touch. "You think I'm hot?"

She cocked her head and grinned at him, her lower lip caught between her teeth. "Eh, you're not bad."

"Not bad." He huffed. "I'll show you not bad."

With that, he reached over and dragged her onto his lap, enjoying the soft exhale that proved he'd caught her by surprise. She settled onto him, and he looped his arm around her waist, holding her close. Those glistening lips parted, taunting him.

He grinned at her. "What do you say to that?"

"I say Bear Grylls better kiss me before I tell him off for taking liberties with my body."

Taking liberties with her body? Who talked like that?

He wondered what part of New Zealand she came from; he couldn't pick up her accent or way of speaking. Then his brain refocused on the pertinent word—*kiss.* She wanted him to kiss her. His erection leaped gleefully beneath her bottom. Whoever she was, and wherever she was from, tonight his Khaleesi was up for some fun, and he was more than willing to assist.

Brooke couldn't believe this was actually happening. After making goo-goo eyes at Jack Farrelly for two years, he'd finally noticed her. All it took was an inch of makeup, eyelash extensions, and a first-rate costume she'd been waiting for the perfect opportunity to show off.

A little effort, a few flirty words, and here she was, in his lap.

Oh, happy days.

His big, calloused hand went to the back of her head, and she reveled in the feel of it. He was such a vital guy, almost larger than life. Brooke wasn't one to play the role of delicate, wilting flower, but she was overwhelmed by his presence. His hand smoothed down her hair, and his face angled toward hers. Her breath caught, then she released a happy sigh as their lips touched.

He groaned against her mouth. "Christ, that sound is sexy. I bet you'd be loud with me inside you."

Heat flushed her neck, but she didn't have it in her to be embarrassed. Not when the evidence of her effect on him throbbed hot and steely beneath her. She drew his mouth back to hers and kissed him again, tasting a hint of beer on his breath. His hold on her waist tightened, and she moaned, loving the sensation of his muscled arm banding around her body.

"Fuck," he murmured, burying his face in the crook of her neck, lips moving against her skin, sending shivers of pleasure creeping down her spine. "What spell have you cast on me, Khaleesi? I'm so damn hard for you, it hurts."

In that moment, Brooke felt as powerful as the queen she was pretending to be. She'd never have guessed Jack liked to talk dirty, but hell *yes*, she could get behind it. She wanted to hear more, particularly as he stripped the clothes from her body, kissed every inch of exposed skin, and thrust into her. She'd bet *all* of him was big and solid. When she wriggled her butt against him, he shuddered, his fingers clenching fistfuls of her hair.

"You tease," he hissed from between gritted teeth.

She started to grin, but then he flicked his wrist and spanked the side of her ass. Her core throbbed in response, and her underwear dampened with her arousal. *Oh, boy.* Her lips parted in shock. She'd never have guessed she liked to be spanked, but she suspected that wasn't the only thing Jack could teach her about herself.

Her head fell back, and he latched onto her neck, kissing the length of it, sucking her pulse point, nipping it with his teeth. Then he raised his head to study his work, his lips curling in a smirk. "Yeah, that's more like it."

"Did you leave a hickey?" she demanded, far less annoyed than she ought to be—secretly thrilled that he'd want to mark her in such a way.

"Mmhmm." He kissed the spot tenderly. "You don't have a problem with that, do you?"

His tongue darted out to lap her skin, and she gasped. "I'll only have a problem if you stop."

He made his way back to her mouth, and their gazes clashed, his dark with intent. "I don't plan to stop until you're screaming, honey."

Hearing that remark, her mind whirred frantically, chaotic thoughts buzzing through it. Did she want that? How far was she prepared to go before she slowed things down?

Her body begged her to go however far Jack wanted, because she'd been craving him for so long, but her brain suggested they get to know each other better before progressing to the bedroom.

Their lips reconnected, and she sighed again. He was kissing her boneless, which didn't help her clarity of thought, nor did his fingers venturing beneath her dress. Their lips clung, then separated, tongues tasting, breath coming in pants. She fisted her hands in his t-shirt and fully committed to the kiss.

Crash!

The door flew open, and a couple stumbled into the room. Brooke and Jack jerked apart, staring at the intruders.

A scruffy blond head lifted, and Logan winked at them. "Sorry guys, the owner needs this room now."

The woman accompanying him hid her face in his chest and giggled. Brooke's sense flooded back. She was sitting on a man's lap, her dress hitched up around her thighs, love bites marring her neck, completely prepared to go to bed with someone who'd never given any indication he even knew she existed before today.

What was she thinking?

Shooting to her feet, she yanked her dress down, stumbled, then righted herself, and raced out of the room. Jack's voice echoed after her, but she didn't stop, and the absence of footsteps behind her indicated he hadn't given chase. Perhaps he didn't want to cause a scene. She was beyond caring.

On the way out, she passed her friend, Kyle, who took in her red face and stricken expression and immediately ushered her into the square.

"What's wrong?" he asked, concern evident in his gray eyes.

"Nothing. Just get me out of here—fast."

Kyle led her to his car, which was parked outside the library where he worked. When they reached her place, he escorted her as far as the bedroom door, where he gave her a hug and promised to call to check on her. Fifteen minutes later, she was in her pajamas, her face scrubbed clean, lying in bed, and replaying the scene in her mind over and over as she stared at the ceiling, wondering if her stolen moments with Jack had been a one-off, or the start of something special. Only time would tell.

1

ONE MONTH LATER

JACK FARRELLY'S four-wheel drive rattled along the road toward Sanctuary, a bed-and-breakfast-style lodge sandwiched between the sea and the national park on the fringes of Haven Bay. He hadn't been sure what to make of it when the owner, Kat, asked him to conduct regular outdoor tours, and the intervening time hadn't clarified his thinking at all. The extra money would be a boon, particularly since his new business adviser, Sterling Knightley, had been giving him a hard time about needing equipment and repairs. That said, Kat's guests tended to be an eccentric bunch, and he wasn't sure what to expect.

He parked in the gravel parking lot and paused, afraid to venture inside and see who was amongst his first tour group. Usually, his administrator, Erica, vetted people before he took them out. This time, he was operating in the dark. Mustering his courage, he got out of his four-wheel drive. If this gig didn't suit him, he'd find another way to get the funds for new equipment. That simple.

"Hey, Jack," Kat greeted him, hurrying down the stairs wearing a massive grin. As usual, the sight of her brought an answering smile to his face.

"Hey, Kitty-Kat," he said, kissing her cheek, which was marred by a pink-white scar that snaked downward disappeared beneath the neck of her shirt—a souvenir from the crash that had killed her husband. "Good to see you."

"You too." She stepped back and tucked her hair behind her ear. "Where do you want your group? Out here? Inside? In the garden?"

The rapid-fire questions had him raising a brow. "Are you nervous?" His lips twisted into a smirk. "Don't you trust me?"

She rolled her eyes. "You're the same Jack Farrelly who got people stranded in a cave on the side of a mountain overnight. What do you think?"

His smirk turned into a grimace. Okay, that was a fair comment. "I'd like to remind you that we were well-prepared and they certainly had an authentic experience."

She snorted. "You can say that again. So, what's it going to be?"

"Bring them out here. I'll need to fit each of them with a helmet and a head torch."

"You're going into the caves?"

"Yeah." She didn't move, so he waved her off. "Go get them. Let me see what I'm working with." Then he turned back to the four-wheel drive and checked that the helmets were arranged by size. He'd already inspected them to make sure the clasps were solid and the headlights were in working order before he left his base in the town center. Now he leaned against the side of the vehicle and crossed his arms to wait.

When Kat emerged with a small group in tow, he eyed them one at a time. There were two older ladies he recognized from around town, a middle-aged couple wearing brand new outfits from the Kathmandu chain store, and a young east-Asian couple. Newlyweds, by his guess. He smiled. The trip might not be as frustrating as he'd feared. Everyone seemed to be walking under their own steam and, with the possible exception of the two elderly ladies, no one appeared as though they might struggle in the caves.

"Hi everyone," he said, straightening. "I'm Jack, of Seafaring Adventures, and I'll be taking you caving this afternoon."

The newlyweds exchanged excited glances.

"Will they be sea caves?" one of the elderly ladies asked.

"No," he said, frowning. "The regular kind."

"Oh." She seemed disappointed. "It's just, with the name of your company, I assumed…"

"Nope. We do stuff on land as well. In the beginning, it was all sea-based, but we've expanded.

A movement behind the group caught his attention. Up at the lodge, a blonde woman hurried out to join them, her cute pink shoes crunching over the gravel. She was one of Kat's friends, but he couldn't remember her name. They'd met once or twice, and she seemed nice enough. Pretty, too, in a delicate way, with blue eyes that tilted down at the corners, slender legs, and wrists he could encircle with one hand. Not the kind of attractiveness he preferred. At least, not these days. She was too similar to his ex, Claudia, for his peace of mind.

"You'll see there are a selection of hard hats behind me. Find one that fits and make sure you can work the head-light. If you press the button to the side of the bulb once, it should light up, and if you press it again, it should change to red. Three presses turns it off."

He stood back while they reached for hard hats, testing different sizes until they found the right one. "When you do them up, the straps should be firm beneath your chin," he continued. "Make sure there's enough room for you to breathe, but not enough to fit your finger into the gap." He waited while people made adjustments, then asked, "Is everyone ready to go?"

Nods all round. He shut the vehicle door, donned a hard hat, and strode toward the lodge, talking over his shoulder. "Today we'll be walking for about half an hour to the caves, and then spending another half hour inside them. Have any of you been to the caves before?" Turning, he paced backward for long enough to see the negative responses, and smiled. "That's great. That means you'll get to see the best parts your first time in."

He scanned their feet, making sure they all had appropriate footwear. Most were wearing sneakers, although the middle-aged couple had professional-grade hiking boots. His gaze settled on the blonde, with her little pink shoes, and he scowled. Up close, he could see they were a brand that Claudia, an Instagram influencer, had been paid to endorse. He recalled this because he'd criticized their functionality, and she'd argued that it didn't matter how grippy they were as long as they looked good. Did this blonde share Claudia's view?

He sighed. Provided she took it carefully—and she appeared to be the type to do just that—they'd be fine. Besides, he shouldn't make snap judgments about the woman based on her footwear. The group passed through the foyer and out the other side, crossing the garden to the base of the forest, where the trees grew tall and cast long shadows. Jack stopped walking and addressed them.

"We're going to take it nice and easy. I'll lead the way, since I'm the only one who knows where we're going, but if you need a break or if I'm going too fast, yell out and let me know. Okay?"

They nodded.

"Will it all be uphill?" one of the older ladies asked.

"Yes, for the most part. The caves we're visiting are set

into a cliff face on a ledge about two hundred meters above us. But don't worry, the climb is spaced out over one-and-a-half horizontal miles, so the incline isn't bad." He grinned. "I have every faith you can handle it."

The two women didn't seem so sure. *Off to a promising start.* By contrast, the other members of the group looked excited and impatient to begin, particularly the blonde, who was bouncing on the balls of her feet. Damn, she might not be his type, but she was cute.

Don't be distracted by "pretty" or "cute." Remember what happened last time?

He'd made sacrifices for Claudia, tried to bridge the gap between their social circles, and in return, discovered she didn't consider him good enough for her. A fact she'd made abundantly clear both to him and her two-hundred-thousand Instagram followers. Talk about a rude awakening.

This woman isn't Claudia, he reminded himself. *Don't treat her like she is.*

"Everyone got water?" he asked, receiving a number of affirmations in response. "Before we get going, does anyone have a medical condition or injury I should know about?"

The old ladies glanced at the blonde, who heaved a sigh.

"I do," she said, smoothing her hands over her pristine white tank top. "But I don't expect it to be a problem."

He scanned her from head to toe. She looked healthy enough, with a flush on her cheeks and all parts apparently in working order. Gesturing for her to come closer so the entire group wouldn't overhear, he asked, "Can you tell me more? Is there medication you need to bring?"

She shifted from one foot to the other and twisted the hem of her shirt as though wringing water from it. The woman was visibly tense.

"I have asthma," she said. "My inhaler is in my pocket."

"Is it bad?" he asked.

"Not great, but it's under control. I haven't had an attack in months."

"Okay then—"

"I also have hay fever, which I took my medication for this morning." Straightening her shoulders, she finally met his gaze. "And I'm recovering from chronic fatigue."

Oh, man. While the hay fever shouldn't be a problem, he wasn't sure how to handle chronic fatigue. To be honest, he wasn't particularly familiar with the condition. But based on the stubborn tilt of her chin and the fire simmering in her clear blue eyes, she expected him to make a big deal of it.

"Is there anything you need from me?" he asked.

Her eyes widened. "No. I'll be fine. I'm used to managing my health, and I'm on the mend."

She seemed to be trying to convince herself as much as him, and for a moment, he wished she hadn't come. Not because she didn't seem lovely, but because he didn't have a clue what to do about her, and her reluctance to be completely open with him wasn't helping. He needed to know she'd speak up if she ran into any problems.

"You'll let me know if you're struggling?"

She pressed glossy pink lips together, and her expression told him she didn't want to agree. He paused. Something about those lips was familiar, but he couldn't quite put his finger on it. Then she tucked her hands inside her elbows and nodded. "I'll let you know."

"Good." Turning back to the others, he gestured toward the forest. "Let's get started, shall we?"

Heading up the slope at about half his usual pace, he started a spiel about the age of the forest, and what native species could be found in it. About fifteen minutes into the walk, he became aware of a faint chattering behind him, the type that seemed like people were discussing something but trying to avoid notice. He looked over his shoulder and saw that the blonde was sucking on an inhaler. She saw him watching, stuffed it back into her pocket, and kept going, but the elderly ladies cast sidelong glances at her as if preparing to catch her should she keel over.

Jack gritted his teeth and resisted the urge to ask if she was okay. She'd said she'd tell him if she needed help, and he had to trust that, even though he was inclined to be mistrustful of her because of her resemblance to Claudia. A few minutes later, he heard a wet sniff, followed by a sneeze.

"Bless you," he called.

They were a couple of hundred meters from the ridge when someone tapped his shoulder and he turned to see the taller of the blonde's fussing companions, Mavis, behind him.

"Yes?" he asked, raising an eyebrow.

"Can we stop for a couple of minutes?" she asked. "Brooke needs a break, but she won't say so herself."

Jack gazed past Mavis, back down the trail at the blonde woman, who was panting heavily. Her cheeks had passed pink on their way to scarlet, her eyes were watering, and her nose was streaming. He bit back his frustration at the way she ducked her head when she saw him, and waited until she was more composed. When she was breathing normally, he continued to lead the way up the ridge, eventually cresting it and arriving at a gaping black hole in the cliff face.

"This is the cave we'll be adventuring into today," he told them. "It's approximately five hundred meters long, and more than five meters tall in most places, but we will come across one point where it narrows and we'll need to climb over an old rockfall to get to the other side, then crawl most of the way to the end." He glanced at the older ladies. "I'm expecting that some of you won't be able to make it over the rockfall, so you'll wait on this side. We'll only be gone another ten minutes or so." He rubbed his palms together. "Does anyone have any questions?"

Mavis's friend Nell raised her hand. "If someone were to, say, have an asthma attack inside, or faint and need to be carried out, is it best if they wait out here?"

The blonde gasped, and glared at her.

"Yes, that would be best, but I'll leave it to everyone to evaluate whether they feel safe coming along." He paced over to the blonde. "Are you doing okay? There's no shame in staying behind."

Her eyes narrowed. "I'm managing fine, thanks. Ignore Mavis and Nell. I know my body, and I know when it's reached its limits. I'm not there yet."

Jack couldn't help but check out the body in question. No denying, she was attractive, and her stubbornness made him grin. Again, he was struck by that sense of recognition. "Remind me what your name is, blondie."

Her mouth dropped open, then snapped shut. She looked utterly astounded by the simple question. And yeah, okay, she was Kat's friend and they'd probably been introduced when they'd met before, but he wasn't the best with names.

Her lips pressed together. "Brooke."

"Brooke," he repeated. "You stick close to me. It's dark in there and I want to know you're safe at all times."

***

IF BROOKE KNEW how to throw a punch, and if she weren't dying a little on the inside, she would have whacked the condescending smirk off Jack Farrelly's gorgeous face.

He doesn't know who I am.

How insulting was that? You'd think a guy would remember a girl's face once he'd had his tongue down her throat. Earlier, she'd thought he was playing it casual, but no, she was so forgettable that even making out with her hadn't got her name to stick in his memory. No wonder he hadn't called. And to think she'd spent the day worrying this entire thing would be awkward because of their kiss. Forget discomfort and uncertainty, she'd just plunged headlong into anger and humiliation.

Her fingers twitched and she clenched them into a fist. The feminist in her demanded she let loose on him. How dare he kiss her and then forget her, as if all women were interchangeable? Yes, she'd been in costume when they'd hooked up, but she hadn't looked that different.

"Fine," she muttered, her fury simmering hotter because, in addition to forgetting her, he was also coddling her. She'd been wrapped in cotton wool most of her life, since before the open-heart surgery she had as a kid, and she was well and truly over it. "I'll stay close."

Everest, she reminded herself. *Think of Everest.*

She had a mission to achieve, and it was bigger than Jack Farrelly and her hurt pride. When she was thirteen, she'd made a pact with her friend Olivia to one day hike to Mount Everest Base Camp. Olivia had passed away eight months ago now, and while she may not be able to fulfill their pact, Brooke would do it for her. After an entire month of feeling human, she was finally daring to set goals.

Bottling up her injured feelings and embarrassment, she put a cork in them. They wouldn't serve her well.

"Great." Jack offered her a hand as he led them into the cave, but she ignored it, and switched on her head torch. It illuminated the space around her. Looking up, she saw that the cave ceiling was high and curved, composed of brown rock. There were no stalactites hanging from it, and she wondered why. A dark tunnel led further into the cliff. Anticipation buzzed through her. She was *actually* here. In a cave in the bush. Inside one of nature's wonders.

She grinned, though no one could see her. Two years ago, she'd never have dreamed she'd ever be in this position, yet here she was. She'd come such a long way, and there was no reason why, in a few months' time, she couldn't be warming her hands on a mug of instant coffee at Everest Base Camp and drinking an extra on Olivia's behalf. That image fired her up more than anything, and she hurried to keep up with Jack. Watching the rocky and uneven ground, she progressed into the cave. It was hard to believe she'd lived within a half hour's walk of this place and never been here. It was amazing. Not at all claustrophobic, like she'd expected.

"How did the cave form?" she asked into the dark.

"Don't know," Jack called back. "Geology isn't my strong suit. "

She'd have to look it up when they returned to the lodge. As they moved around a bend, the daylight faded to a pale slash behind them, and then vanished from view completely. Brooke wondered whether it would be pitch black if they were to turn off their head torches. Detouring to one of the cave walls, she ran a finger along the rock. It was cold and damp, rough to touch. Trailing a finger along, she studied the contours, so preoccupied that she walked straight into someone's back, and had the air knocked out of her.

"Oof," she gasped. The man in Kathmandu gear peered over his shoulder at her, and she apologized. "Sorry."

"That's okay," he said.

Trying and failing to draw a deep breath, she fished in her pocket for her inhaler, which probably wouldn't be any help but was better than nothing, and dragged on it. Then she jammed it back and raised her arms above her head to open her lungs.

A figure appeared at her side. "Are you okay, Brooke? Do you need to stop? Is there anything I can do to help?"

She flushed red to the roots of her hair. Thank God no one could see. She hadn't realized the entire group was waiting, and worse, Jack was hovering over her like a worried parent. Her cheeks burned and she wished the ground would swallow her up. What must he think of her?

Why do you care? He's guilty of a kiss-and-run!

"I'll be okay in a moment."

A light touch landed on her back. "We'll wait."

Seconds ticked by, and despite her mortification, she eventually recovered. "I'm better now."

"Good," Jack said briskly. "But please tell me if that changes. This second part is a bit harder." He aimed his headlight further into the cave and raised his voice. "Behind me, you'll see that there's a pile of rock that reaches nearly all the way to the cave ceiling. What you'll need to do, if you want to go on, is climb over the rock pile, and from there we'll be crawling." Was it Brooke's imagination, or did he look pointedly at her when he said that? "So, who'd like to go first?"

"Me," she said, so softly no one seemed to hear. "*Me*," she repeated, more loudly.

Jack's face twisted in concern. "Are you sure that's a good idea?"

She stood firm. She didn't want to give him any reason to look at her with pity. On top of everything, she didn't think she could handle that. She wanted him to see her as a desirable woman, an equal, not someone he needed to fuss over.

"You won't have to carry me out, I can promise you that." It was a bold promise, but one she intended to keep. If she couldn't leave under her own steam, she'd hide in a corner and hibernate until she recovered.

"Okay," he said, clearly dubious, but willing to give her the benefit of the doubt. "Away you go. I'll be right here. If you run into trouble, yell out."

Brooke summoned her strength—what little of it she possessed—and clambered up the pile of rocks, which shifted and wobbled beneath her feet. It was hard work. By the time she reached the top, her breathing was shallow and her arms and legs felt weak.

"Are you okay up there?" someone asked. Not Jack.

"I'm great," she replied, then dropped over the other side of the rock pile, where they couldn't see her, and switched her light off while she rested.

When she heard another person scaling the rocks, she flicked it back on and scrambled down until she reached the cave floor. At this point, it was about four feet high—enough to crawl comfortably, but not enough for a grown person to walk upright. Shuffling to the side, she waited. First over the pile was the man she'd bumped into. His wife followed, and then the younger couple. Jack came last. Mavis and Nell must have opted to wait on the other side.

Jack crawled to the front of the group. "Nice and roomy over here, eh?"

Someone sniggered. Meanwhile, Brooke thanked her lucky stars she hadn't been cursed with claustrophobia as well as every other malady.

"The tunnel continues for another hundred meters," he told them. "It opens up into a cavern at the end, so you'll be able to stand again."

With that, he started into the dark. Brooke trailed close behind, recalling her promise not to venture far from him. She was so caught up in the wonder of the place that she hardly noticed her palms scrape on the ground as she moved, or her knees knock into pointy stones. She was in a *cave*. Surrounded by rock on all sides. *Adventuring*. She laughed. It echoed around them, sounding slightly maniacal. Jack glanced over his shoulder.

"It's so awesome," she said by way of explanation.

He grinned. "Sure is."

After a while, they came to a low-hanging rock, and she had to drop to her belly to fit beneath it. On the other side was the cavern Jack had mentioned. It was easily the size of the communal living room at Sanctuary. She got to her feet and strode around the perimeter. After a few minutes, Jack called them to attention.

"Everyone, turn off your lights. Three clicks."

Brooke felt for her button and did as he said. The lights flickered out, one by one, leaving them in total darkness. *Wow*. Even in the dead of night, with the forest on one side and the sea on the other, she'd never been in darkness quite as inky and perfect as this.

"Amazing," a female voice said.

"Nowhere else is as dark as the inside of a cave." This voice was Jack's, deep and rumbly. Strange, how she'd never noticed how sexy a voice could be. It matched the man. Unfortunately, however sexy he may be, he was also a jackass.

Trying to put him to the back of her mind, she focused on the darkness cocooning them. If she stared into it for long enough, she imagined she could see patches of light and the outline of shapes, but she knew that was just her brain filling in the blanks, deceiving her. The flashes of texture in the dark reminded her of the 1915 painting, The Black Square, which was quite literally a square painted black. Something she'd never understood, until now.

"Lights back on."

Reluctantly, she switched hers on, and the cavern was illuminated once again.

"Everyone ready to go?"

They headed back the way they'd come, over the rock pile to rejoin Mavis and Nell, then out into the bright sunlight. Brooke couldn't stop smiling. They'd gotten off to a bumpy start, but aside from a few moments of awkwardness, she'd had the best time.

Halfway down the hill, Nell complained that she couldn't carry her bag any longer, and Brooke took it from her, ignoring the woman's protests. She was exhausted, but also on cloud nine. Nothing could stop her. At the bottom of the hill, she handed the bag back but didn't sit with her friends. Her legs were like jelly and she was afraid that if she did, she wouldn't be able to get back up again. Instead, she waited for Jack to thank the group and instruct them where to leave the equipment, then lingered midway between her friends and the lodge. Jack glanced her way and she found herself hoping he'd come over to chat.

But then Tione emerged from his cabin, his Chihuahua, Pixie, tucked into the crook of his arm and his cross-bred bull terrier, Zee, on his heels, although his other two dogs were nowhere in sight. Jack waved him over. The two men started chatting, and even though Brooke edged closer, under the pretense of pulling a weed from a flowerbed, she may as well have been invisible.

2

___

Jack noticed Brooke lingering nearby. She glanced his way a few times, and he wondered if she wanted something. But when she didn't approach, he decided he must be mistaken, and took the opportunity to evaluate her instead. Brooke intrigued him. She was pretty, and stubborn to boot. He found he liked her very much, but he wouldn't let himself act on that attraction. With her designer activewear, sun-kissed hair, and graceful movements, she was too much like Claudia, and regardless of whether or not she seemed nice, he'd learned his lesson about staying in his lane when it came to women. Still, he couldn't shake the feeling that there was something familiar about her, beyond her simply being Kat's friend.

When she reached for a weed in the garden, he noticed that the porcelain-pink polish on her fingernails was chipped from scrabbling around in the cave. Those delicate nails and her pale skin screamed of long days spent inside. Claudia had always been perfectly manicured—including in the dozens of Instagram photos where she appeared to be rock climbing or caving or hiking. That should have been a red flag from the start. And okay, maybe it wasn't fair to compare the two, considering how little he knew about Brooke, but she struck him as the kind of girl who wouldn't understand his choices. Eventually she straightened and hustled away. Jack looked from her to Tione, and caught his friend frowning at him.

"What?" he asked.

"That was a dick move," Tione replied.

Jack shrugged. "Don't know what you're talking about."

"Brooke. She clearly wanted to talk to you."

Did she? He hadn't been sure, and part of him had believed he was reading too much into her presence because of the inconvenient pull of magnetism he felt toward her.

"Huh. Couldn't tell."

To his surprise, Tione's eyes narrowed. "Bullshit. You could have made a polite excuse instead of ignoring her. That was rude."

Jack's arms crossed defensively. "I didn't realize she wanted to talk," he reiterated, guilt prickling his skin because the statement wasn't entirely true.

"Seriously?" Tione demanded. "Do you have a problem with her or something?"

Uh-oh. Jack got the feeling he was treading on thin ice here.

"No," he said, looking out over the garden so he didn't have to make eye contact with the tattooed tank of a man who seemed to have taken exception to him. "I barely know her. I know her type though—bubbly and well-meaning, but high maintenance. She belongs at a fancy brunch or in a high-end club, not in the bush."

"Brooke?" Tione asked. "In a nightclub?" His lips twitched, then he scrubbed a hand over his bearded cheek.

"What's so funny?"

"Just wondering when you got so bad at reading people."

Around about the time he'd hooked up with Claudia, Jack would guess. "What do you even know about her?"

Tione wasn't a ladies' man. His stocky build, beard and glower tended to frighten women away. And if that didn't do it, his hundred-pound bull mastiff, Trevor, did. Right now, he was frowning like he couldn't quite believe what he was hearing.

"Brooke lives here, asshole. Has done for two years. So it happens that I know her quite well."

"Oh." Jack had known she lived in the area. He wasn't a total idiot, but he'd never made the connection that she actually resided at Sanctuary, with Kat and Tione.

"Yeah, 'oh.'" Tione was on a roll now. "She's a great girl. Kind, funny, and really damn smart." Coming from him, that meant something. Not that you'd know it to look at him, but Tione was a certified genius. The kind who could join Mensa if he wanted. "You'd be lucky if she wanted anything to do with a grisly old bastard like you. But for the record, you've got her all wrong."

Jack fell back a step, startled by his friend's vehemence. He studied Tione's expression—which to be fair, wasn't much different from usual. A dark scowl, lowered brows. He'd squared his shoulders, like he was considering flattening Jack with a solid punch if he said anything else less than complimentary about Brooke.

Jack laughed to mask his stab of discomfort when he reached the only logical conclusion. "You have a thing for her."

If possible, Tione stiffened further. "Do not."

"Come on, you're ready to lay into me."

"Because she's my friend. You ever heard of that? Being friends with a woman?"

"I have female friends."

One of Tione's bushy black eyebrows went up.

"I do," Jack insisted. "Kat, for instance." He wracked his brain for more examples, but other than women friends he'd fallen out of touch with, and Erica, who was forced to spend time with him, he couldn't think of any. Perhaps Bex, his personal trainer, but they never got together outside the gym. "Okay, so you don't have a crush on Brooke. But her being a great girl doesn't mean she's right for me, or that I'm right for her."

"Fair call. You're probably not up to her standards."

He flinched. Well, if that didn't just hit the nail on the head. Time to change the subject. "Have you heard from Sterling today?

"Yes." Tione eyed him suspiciously. "I think he and Kat will be moving in together any time."

"Good for them." There had been a time when Jack had considered dating Kat himself, because she was exactly the sort of person he could trust, but she'd found love elsewhere and he'd discovered he didn't mind. They were great friends, and crossing that line would have been a mistake.

Tione chuckled and clapped him on the shoulder. If Jack had been less well-built, he'd have gone flying from the force of it. "Don't worry, we'll find you another woman who likes climbing mountains and has no standards."

"Whatever you say, Tee." He glanced at his chunky waterproof watch. "I'd better head back and prepare for the group I've got first thing tomorrow. Catch you later."

"See you."

Jack nodded farewell, gathered the discarded helmets in a box, strolled across the garden, and paced through the foyer of Sanctuary and out the other side to the parking lot, where his four-wheel drive was parked. He packed the box into the back and drove to his storefront in the town square, located beside the medical center and across the road from the glass and pottery studio. Once he'd unloaded the helmets, he checked that the headlights still worked and that nothing had been broken, then assembled everything he'd need for the next day. Preparation complete, he debriefed Erica and headed home.

The house was silent when he let himself in, everything exactly where he'd left it, and the place smelled of dirty laundry. Ignoring the state of the living room, which he hadn't tidied in weeks, he microwaved a bowl of leftover chicken and vegetables, grabbed a beer from the fridge, and took his dinner out to the deck, where he could bask in the dying sunlight without facing the mess and emptiness of his living quarters. It was supposed to be home, but most nights, it felt more like a place to crash than anything else.

BY THE TIME Brooke had showered and changed into her pajamas, which read "Geek is the new sexy," her natural buzz had worn off and she was exhausted. The only energy she held onto was the rage that seemed to grow exponentially the longer she allowed it to fester. How dare that heinous man kiss her until she couldn't even remember who Rosa Bonheur was, or why she'd been so important to future generations of female artists, and then forget all about it? How dare he make her feel beautiful and desirable and then squash that feeling with cold, hard reality?

As she wondered how many other women had suffered the same indignation, her pulse picked up, drumming in her throat like the marching anthem for the sisterhood of women Jack Farrelly had forgotten. She had no reason to believe there had been any others, but she preferred to think he was an asshole than admit she just hadn't made that much of an impression. Grinding her teeth together, she made those theoretical and possibly imaginary women a promise. He wouldn't treat any others like they were disposable and get away unscathed. Not on her watch.

Grabbing her laptop, she shimmied into bed beneath the covers, switched it on and loaded up her blog, the one she'd chronicled her journey on since her second heart surgery at fifteen, when she'd decided she needed to take ownership of her health issues and stop living in denial. Her parents may have wanted to hide her from the world forever, but she'd long since known she'd only be happy if she wrestled everything from life that she could. Opening a new post, she vented her fury to the web, not filtering the words as they spilled from her brain to her fingertips and appeared on the screen.

Brooke v. *World: Monday 3 February (evening)*

You might be wondering why I'm posting twice in one day. Today has taken a nosedive and I really need your support. You remember how I finally got up the guts to kiss Jack at the New Year's Eve party and then he didn't call? It turns out, he doesn't remember me. How freaking humiliating is that?

He and I shared a toe-curling make out session—the best of my life—and it was apparently so unmemorable that he doesn't even recall my name.

Please tell me there are men out there who would appreciate my ability to recite the actors from Doctor Who in chronological order, admire my collection of cosplay outfits (and preferably have their own), and who possess a modicum of common decency. Please tell me Jack is the exception to the rule.

Also, sigh. I'm just realizing, I must have terrible taste in men. Tell me I'm not the only one who's been so stupid. I don't know what to do with myself—or him. Any and all advice appreciated.

Brooke XX

•   •   •

SHE READ over what she'd written. The simple act of venting was cathartic and eased the pressure in her chest. She didn't even need to post it. No one else had to know about her private humiliation. But man, giving words to her feelings really helped, regardless of whether anyone would ever see.

She yawned, her limbs heavy, her mind beginning to turn fuzzy. Time to rest. She hit the delete button, closed her laptop, rolled over, and was asleep within seconds.

3

SOMETHING thudded in the back of Brooke's consciousness. Thud. Thud. Thud. The thudding was followed by the sound of two bits of metal scraping against each other. Ick, what *was* that?

"Brooke, you up?" a voice called.

She groaned and tried to open her eyes, but she was lying face down and they stayed sealed tight.

A hand touched her shoulder. "Brooke, it's lunchtime."

"Mmph," she replied, her mouth pressed against the mattress. Couldn't they just go away? She was so tired, her legs like chunks of lead, her arms void of strength. Her head was foggy, her thoughts sluggish. She needed to rest for longer.

"You can go back to sleep later," the voice said. This time, she placed it as Kat. "But you didn't have dinner last night, or breakfast this morning, so you need to refuel."

Brooke lifted her face so there was enough space between her lips and the bed for her to mutter, "Fine."

"Good." The weight of the hand left her shoulder. "I'll send Tee to get you if you're not out in fifteen minutes."

"Mmkay."

Once the door clicked shut, Brooke raised herself up, slowly and carefully. She cleared her throat, which felt scratchy, and pressed her fingertips to her lymph nodes—firm and slightly swollen. Letting her head drop to her chest, she rubbed her bleary eyes. She'd overdone it yesterday. Most days, she no longer experienced any of the symptoms of chronic fatigue, which had struck her down a year ago after a nasty bout of glandular fever, but the symptoms returned when she overexerted herself.

"Stupid," she grumbled. She'd been determined to put on a good front for Jack, and it hadn't done her any favors. Raking a hand through her hair, she winced when it snagged on a knot. She grabbed her brush from the bedside cabinet and dragged it through her hair with one hand, using the other to open her laptop. Immediately, something unexpected caught her eye and she froze, brush halfway down the length of her hair.

Her heart stuttered, and her lips parted. *Oh, shit.*

The post she'd written yesterday. The one about Jack. She must have been so exhausted she'd hit the wrong button. Instead of deleting it, she'd published it, and already more than thirty of her readers had commented. Spots flashed in front of her eyes, and her head spun. She was going to be sick. Hands shaking, she refreshed the page, then checked it to make sure her eyes hadn't deceived her.

No such luck. The post was still there, along with the comments. She heard a sound and realized she'd whimpered. Sweat beaded on her upper lip. With a growing sense of dread, she scrolled down and started reading. Most of the comments were sympathetic, but some offered suggestions about how she could force Jack to remember her. Her breath caught in her throat. Jessica, 15, from Auckland, went as far as to suggest that she should seduce him, make him fall in love with her, and then reject him for revenge. Jessica's suggestion had more than a dozen likes. Her readers were loyal and vindictive. Another woman, Amber, recommended she become his girlfriend, make him crazy for her, and break up with him publicly in a way that would make sure no one else would ever want him.

Brooke clutched at her cheeks. Why oh why had she felt the need to vent? Even if she'd had no intention of posting her rant, she should have known better. Nothing died on the internet, and nothing could truly be deleted. She glanced at the clock. She had ten minutes before Tione came looking for her. With clumsy fingers, she replied to Amber's comment.

Haha, great suggestion! Thanks for having my back. XX.

She wasn't about to take either Amber or Jessica up on their advice, but they cared about her enough to be angry on her behalf, so she owed them gratitude for their support. That done, she tapped out a brief update.

BROOKE V. World: Tuesday 4 February

Thanks to everyone for the comments and suggestions. I'm a bit embarrassed about venting to you all. I appreciate your thoughts and well wishes, and I'm going to do my best to take the high road. I'll try to forget what happened and focus on the important thing. I need Jack to help me get in shape and tackle some big challenges on the horizon. I'm excited for them, and I'm sure you will be too when you hear what I've got planned.

I'd love to hear how you're doing and what challenges are coming up in your life. Leanne shared with me that she's going through another round of chemo, so let's keep her in our thoughts today.

Brooke XX

. . .

ONCE SHE'D PUBLISHED the update, she finished brushing her hair and showered so she didn't smell like she'd been in bed for eighteen hours, then dressed and went to lunch. She'd hoped to find Kat in the dining hall to discuss her mission to hike to Everest Base Camp, but her friend was nowhere in sight. Instead, Brooke ate alone beside the window overlooking the garden, where Betty, Nell, and Hugh MacAllister, the town councilor, were eating a home-made picnic. Betty was the leader of the Bridge Club, which many of the local retirees—including Nell and Mavis—belonged to. The club had a reputation for meddling in other's lives as much as they played bridge, if not more so.

When she'd finished her chicken salad, she cleaned her plate and leaned over the counter to call to Tione.

"*Kia ora*, Brooke," he greeted her, his lips tilting up at the corners into what, for him, passed as a smile. "How are you feeling today?"

She bit her tongue. When people asked that, her first instinct was to get defensive, but they only asked because they cared. "I'm all right," she said. "A bit tired, but I'll live."

"Great. Glad to hear it."

"Have you seen Kat around?"

His grin spread until no one could possibly mistake it. "Yeah, and I think you should give her some time alone."

"Why?" she asked, curious.

"She left nearly half an hour ago, and just before you got here, she came back—" he leaned close and lowered his voice "—with Sterling. They looked like they were in a hurry to get somewhere private, if you know what I mean."

"Good for her!" Brooke beamed, delight fizzing through her. She liked Sterling Knightley, the new business consul-tant in town, and was pleased Kat was no longer letting the pain of losing her late husband get in the way of her future happiness.

Tione nodded. "She deserves a bit of fun."

"You're right. I'll give them some time." Like, a lot of time. She could wait a day or two for Kat's opinion. It wasn't like she was ready to set out for Everest tomorrow, and she needed to write more of her doctoral thesis.

ON WEDNESDAY, Jack returned for his second session at Sanctuary a little warier than he had for the first. He hoped he didn't have to deal with Brooke again. He didn't want to see her cute face and remember how Tione had raved about her while trying to remind himself that she wasn't for him. Whatever Tione had said, Jack was too rough around the edges for a girl like her. Not that she'd expressed any interest. He was making all of this more complicated than it needed to be.

Today, he'd planned an easy hour-long hike, followed by an abseiling lesson. He'd need some of the participants to carry equipment, but provided they had the same number of people as Monday, it would be a breeze. He parked. Kat was waiting on the doorstep and headed over to greet him.

"Beautiful day, isn't it?" he asked as he got out of the vehicle.

"We need to talk," she replied.

Uh-oh. He swallowed hard and pulled up his big boy shorts. "About what?"

She crossed her arms and her lips formed a thin line, her eyes like daggers. Shit, he was really in trouble. He mentally scanned back over the past two days and wondered what he'd done.

"When we agreed to this arrangement, I specifically asked you if you could work with people less capable than yourself, and you said yes."

"If I remember correctly, I said I'd try my best."

Her eyes narrowed. "Semantics. The point is, Brooke slept for eighteen hours after you finished with her on Monday, and she should never have been allowed to work herself into a state like that."

Jack deflated, guilt pinching his soul. "She did? I'm sorry. She seemed okay at the time." More or less. He'd sensed she was putting on a brave face, but he hadn't thought she'd been in poor enough condition to sleep for nearly a day.

"That's not acceptable," she said, unfolding her arms and placing her hands on her hips. "I need you to do better."

He blinked. "You're really angry at me."

She nodded, the movement jerky. "Brooke doesn't like to admit when she's having a hard time. Especially not to people she's uncomfortable with. As her best friend, I know this. Just like I know she'll act like she's fine if she can get away with it, but you're paid to keep an eye on people, and you should have noticed something was wrong."

"Like I said, I'm sorry." Jack squared his shoulders. "I should have watched her more closely, but you need to remember, she's an adult and she's responsible for communicating with me when she's struggling. If she doesn't do that, there's not much I can do for her."

Kat nodded, lips pursed. "I know. She should have been more open with you. I guess I expected you to ease her into it because of her borderline health, but if she was being her usual stubborn self, you couldn't have known."

He frowned, something in her words catching his attention. "Tell me more about what's wrong with her."

Kat stared at him. "Are you being serious?"

Why would he joke around about this stuff? A woman's safety was at risk. "Do I look like I'm kidding?"

Her hands fell from her hips. It seemed he'd taken the

air out of her sails. "Brooke has lived here for two years. How is it possible you don't know her background?"

Jack flinched at the quiet rebuke in her eyes. Damn, now he really felt like a tool. "I know a little," he said. "Asthma, hay fever, chronic fatigue. Is there more to it than that?"

Kat sighed, rubbing one eye and then the other with the heel of her hand. "There's nothing seriously wrong with her —*now*. But she has the world's worst track record. Something wasn't right with her heart when she was younger. That's healed—she had some kind of open-heart surgery to fix it—but she also has eczema, gets motion sickness, you name it. A year ago she got glandular fever, and the chronic fatigue is a hangover from that. She's more or less recovered, but it still rears its ugly head from time to time."

"Oh." Yeah, okay, he'd thought she looked like an indoorsy type, but he hadn't thought she seemed as frail as Kat described. Open-heart surgery? That was a big deal. "If her health is that bad, she shouldn't be coming on my trips. It's too risky. I don't want her getting hurt." He didn't want to see her pretty face pale and unresponsive.

"Try telling her that."

Kat turned to go inside, but he caught her by the arm. "When I agreed to this, I reserved the right to turn people away. I'm using it now. If she's that unwell, she shouldn't come."

Kat gave a saccharine smile. "Like I said, *you* can tell her."

He watched her go, exhaling slowly. *Wow.* He'd never seen Kat go mama-bear over anyone before. She was usually a busybody, but not a fierce one, and to be honest, it was a little frightening. Slamming the car door shut, he strode to the foyer, where the group was waiting. The Kathmandu couple had come back for more and greeted him with eager smiles. Mavis had also returned, but she'd brought Betty rather than Nell. Three fit guys in their twenties lounged against a wall, talking quietly between themselves and stealing occasional glances at the final member of the party. *Brooke.*

If Kat hadn't shared what she had, he wouldn't have believed that Brooke had been anything other than perky and energetic since he'd seen her last. She looked vibrant standing behind the desk, a smile flirting with the corners of her mouth and a rosy flush on her cheeks. Lust speared through his gut and he bit the inside of his lip to stifle a groan. Why did she have to be so appealing, with her electric blue eyes and dewy complexion? His body reacted to her instinctively, going on an all-systems-alert. Strange, when he was rarely affected this way by a woman. Ruthlessly squelching his response, he reminded himself that he couldn't think of a girl less suited to his lifestyle, and he was sure the same could be said when it came to his suiting her. Unfortunately, his mind and his body had different ideas.

"Hi, everyone," he said, once he had himself under control. "I'd like you to all head into the parking lot. I'll join you in a moment." When they started moving, he pointed at Brooke. "Except you."

Mavis and Betty tittered and exchanged glances, like they didn't want to leave her alone with him. He raised a brow and they hustled away, casting dubious looks over their shoulders. He scowled. Did they really think he posed a risk to her?

"You wanted me?" Brooke asked, coming around the desk to stand in front of him. He tried not to notice the way her slim-fitting tank top outlined slender curves. *Not appropriate.* Even if she wasn't all wrong for him, she was probably too young to be interested. It was hard to gauge her age, but he put her somewhere in her early twenties. Compared to his thirty, that was a big difference in life experience.

"I think it's best if you stay here," he told her, noticing that Kat hovered a few feet away.

Her jaw dropped. "Why? I managed all right the other day. I didn't hold anyone up, or get in the way."

He sighed. Did she really want to go down this path? "No, you didn't. But you slept for eighteen hours afterward."

Her gaze slid over to Kat and she glared. "I was fine," she insisted through gritted teeth.

He softened his expression. "Be honest with me, Brooke. You're not doing either of us any favors if you pretend to be fine. I'm not a mind reader. If you come with me, I need to be able to trust you to let me know how you're doing at all times."

"Okay, maybe I overdid it," she conceded. "I should have taken it easier, but I've learned my lesson, and I promise to be more up-front with you and pace myself."

"I'm not sure I'm willing to take that risk," he said. "We're walking farther than we did last time, and I don't have time to figure out how we can make it work for you."

She crossed her arms and looked somewhere over his shoulder, blinking rapidly as though holding back tears. "If I need to stop, I will, and you can collect me on the way back. Please." A note of pleading entered her voice, and it twisted Jack's gut. "I need to do this. It's important. I could explain why, but it'd take more than a couple of minutes and I know you want to get moving."

"Brooke, honey," Kat said, laying a gentle hand on her arm. "It's one trip. There will be others."

Would there? Because Jack wasn't sure.

Brooke closed her eyes. "Sorry. Of course there will." She released a shuddering breath. "I'm being unreasonable."

"Maybe a little," Kat confirmed, a smile creeping over her face. "Why don't you sit this one out so Jack doesn't get off schedule, and then we can have a talk about what to do in the future once he returns."

Jack could see the emotions warring within her. Apparently joining the group meant a lot to her.

"Okay." Her shoulders drooped, and oddly, his mood dropped with them. "I guess that will be fine."

"Great," he said, before she could change her mind. "I'll come by once we're back." He didn't know where he'd find her, but considering he didn't plan to go anywhere near her without Kat to play mediator, his friend could show him where to go.

"Don't forget," Brooke warned, and from her expression, he could tell that if he did, she'd hunt him down.

He nodded, then followed the others outside, finding them waiting beside the four-wheel drive.

Betty waved a hiking pole as he approached. "Did you scare that poor girl away?"

"We decided she's better off not joining us today," he replied.

She harrumphed, in that way only little old ladies could. "I don't suppose that was *her* idea."

He didn't say anything, just handed bags to the three young men. Once they'd all geared up, he issued directions, then fell into step at the back.

Betty joined him. "You know what I think?" she asked.

"I'm sure you're going to tell me whether I want to know or not."

She thwacked his leg with the end of a pole. "You're a cheeky devil, Jack Farrelly. I think you don't want Brooke coming because you don't like the way she makes you feel."

Huh. Well, there's a thought.

"And how's that, Betty?"

"Aroused."

Jack tripped over his own feet. *Dear God, what?*

He glanced at Betty. Had he heard her correctly? Had the God-awful word "aroused" just passed between her prune-like lips?

She hooted with laughter. "I hit the nail on the head, eh, Jack?"

She... He...

He shook his head, both amused and dismayed. It wasn't as though he could deny it.

"Don't be ridiculous," he said, then added fondly, "and get your pointy little nose out of my business."

4

———

Brooke bashed at her laptop keyboard, hammering out an opinion piece about the sexual objectification of women in art that she was writing for a well-regarded magazine. The keys were taking the brunt of her frustration at being cooped up inside, and any minute now, she expected her screen to go black as her computer gave up beneath the onslaught. Reaching the end of a particularly scathing paragraph, she hit the return key and was about to launch into a new argument when there was a knock on the door.

She growled under her breath. She was on a roll and didn't want to be interrupted, but a quick glance at the clock told her it might be Jack. Stretching out the kinks in her shoulders, she sighed. She almost hadn't thought he'd bother coming to talk to her. He'd seemed ready to dismiss her earlier, and she'd been prepared to get on her knees and beg. Securing his help was step one in the plan to get to Everest—a task she needed to complete, to honor Olivia's memory and prove that her friend's life had meant something. She got up and went to the door, opening it just enough to peek out. A pair of cocoa brown eyes looked back at her. Through the sliver of space, she saw Jack Farrelly crack a grin. Her pulse skipped, and she had to remind herself she was mad at him.

"Hello," she said, yanking the door all the way open and leaning on the frame so he couldn't get past. She didn't want him under any illusion that he was welcome in her room.

"Hey," he said, more softly than she'd expected.

"Mind if we come in?" Kat asked from somewhere behind him.

Brooke stepped aside, aware that her room was cluttered and probably not anything like the women's bedrooms Jack usually visited.

It doesn't matter. He's not here for that.

He brushed past her, and their chests came within a couple of inches of each other. Her breath caught and she ducked her head to hide her expression. Though he was a broad-shouldered, virile man, who most women were probably attracted to, she didn't want to be lumped amongst the ranks of his admirers. Especially not when he'd forgotten her. How many women did the guy passionately make out with, if they dropped from his mind so easily?

Jack sat on the edge of her bed, and she crossed her arms protectively over her chest. Seeing him there disturbed her, and she pulled out the chair behind the desk because she knew she couldn't concentrate if she joined him. Kat, who had no qualms whatsoever, plunked down on the bed beside him. He glanced around the room and Brooke resisted the urge to squirm. Cataloging his features, she noted the fine sheen of perspiration along his hairline, dampening his chestnut-colored hair. Her fingers wanted to run through those thick, lush locks. She curled them into her palms. Why did she have to find the man so annoyingly attractive?

"How was it?" she asked, although she'd rather not know.

"Good," he replied. "Had a nice time. Didn't run into any problems."

She stifled a sigh. She'd dearly have loved to accompany him. "Glad to hear it."

See, she could be an adult. Kat gave her an encouraging smile.

"Here's what I don't get," Jack said. "If you're not healthy, why do you want to make things worse for yourself by joining my trips? Why do you care so much?"

Brooke fought the pull of his deep, irresistible eyes and rallied her thoughts into some semblance of order. "I'm almost recovered," she told him. "It's very rare these days that I'm unwell." She waited until he nodded, confirming he was actually paying attention, before she continued. "I have a few chronic conditions—like the asthma and hay fever I told you about—and they're a pain in my butt, but they're totally manageable. The other day, on the walk to the cave and back, I felt pretty good. A bit worn out, but nothing compared to how bad I used to be. To be honest, overall, I think I feel better now than I ever have in my life."

Better, and more determined to take advantage of that fact. She nibbled the inside of her lip, afraid to voice her dream, but knowing if there was ever a right time to do so, it was now. She summoned the same courage she'd had to call on countless times before, every time she faced a new and unknown treatment.

"I have a goal. Well, more of a promise to keep, actually, to someone who meant a lot to me. For the first time, I feel like maybe it's possible."

"What's that, Brooke?" Kat asked, leaning forward, eyes alight with interest. "And who did you make the promise to?"

Brooke hesitated. She hadn't spoken this aloud since she

and Olivia had made the vow, afraid she'd be laughed out of the room if she ever did. "Promise you won't think it's silly?"

"I promise," she said.

"I want to go to Everest Base Camp."

She could have heard a pin drop.

"I want to go to Everest Base Camp," she repeated, more firmly. Now that she'd voiced the words once, it became easier. "And I truly believe I can."

"Good for you," Kat said, although Brooke could tell from her tone that she had doubts.

"I need to try. It was something I was going to do with an old friend of mine." She looked at Kat meaningfully. "Olivia."

Kat's expression softened. She knew Brooke had attended the funeral a while back. "Oh, sweetie."

Meanwhile, Jack scrutinized her as if trying to see right into her mind. She held his gaze and let him see whatever he needed to. Finally, he said, "You've got a long way to go."

"I know." Did she ever.

"I can't promise you'll make it that far."

"No one can." The words were hoarse, and she swallowed. "Be straight with me. I don't have my head in the clouds."

A smile curled the edges of his sensual mouth. That smile did funny things to her insides. She tried to ignore its effect on her, feeling oddly like she was suspended in midair while she waited for his verdict. Suddenly, the waiting was too much.

"It's not only for my sake," she said hurriedly. "Or Olivia's." Not that he'd know anything about her friend. "It's for my readers. I have a blog and I want to show people what's possible if they work hard and believe in themselves."

Jack blanched. "You're a blogger?"

She nodded eagerly. "Have been for years. For a while,

the internet was my only connection with the outside world, and I was determined to take ownership of my life however I could."

A little color seemed to return to his cheeks, and he asked cautiously, "What kind of blog is it?"

She shrugged. "Motivational. Aimed at people like me, who have illnesses or aren't as able as the average person."

"That's... admirable."

She sensed he had a hard time saying as much, although she didn't understand why. "Thanks. So, will you help me?"

He nodded. "I will. I like your determination. You'll need to hold onto that." He leaned toward her, his forearms resting on his thighs. "My next session is on Friday, and you're welcome to come."

A grin spread over her face.

"But," he added, holding up a finger, "I call the shots. You have to follow my instructions, even if you don't like them, and we need to have open and honest communication about how you're feeling and what you can handle. I can't have you in my group if you hide things. Do we have a deal?"

"Yes," she exclaimed. "Absolutely."

It wasn't in her nature to let a man like Jack—*especially* Jack—see her weakness, but for the sake of realizing a dream, she could get over that. It was a small hurdle to leap.

"Great." He stood, and she did the same, then backed off quickly when she noticed it put her chest-to-chest with him again. "I'll see you Friday." He paused in the doorway. "Bring your inhaler, your eye drops, whatever medication you need, and for God's sake, bring some decent footwear. Not those silly little pink things you had on the other day."

"Sure." Apparently her vanity hadn't gone unnoticed. "And Jack? Thank you."

He nodded. "Just don't make me regret it."

"I won't."

"Oh, and no photographing me—or anyone else in the group—for your blog."

"Deal."

He left, and Kat started to follow him, but Brooke stopped her.

"Hey, Kitty-Kat, just so you know, I'm really happy for you and Sterling."

Kat's cheeks flushed. "Thanks." She gathered Brooke into a hug. "So am I."

"Will he be moving in?"

"Soon, but we're not in a massive hurry. We want to do this right."

Brooke smiled. "I'm sure you will. I'm glad you're letting yourself be happy."

"Me too. I think it's what Teddy would have wanted." Kat gave her one last squeeze and headed out. "See you at dinner."

When the door shut behind her, Brooke sat at her laptop, opened her blog, and added a new heading.

Brooke v World: Wednesday 5 February

Next Goal: Mt. Everest Base Camp. Bring it on.

JACK'S NERVES were unsettled as he waited in the foyer for Kat. He paced to the window and gazed out over the garden, which was empty except for Tione's border collie, Bella, who was sprawled in one of the last patches of late afternoon sun, and his Chihuahua, Pixie, who was digging in the garden, barely making a dent in the soft earth.

Footsteps sounded behind him and he turned. Kat joined him, wearing a soft smile, her black hair hanging in a ponytail over one shoulder. He waited for a moment to make sure Brooke hadn't followed, then said, "Please tell me she isn't serious about getting to Everest."

Kat sighed and pressed her lips together. "It's the first I've heard of it, but she doesn't tend to say or do anything without thinking it through."

"Come on. You think this isn't some random impulse?" Jack could admit he might have misjudged Brooke because she reminded him of Claudia, but regardless of that, a rational person didn't push herself to exhaustion.

"She's not reckless," Kat said. "More like mule-headed. Once she gets an idea in her mind, she's stubborn as hell, but a lot of people don't notice because she's not in your face about it, she's just quiet and determined and gets things done."

"But she can't think she'll make it all the way there."

The woman was a far cry from being in top shape. He'd even go as far as saying Claudia had more chance of hiking to Everest than Brooke did, and his ex hated anything that required her to sweat or get muddy.

"She does," Kat said. "And don't go getting it in your mind that she's an airhead, either. She's clever. Probably more so than you or me. You know she's doing a PhD, right?"

"Huh." He frowned. "I wouldn't have guessed that." For one thing, he hadn't been sure she was old enough. "What subject?"

"Art history."

Okay, that made sense. His world realigned. He hadn't been entirely off-base—she was a cultured, arty type.

Kat broke into his thoughts. "I hope you meant what you said."

"About what?"

"Helping her."

He swallowed. "Yeah, I did." Kind of. "I doubt she has a

snowball's chance in hell of making it to Everest, but I won't stand in the way of her coming on my trips or doing whatever training she thinks she needs, as long as she's sensible about it." He may not believe it was within her ability, but that didn't mean he wanted to be the reason she lost that spark in her eye.

"Good."

"I'd better be off."

"See you around."

He tipped his head to Kat and wandered outside.

During the drive, he found himself pondering Brooke's declaration, and wondering if she had the slightest idea how much work and planning it would take for her to get to Everest Base Camp. It wasn't the kind of thing a person just decided to do to inspire others, however noble that may be. Perhaps he needed to show her how much dedication it would take. Surely it was better she realize now rather than after she'd put her whole heart and soul into it, only to fall short.

He stopped at Café Oasis to buy a mini quiche for dinner, then went home. Taking his quiche to the outside deck, he ate alone, as per usual, turning over the situation and examining it from different angles. It seemed to him that the kindest thing to do, in the long run, would be to show Brooke what kind of targets she'd need to meet to fulfil her dream. That ought to bring her well and truly back down to earth. She needed to realize mountaineering was not a glamorous pursuit. When the quiche was gone, he grabbed his phone from his pocket and devised a list of tests. Ones that would force her to get real about things. Once he'd finished, he jotted it on a piece of paper and tucked it away.

5

THE 6TH of February was a public holiday, and a large number of tourists visited Haven Bay to surf, bask in the sunshine, and sample the quirky ice cream flavors at The Shack. Subsequently, many locals stayed home or went to the less popular parts of town. First thing that morning, Brooke had called her friend, Kyle, who worked at the library, and arranged to visit his place. She hadn't seen him for a week, and needed a dose of his optimism. As soon as she'd gone public with her long-term goal of reaching Mt. Everest, she'd started having doubts.

Who was she kidding?

Yeah, she was healthier than she'd been in ages, but she was still unfit, unconditioned, and inexperienced. Just look at how tired she'd been after a short hike and a scramble through a cave. Who was she to think she could make it to Nepal? To the highest mountain in the world?

But she'd said it now. Put the words out there in the universe, and she was committed. She couldn't take it back. What's more, she didn't want to. She owed it to Olivia to do as she'd said. She owed it to both of them. But before anything else, she needed to figure out the steps to take to achieve her goal. Once she'd done that, she could break them into manageable chunks. That was why she needed Kyle. Besides being a beacon of hope and never-ending support, he also possessed the kind of mind that thrived on to-do lists and deadlines.

Driving past the beachgoers, she edged around the town square and arrived at his shoebox-sized flat, which was located in a building on the fringe of the commercial area. She hopped out of her car, grabbed her purse, and let herself in. She and Kyle didn't bother with knocking. They had no secrets from each other, and it wasn't as if either of them liked to hang around in their underwear. Even if she had walked in and found him in the nude, it wouldn't be anything she hadn't seen before. The two of them had been roommates during her undergraduate. In fact, she'd moved to the bay because he'd sold her on the healing power of the sea breeze.

"Hey, Kyle." She strolled down the hall. "Where are you?"

"In here," he called from the living room. She followed his voice and found him sitting on the couch, a mug of coffee in his hand and a mound of bacon and eggs on a plate in front of him. He waved to her, swallowed a mouthful, and gestured for her to join him. "Do you want some breakfast?" he asked. "I made extra."

"No, thanks. I already ate." Besides which, cooked breakfasts weren't really her thing. When you'd spent as much time on bed rest as she had, you learned to eat light meals so they didn't go straight to your hips.

He shrugged and helped himself to another spoonful of eggs. "Suit yourself."

Kicking back, Brooke looked at the TV screen. An episode of *Battlestar Galactica* was playing, and they both watched while he finished his breakfast. When he was done, he opened the curtains to let the sunlight in, and tugged off his hoodie, lifting his t-shirt to reveal a strip of toned abdomen that would have surprised her had she not seen his body before. Kyle might be a gaming librarian, but he was a sexy one.

"So," he said, angling his body toward her. "What's up?"

She reached over and grabbed his hands. "I need to borrow some of your undying optimism."

His lips quirked. "Okay, sure thing. What am I being optimistic about?"

She inhaled slowly, then released the breath. "I've decided I want to hike to Everest Base Camp."

He cocked his head. "As in, the Everest that's located in Nepal, on the other side of the world?"

At least he hadn't laughed in her face. "Yeah," she said. "That's the one."

"And when did you decide this?"

She raised a shoulder and dropped it. "I've been thinking about it ever since Olivia passed away. When we were girls, we talked about going together, and thinking about that was something that got me through some hard times. We always knew it was a long shot, but now it's impossible, at least as far as she's concerned. It just struck me that life is so short, you know, and if I want to go, I can't just wait around and expect it to happen." She sighed. "Last night, I blurted it out in front of Kat and Jack, and now I'm committed."

"Why is that a bad thing?" he asked, his tone teasing. He still hadn't laughed. Thank the heavens for Kyle Pride.

"Because I don't know if I can do it," she whispered.

"Of course you can," he said, as if it were really that simple. "You, Brooke Griffiths, can do anything."

She laughed, the sound weak. "Be real, Kyle. I can't even run a mile without stopping for a breather."

"So you'll start small and work your way up." He grinned. "Jog half a mile and walk the rest."

Already, his optimism was infusing her. Her lips curved up.

"That's it," he encouraged her. "That's my girl. Now, tell me, if this were a project you had to do for your thesis, where would you start?"

Her brows knitted together. "I'd break it down, set deadlines for each component, and then take bites out of that cookie until I'd eaten the whole thing."

He nodded. "So, what are you going to do?"

Reclaiming her hands, she pumped her fist. "I'm going to do my research and make a plan. Thanks, Kyle." She gave him a quick hug. "Are you going to be my research buddy?"

"Hell, yeah. I'll grab my computer and let's get to work."

TWO HOURS LATER, they were sitting side by side on the couch, and Brooke had a complete packing list for Everest, which included things like thermal socks, a low temperature sleeping bag, hiking boots, and a hydration bladder. Before now, she'd never even realized that different sleeping bags suited different temperature ranges. They'd also figured out the best time of year to make the trip, and the dates brought the realness of her mission home. Made it feel like something that could actually happen. She stared hard at the screen. October to December, that's when she was hoping to be ready. If not, she'd have to put it off until the following year.

"All right." She rubbed her palms together. "Let's see how hard this is going to be."

Kyle's fingers flew across the keyboard. "I've found a complete itinerary published by *National Geographic*. It looks like you need to be able to walk an average of five hours per day, consistently uphill, for about two weeks, carrying your pack."

Brooke exhaled, her breath whistling between her teeth. A one-hour uphill hike with no bag had exhausted her. "I'm so far from being able to do that, it's insane." She ran a hand through her hair. "Am I crazy?"

Kyle squeezed her knee. "You'll get there."

"But I'll need help. Jack has already promised to assist, but I think it'll take more than just him to get me there."

"That's unlike Jack. You must have been quite persuasive." He emailed her the link and shut off the screen. "But you don't need to worry. You have all your friends behind you. We'll get you there, Brooke. In fact, let's get started on your exercise program right now, with a walk to The Shack."

She giggled. "You want to battle the tourists for ice cream?"

"I don't want to," he said. "But for you, I'm willing to try."

She snorted, then clapped a hand over her mouth, mortified. "Oh, my God."

Laughing, he offered her a hand. She grabbed it and let him hoist her upright. As they left his home, her spirit felt lighter, and her steps were springier.

She was lucky to have a friend like Kyle.

"Is this your first time?" Jack asked the couple who'd booked him to take them rock climbing.

"It is for me," the man—who was slender and balding—replied. "Cameron has been climbing a few times." He grinned wryly. "You might be able to tell, she's the athletic one in our relationship."

Jack glanced at Cameron, a fit brunette who carried

herself with confidence. Yeah, he'd been able to tell. Cameron wouldn't have been out of place working as a guide herself, whereas Darrell, her boyfriend, had a computer tan. Jack studied the woman. She was the kind of person he should date. Someone authentic, who cared more about personality and having fun than maintaining appearances. So why wasn't he attracted to her? Besides the obvious—that being the man he was fitting into a harness. Cameron was the antithesis of Claudia. Of Brooke too, if he were being honest. He shook his head. It seemed he was destined to desire women who'd only hurt him.

Cameron laughed. "Darrell agreed to come because I'm learning squash so we can play together. He had to return the favor."

Jack glanced between them again as he checked Darrell's helmet. It was no business of his, but the couple seemed ill-suited. He doubted they'd last long. They were probably in the honeymoon stage, when they found their partner's differences endearing, but he knew from experience that wouldn't last forever.

"Do you climb often?" he asked.

"Maybe half a dozen times each summer. Not a heap, but enough that I don't get too rusty."

"So you'll be comfortable without much of my help." He checked her harness anyway, because this was his business and he was responsible if anything were to go wrong.

"Yeah," she agreed. "I probably could have taken Darrell out on my own, but I wanted to relax and enjoy myself. We've been together for long enough now that we thought it was time to try each other's hobbies."

"Oh." His brows shot up. "How long have you been together?"

"A little over five years," she said. "And there are some things we enjoy together, but we thought it was time to shake things up a bit and do things we wouldn't usually do together."

Huh. So he'd been mistaken. No honeymoon period here. Was it possible they'd managed to maintain a happy relationship despite their differences? Or were there tensions simmering beneath their smiling exteriors that they kept hidden from view?

"Fair enough," he remarked.

Once they were ready, he steered them to the rock face he preferred beginners start on. "Show me what you've got," he said to Cameron. She rubbed chalk on her palms and moved up the rock, as agile as one of the lizards that darted across the surface from time to time. He nodded approvingly. "You're okay to get yourself back down?"

"Yep."

He turned to Darrell, wondering once again how he'd managed to woo—and hold onto–a woman who was clearly different to him.

"Isn't she amazing?" Darrell asked, admiration in his voice.

Jack didn't answer. "You ready to give it a go?"

Darrell nodded, his jaw squaring with determination. Jack explained how to begin, then kept an eye on him as he falteringly climbed the first two feet. Then he seemed to get stuck. By this time, Cameron had abseiled down the cliff and stood beside Jack.

"There's a handhold to your right," she said, and Darrell clung to the rock with his left hand while his right skimmed the surface, searching for a place to grip. He found the spot she mentioned and held on, digging his foot into a crack while he edged upward.

"You're doing great, honey," Cameron called. "There's a hollow about half a meter above your left foot."

With Cameron's encouragement, he painstakingly made

his way halfway up the cliff, until he was well and truly stumped.

"Good work, mate," Jack yelled to him. "Now, bend your knees, push off the rock face, and I'll belay you down."

When Darrell reached the ground, Cameron hugged him, pressing a kiss to his sweaty cheek, and then released him, beaming. "That was brilliant, babe. I'm so proud of you."

"I think I nearly pissed myself," Darrell said.

Jack resisted the urge to chuckle. He'd never admit such a thing to a woman, especially not one he was hoping to take to bed later. But Cameron just kissed him again. It seemed they were crazy about each other, despite all odds.

"I appreciate you making the sacrifice," she said. "Did you enjoy yourself?"

"If I say no, will you make me do it again anyway?"

"Yes," she said, with a smug grin. "That's the deal."

"Then yeah, it was kind of fun, but my fingers are cramping."

The couple continued chatting while Jack scoped out the next spot for them. They continued for another couple of hours, by which point Darrell looked like he might collapse.

Later, Jack was driving to his office when he caught sight of a shock of blonde hair atop a slender body at the beachside pavilion. The way the woman's neck curved into her shoulder was familiar, but it took him a moment to place it. *Brooke.*

He'd become so accustomed to seeing her only at Sanctuary that he'd forgotten she had a life outside of the lodge. And right now, she was clearly enjoying it, with an ice cream in one hand, strolling side by side with Kyle Pride. They were near enough to each other that their arms brushed as they walked, and Jack's fists clenched around the steering wheel. Kyle was talking, waving his hands, the most animated Jack could recall seeing him, and Brooke was smiling—a wide, open smile that lit her face and hit him with the force of a punch in the gut. He'd never seen her smile like that. Nor had he realized how much he wanted to.

There was a lot to like about Brooke, and apparently Kyle had already figured that out. The guy ducked his head and licked her ice cream, a particularly intimate move. The kind a lover might make. Jealousy flared, hot and sharp. Jack wanted to stop the car, stomp over there and drag Brooke a respectable distance away. While it made no sense, he couldn't get over the feeling that Kyle was encroaching on his territory by being with her, when in actuality, it was none of his business.

Jack sighed. He shouldn't be disappointed. He had no right to be. And yet, he was.

"Don't be a dipshit," he muttered to himself. "She's all wrong for you anyway."

6

BROOKE V WORLD: Friday 7 February

It's official. I'm aiming for Everest—a journey in honor of my dear friend Olivia—and today is the first step. Jack is letting me join his outdoor adventure sessions to build fitness and learn new skills, and Kyle has helped me put together a plan of action. I'll need to do other things to prepare as well, like get a gym membership—shock horror—but today, I'm on my way.

Wish me luck. XX

THIS TIME, Brooke dressed for her afternoon trip with more care. She wore sturdier shoes and practical clothing. She wanted Jack to see that she was taking his advice seriously. She slathered on sunscreen so she wouldn't burn, which she tended to do easily, courtesy of her fair complexion, and tied her hair in a tight ponytail. Finally, she filled her water bottle and placed it in a backpack along with her inhaler, pain meds, allergy pills, insect bite cream, a spare sweater, and two granola bars. Then she headed down the hall to the foyer.

"Hi." She greeted Jack with a smile. He was leaning

against a wall looking rugged and manly and delicious. Heat curled through her, and she tried not to let it show on her face. The last thing she needed was for him to think she had a crush on him—especially after the beating her ego had taken when she realized he didn't have a clue who she was.

"Hi, Brooke."

At least he'd remembered her name. She scanned him from head to toe, noticing boots that looked like they'd seen a few summers, shorts that stopped at mid-thigh, and a camouflage t-shirt that somehow made his skin seem even more deeply tanned. Touching the side of her mouth, she confirmed she wasn't drooling, and mentally scolded herself for checking him out. He was here in a professional capacity. But oh boy, did he fill those clothes nicely.

"You don't have any gear," she said, as if to justify why she'd been staring at him.

"Won't need it today," he replied. "We're walking up to the waterfall."

Oh. She deflated. Here she was, ready for adventure, and they were going somewhere she'd been a dozen times before.

"You're disappointed?" he asked, crossing his arms over his burly chest.

"No," she said quickly. "The waterfall is great."

His thick brows drew together. "You've been up there?"

"I've been to the waterfall pool, yes."

A cocky grin crossed his face. "Well, then, you haven't done the waterfall the way I do it. Prepare to have your mind blown."

"Really?" She sounded dubious. She couldn't help it.

He winked. At *her*. Brooke swallowed. Jack Farrelly had winked at her. Now, her mind was blown.

"Just you wait," he said. "You'll see what I mean."

The door to the dining hall opened and they both

glanced over. The Kathmandu couple came through, with Kat right behind them. When she saw Brooke and Jack standing together, she stopped short, then came to them with purposeful strides.

"Please tell me you two are getting along," she said. "I don't want to play mediator today."

"We are," Brooke assured her. "Don't worry about us, Kat. We're going to have a great time. Aren't we, Jack?" She bumped him with her elbow.

"Yes," he agreed, sounding less than confident. "Of course."

"Good." Kat's voice was laden with suspicion, and while it was sweet that she worried, Brooke could take care of herself. "There's one more person joining, I think," she continued. "Tina—she's an artist," she added for Jack's benefit. "She's looking for a little inspiration."

Jack muttered something under his breath but both women paid him no heed.

"Tina is more than welcome to use my wall for practice," Brooke offered. "I adore what she did last time." While she'd been laid up in bed with chronic fatigue, Tina had painted a mural of a Nordic village scene across one of her walls. It was peaceful. Serene. Brooke had watched as it came to life, one stroke at a time, and had dreamed that she'd be able to visit that village one day.

"Thank you," a woman said from behind them. Brooke turned. While they'd been talking, Tina had arrived. "I'm pleased you liked it."

"How could I not? It's breathtaking. But if you want to cover it up and start over, you're more than welcome to."

"I'll keep that in mind."

"If this is all of us, shall we head out?" Jack asked, leading the way outside. They trailed through the garden, past Tione's cabin, and into the forest. As they walked, he explained that their first stop would be at the waterfall, twenty minutes up the track.

First stop? Brooke frowned. He hadn't mentioned a second stop to her earlier. At the base of the hill, she paused and drew on her inhaler, in preparation for the climb. She'd made the trek to the waterfall a few times over the years, but it never paid to get complacent and she didn't want to risk anything going wrong.

She could totally handle this.

And the fact that no little old ladies were here to dote on her? So much the better.

She fell into step behind the Kathmandu couple—whose names she'd learned were Sylvia and Brian—but stayed in front of Tina, who was meandering along, pausing to stare into the distance or examine patterns on tree bark that no one else could see. Her calves burned, and she loved it. When they reached the waterfall, she rested her hands on her hips and tilted her head back, sucking in breaths. She felt *good*. Once her breathing evened out, she wandered to the mossy edge of the pool and dipped a finger in the water. It was cool, but not freezing.

"Want to see where it comes from?" Jack's rumbly voice did funny things to her insides.

"It comes from the mountains, right?" she asked.

He raised his eyes to the sky. "Technically, yeah, Little Miss PhD." It was the first time he'd given away the fact he knew anything about her. She should be annoyed to learn that he'd asked around, but instead, pleasure tingled low in her belly. If he was asking around, he must be interested in her, at least to some extent. "But there's also a tarn on the ledge above our heads, which is where the waterfall begins."

Brooke's mouth fell open. "Are you kidding me?"

She knew from books that a tarn was a small mountain lake. Loosely, she assumed he meant that the waterfall was fed by a high-altitude lake. Or, more likely, based on what she knew of the terrain, a large pond.

"Hand on heart," he said, doing just that. "I'm one hundred percent serious. Want to see?"

"Is Spock a Vulcan?" When he looked baffled by the *Star Trek* reference, she rolled her eyes. "Uh, *yes!*" Had she just been thinking she was worn out? Pfft. She rallied.

"Great." An emotion flickered in his dark eyes. One that intrigued her.

No, don't be intrigued by his panty-melting hotness. He's a means to an end. And he didn't even remember who you were.

But heck, she wanted to lick him like he was her favorite chocolate bar. A bead of sweat trickled down a cord of his throat and she stared at it, mesmerized. It would be so easy to lean forward, flick her tongue out and taste it.

Taste his sweat? Whoa, girl.

She should be disgusted. Unfortunately, disgust wouldn't explain the pulse between her legs. She looked down, hoping her expression hadn't given her away.

"Is everyone up for a bit of a climb?" he asked the group. The answer was a resounding yes. "It's a bit of a scramble," he continued. "And it's quite steep. There are times when you'll need to use your hands as well as your legs to keep stable. If anyone wants to stop or slow down, that's perfectly fine, just yell out. Communication is key. Got it?"

"Yes, sir." Brooke wrapped her hands around her backpack straps so she didn't salute. This was not the time to give him cheek.

"Sylvia, I want you to go first," he said. "Brian will be behind you, then Tina and Brooke. I'll be the tail-end Charlie so I can keep an eye on you all. Take your time. It's not a race."

With that, he dropped back while Sylvia started up the narrow trail he'd pointed out, which was nearly indistinguishable from the surrounding bush. A "game trail," he called it. Brooke watched Sylvia's progress, trying to determine the best places to put her feet.

A moment later, a voice at her ear said softly, "Is there anything in your bag you'll need for the hike?"

She shivered, the intimacy of his breath on the back of her neck startling her. "Y-yes. Lots of things."

"Anything you can't live without for an hour?"

She sidestepped to put some space between them. "My inhaler."

"Pass me your bag," he instructed. "Leave everything else behind. I'll keep it in my pocket in case you need it, but I don't want you carrying anything you don't need."

She didn't argue, although this felt a whole lot like being coddled. She handed over her backpack and he shouldered it, then it was her turn to climb.

She could sense Jack behind her, and stumbled when her foot landed on a patch of moss. She heard his quick intake of breath, but he didn't say anything, and for that, she was grateful. Slowly, she put one foot in front of the other—onward and upward—and forced herself not to look back. His gaze burned into the spot between her shoulder blades, and she didn't need to look to know that he was watching her as closely as an unpinned grenade. She promised herself she wouldn't do anything to justify his caution.

Every few minutes, the group stopped to rest. None of them spoke, but when the brush became sparser, they paused for a while longer. Brooke planted her butt firmly on the ground and gazed out over Sanctuary and the beach. They'd gained enough altitude for her to see the roof of the lodge and the chimney of Tione's cabin, but not enough to make out the gardens or any people who might be lingering in them. After a while, they continued. Finally, at the top of their climb, she hauled herself over the edge of a thinly vegetated ledge and lay on her back, gasping.

"Everything all right?" Tina asked, squatting next to her.

"I'm fine," Brooke huffed. "Just communing with nature."

"Okaaay." She sounded doubtful. "You need anything?"

Brooke shook her head, too puffed to talk. She watched a fluffy white cloud glide overhead and focused on it while her breathing settled. Then she sat up. The world spun as vertigo overcame her. Squeezing her eyes shut, she clutched her head. When she opened them again, a calloused hand had materialized in front of her. She stared at it blankly.

"Take it," Jack ordered, his voice gruff. She grabbed the hand and he hoisted her to her feet, steadying her when she wobbled. "How are you doing?"

She considered smoothing over the truth, but decided it wouldn't be in her best interest to do so. "Not terrible, but a little borderline."

He nodded, and she wished she could read his thoughts. "Thanks for your honesty."

"No problem."

He squeezed her hand once then released it and strode over to Tina, who was standing precariously near the edge, looking out at the view. The bout of vertigo passed, and Brooke headed in the other direction, more interested in the beautifully clear tarn. It was shallow, probably no more than three feet deep, but its transparency made the layer of water appear so thin, she guessed she could reach straight in and grab a handful of pebbles from the bottom.

Sylvia joined her, a hand over her eyes to shield them from the sun. "I've never seen anything like it."

"It's magical," Brooke agreed. "The kind of place that looks like it hasn't changed since the first people moved here. It looks untouched, you know?"

Sylvia nodded. "It's remarkable. I almost feel like it would be wrong to disturb the water because it seems so pure."

Brooke agreed wholeheartedly. Crazy to think this place had been nearby all this time and she'd never known. She could have gone her whole life without seeing it, without feeling the beauty of this place in her heart, filling it so full she wanted to sing and cry and dance.

This. This was what she wanted for herself. A lifetime of discovery and wonder.

"Some of the cleanest water in New Zealand."

She tilted her face up to Jack's, and found him frowning down at her.

"Are you sure you're okay?" he asked. "You're not gonna flake out on me, are you?"

She touched the corner of her eye and felt the wetness there. "No," she told him. "I'm wonderful. Truly. Thanks so much for bringing us here."

***

JACK DIDN'T KNOW what to make of Brooke. Not only had she been open with him about how she was doing, but now she looked like she might cry and he had no idea why. Surely if exhaustion was going to overwhelm her, it would have happened halfway up the side of the hill.

Even more disconcerting than her tears was her expression as she stared into the water, as though she'd never seen anything so beautiful. Of course, it could have just been that she had dust in her eye, but he didn't think so. In this, at least, she differed to Claudia, who'd have had her phone out, snapping photos within seconds—or demanding someone else take them so she could be front and center of every shot.

"You're welcome," he said, realizing she expected a response. "Another five minutes, then we'll head back. Can you manage that?"

She nodded. As he turned away, she snagged his arm. "Hey, Jack?"

Her hand was small on his bare elbow and his skin seemed extra-sensitized to her touch. His throat went dry and he swallowed with difficulty. "What?"

Her big blue eyes blinked at him, and he realized he'd been too abrupt. What was wrong with him, reacting to her this way? It wasn't her fault he was inconveniently attracted to her, and that his hormones weren't getting his cease-and-desist messages.

He softened his tone. "What is it?"

"Is anybody allowed up here?" she asked. "I mean, could I come back here without you, or do you have a special permit that gives you permission to come here?"

She wanted to come back? To huff and puff her way to the top of the ridge again? He was tempted to lie. He didn't want her putting herself at risk, but she could find the information with a simple Google search.

"It's open to the public," he told her. "Most people don't know it's here, that's all."

She beamed. "Awesome. Thank you."

He was starting to get sick of her thanking him. Especially when he'd devised a list of exercises intended to knock some sense into her about her physical capability—or lack thereof.

Turning away, he called out, "Another two minutes everyone. Take your photos, have a drink, and we'll head back down."

He waited at the head of the trail while the small group assembled. Brian began descending first, since he'd come equipped with hiking poles to help him find the most stable places to put his feet. Once again, Jack took up the rear. As Brooke passed him on her way down, he noticed some of the color had leached from her face, and he kept close to her, but once they reached the flat, she started chatting with Tina and seemed to regain her energy. He was glad. He didn't like the thought of her wearing herself out.

When they emerged from the forest into the sun-soaked garden, he farewelled the others in the group, but asked Brooke to stay behind as he returned her backpack. They sat cross-legged on the lawn and she plucked daisies, twining them together, even though her eyes were visibly watering and her nose was sniffly.

"I've been thinking about your situation," he told her.

"Yeah?" She sounded cautious, and he couldn't blame her.

He cleared his throat to dislodge a lump. "Actually, I came up with some challenges for you, if you're serious about making it to Base Camp."

She dropped the daisy chain and gave him her full attention. "I'm perfectly serious."

God, those eyes. Bright and intense. If she ever wanted to manipulate a man, all she'd need to do was widen them and pout. He shook himself.

"Good." He took the list from his pocket and scanned it. "Number one: complete half an hour on a stair climber wearing a thirty-pound pack. Number two: walk seven miles with a ten-pound weight vest. Number three: jog four miles without stopping." He raised his eyes. "It's important that you have good endurance." She nodded, but the rosy hue had vanished from her cheeks. "Number four: swim half-a-mile without stopping. You need to work on regulating your breathing, and swimming is one of the best ways to do that. Number five—"

"How many things are on this list?" she interrupted,

fiddling with the daisy chain again, and avoiding eye contact. Her earlier blind optimism was gone, and he felt like an asshole.

"Ten," he said. "But it's just a starting point."

She nodded and held out her hand. "May I read it?"

He handed the paper over and watched as she grew more and more pale, but then her chin jutted out and her shoulders squared, that stubborn streak rearing its head.

"Where would you recommend I start?"

"Uh..." The question was so unexpected he didn't have an answer. The way she'd been crumpling in on herself, he'd expected her to tell him his list was crazy. "If I were you, I'd start with a short hike."

That was the easiest item on his list, and something he didn't expect her to particularly struggle with.

"Okay." Her tone was decisive. "What should I do to prepare?"

He wracked his brain. "You'll want a new pair of boots, but before you invest in those, I'd suggest you make an appointment with Bex at The Hideaway and get her to write an exercise plan for you. She can help you build up muscle in your legs and shoulders."

"True. I'll do that tomorrow."

Shit, this conversation was not going as he'd intended. He'd expected her to be daunted. Had prepared himself for a heart to heart about starting with small goals before leaping to the big ones.

"That's a great idea," he said. She smiled, and he found himself adding, "Maybe we can do a few private trips together when I don't have anything else booked."

"*Really*?" She lit up like someone had turned on a lamp inside her soul. She was radiant, and he felt it like a kick in the solar plexus. "You'd do that for me?"

He wanted to bury his face in his hands. Why had he

opened his big stupid mouth and made an offer like that? He could hardly take it back. Not when she was looking at him like she was a five-year-old and he'd promised her a new kitten.

"Yeah, I guess so." He didn't like the way her smile made him feel. Getting up, he brushed himself off. "I'd better get going. Bye, Brooke."

Without a backward glance, he left, wondering why it was that he couldn't behave like a normal person around this woman.

7

―――――

CONFUSED by Jack's abrupt exit, Brooke glanced around to confirm that no one had chased him away. Nope. Weird. She reread the list of challenges he'd given her. Some would be very difficult. Thirty minutes on a stair climber with a thirty-pound bag? She could barely manage five minutes without a weight last time she'd tried, which had been a good eighteen months ago. But she wouldn't let this list defeat her. She'd known achieving her mission wouldn't be easy, and now she had a series of steps to get her there. Nothing motivated her like the satisfaction of crossing something off a list. Except, perhaps, the satisfaction of proving someone wrong. She'd spent her whole life doing that, and didn't intend to stop now. Especially not when her legion of readers were counting on her to pave the way and show them what they were capable of.

She made her way to her bedroom, unloaded her backpack, and tidied her gear away. Then she shrugged into a light jersey and returned to the garden with her phone, tapping in Bex's number. While the phone rang, she plucked weeds from amongst the roses.

"Hi, Brooke," Bex said when she answered.

"Hey!" Brooke winced at the high note in her voice and dialed it back a notch. "I have a favor to ask. I'd like some help with a personal training program."

"Okay, sure thing. Have you run this by a doctor?"

"Yes, months ago, and it's fine, as long as someone monitors me. What time does Izzy go to bed?" Izzy was Bex's epically cute diva of a daughter. Six-years-old and enough sass to give any Hollywood leading lady a run for her money. "Perhaps I can come over and we can talk?"

"Better idea," Bex said. "I'm teaching an art class at Sanctuary tomorrow. I can come over early, drop Izzy off with Shane and Hunter for DIY Saturday, and we can catch up then."

Brooke would rather do it tonight, but she also didn't want to be pushy. "That sounds great."

Bex chuckled, the sound low and husky. "Girl, the best things come to those who wait."

Apparently, her low-key act wasn't fooling anyone. "If you say so. I'll see you tomorrow. Kiss that sweet girl of yours for me."

"Bye, now."

They hung up and Brooke stayed in the garden for a while longer, until it was time for dinner. She inserted herself into a group of travelers—the better to distract herself—and later worked on her thesis before bed. Unfortunately, it didn't seem to matter how tired her body or her mind was, she was too worked up about the coming day to fall asleep.

JACK WAS the last to arrive at Logan's apartment above The Den for poker night. Seated around the table were Logan, Sterling, Tione, Shane, and Kyle. Logan, with his shaggy mane of gold hair, owned the pub and was Jack's best friend. Shane taught at the local school, and was permanently frazzled. Jack dropped into the empty chair between Shane and Kyle—Logan's younger brother. The men fell silent.

"What is it?" he asked, glancing from one face to another.

Logan cleared his throat. "We were just congratulating Sterling on how well things are going with Kat," he said, looking awkward.

Oh. Suddenly the furtive expressions and lowered voices made sense. They feared he'd take it badly because he'd never made a secret of the fact that he wanted a chance with Kat if she was ever on the market. Fortunately, he was long past any misguided thoughts of he and Kat as a couple. They had a lot in common and got along well, but the truth was, she didn't set him on fire. Not like her frustratingly unsuitable friend did.

"Yeah, congrats," he said, reaching out to grab Sterling's hand and give it a brisk shake. "Good for you. You'd better treat her well."

"I will," Sterling said, expression earnest. He'd changed so much since the first time he'd come to poker night, all closed off and icy. "I know how lucky I am."

Tione clapped him on the shoulder. "He also knows that he'll answer to us if he doesn't. Right, mate?"

"It won't come to that," Kyle said. "He knows a good thing when he's got it."

"Great." Logan held up the pack of cards. "Now that the celebration is over, who's dealing?"

Shane took them and started shuffling. "You're seriously not bothered about Kat and Sterling?" he asked Jack, quietly enough to avoid being heard by anyone else. Not that they were listening. Logan was handing out beers while Tione emptied bags of popcorn and pretzels into bowls.

Jack shrugged. "Nah, I'm really not. Shocker, right?"

Shane smiled. "Glad to hear it. Couldn't tell if you were putting on a brave face."

"Can we not talk about our feelings please?"

"You'd rather just grunt and drink beer?"

"Uh, yeah."

"Suit yourself." Shane dealt the cards, and Jack and Kyle laid out the small and big blind. Then the game began. Three hands later, only Kyle and Sterling remained in play. Giving into impulse, Jack finally asked the question he'd been dying to since he arrived.

"Hey, Kyle, I saw you out with that pretty blonde the other day. Is she your girlfriend?"

Four pairs of eyes shifted to Kyle, who stared at Jack in the strangest way. Almost like he could see right into his mind.

"You mean Brooke?" he asked.

Jack sensed Tione peering at him and ignored it. "That's right."

"We're not dating," Kyle said. "We're just friends."

Just friends. Yeah, how many times had he heard that before? Usually when one of the people in question had been hopelessly friend-zoned by the other. He wondered, in this case, who'd friend-zoned who.

"You seemed pretty close."

"We're *close* friends," Kyle said, his gaze becoming wary. "We're both addicted to sci-fi shows, so we like to watch them together." Some of the tension eased from Jack's shoulders, then Kyle added, "And we did share a place for a while, which is a surefire way to either cement a friendship or end it."

They'd lived together? Why hadn't he heard about this? Surely he'd have known if Kyle was rooming with a woman. Heck, the whole town would have known.

"Are you pulling my leg?"

Kyle's head tilted to the side and he studied Jack. Behind his wire-framed glasses, it was impossible to tell what he was thinking. "Why would I do that?"

"For the hell of it," Tione suggested.

"Brooke and I roomed at university," Kyle explained. "We were in the same hall of residence and a group of us moved in with each other afterward."

"Kyle, it's your turn," Shane prompted. Kyle called, and so did Sterling.

"Kyle's playing the long game," Logan said, snatching a handful of pretzels and crunching into them. "The *really* long game."

"I'm not playing the long game," Kyle muttered as he turned over his cards.

"Then why did you forbid me from making a move on her?" Logan demanded. "Wasn't that you staking your claim?"

Jack's stomach lurched and his beer bottle slipped from his grip. He caught it before it hit the floor, and when he looked up, Kyle was staring at him again.

"You know," Kyle said, not taking his eyes off Jack, "maybe you're right. She's an awesome girl. Beautiful, too."

Logan swilled beer and nodded. "If I had a friend who looked like her and was half as sweet, I'd snatch her up before someone else did."

"Good point, man," Kyle said, as if the thought had never crossed his mind. "You're right. I should take a shot with her."

Jack ground his back teeth together. How could any man be friends with Brooke and not want to touch her, kiss her, or taste her? He couldn't, simple as that. Which meant that Kyle really *was* playing the long game, and Jack, with his stupid questions, might have just pushed him into action.

How typical. He'd accidentally encouraged another man to ask out the girl he was lusting after. He cracked his knuckles and forced his jaw to unclench. Tione frowned at him.

"What?" Jack snapped.

"Nothing." Tione held his palms up in a gesture of peace. Jack glared at him, then glared at Kyle for good measure. Kyle held his gaze with something a lot like defiance. What was that about?

"Sterling, what have you got?" Shane asked.

Sterling turned over his cards, and everyone groaned. He'd won, as was becoming the norm. They continued playing for a while, and no one mentioned Brooke again. Jack drank more than usual, determined to wipe the image of her flushed face this afternoon from his memory, and determined not to care if Kyle decided to pursue her. She was all wrong for him anyway—she had a *blog* for God's sake, and that alone made her far too similar to Claudia for his peace of mind. He wasn't about to chase after her because of a short-term infatuation. Especially not when she hadn't given any indication she wanted him to.

By the time they wrapped up, he was unsteady as he staggered down the stairs and made the short walk home.

8

———

SINCE BROOKE HAD BEEN TOO excited to sleep, she was up at dawn. She made herself a coffee, reheated one of Tione's muffins from yesterday's breakfast, and dressed in leggings and a tank top. Then she headed outside and inhaled a lungful of fresh morning air.

"What a beautiful day," she said, to no one in particular.

Bella wandered across the lawn and Brooke knelt to ruffle her fur and scratch the scruff of her neck, her favorite place to be petted.

"Good girl," she crooned. "Do you want to come for a walk with me?"

She knocked on Tione's door and told him she was taking Bella up to the waterfall. He grunted something unintelligible in response. She grinned. Yesterday had been the men's weekly poker night and he was usually a little worse for wear the next morning. She and Bella started into the forest together. Her muscles were stiff, and it was slow going, but she persisted and after ten minutes, they'd loosened up enough for her to enjoy herself.

Dawn in the forest was a glorious experience. Birds tweeted and chirped from above, and crepuscular insects and animals—those that were active at the beginning and end of the day—rustled in the undergrowth. Light filtered through the branches and speckled the track with patches of gold. It felt like a new beginning.

She sat beside the waterfall pool while Bella leapt in, spraying water everywhere. The border collie's head broke the surface and she paddled across the pond, staying well away from the waterfall, emerging on the other side to shake herself dry. She sniffed a few rocks, then trotted into the bush. Brooke wasn't worried about her straying. Bella probably knew the way to Sanctuary better than she did. Tione never bothered to keep her fenced in, and she still found her way back to him every night.

Eventually, Brooke rose and headed back. A moment later, a twig cracked, and then Bella rejoined her. Once at Sanctuary, she left the dog in the garden and went to her room, where she decided to investigate how to build her core strength. She switched on her computer and watched a demonstration video about how to do a prone hold. It looked easy enough. She set a timer for three minutes, assumed the position, raised her knees from the floor, and flattened her back. Almost immediately, her abdominal muscles started to burn. Squeezing her eyes shut, she held the position until she didn't think she could stand it any longer, then opened them. Twenty seconds had passed. Apparently, her core needed a lot of strengthening.

Her phone rang, and she dropped out of the prone hold with a sigh of relief. Excellent timing.

"Good morning," she said into the speaker.

"You're welcome," Kyle replied enigmatically.

"Huh?"

"You owe me," he continued, as she shifted onto the bed and kicked her feet up. "Last night, Jack was angling for information about you. I think he was trying to work out if we're a couple."

Her heart gave a skip and a hop. What would have given Jack that idea, and why would he care?

"I said we weren't, but I may have given him the impression I was interested in you, so if you could just go along with that and hang on my every word, it would be great."

She hid her face in a pillow and groaned. "Why would you do that?"

"Because it seemed like he was trying to scope you out."

She straightened. "I think you misread the situation. He couldn't be less interested in me if he tried. Even if, by some miracle, he was, he's not going to do anything about it now that he thinks you and I might be together."

Kyle laughed, and her hands twitched with the urge to strangle him. "I beg to differ. Men love a bit of healthy competition."

She gaped. "Excuse me? I'm a woman, not some trophy for you and your friends to arm-wrestle over."

He stopped laughing. "I know. You're an intelligent, classy woman with good taste in friends."

Classy? That was pushing it. He'd seen her shoveling lime-swirl ice cream into her mouth while wearing fluffy slippers and a baggy hoody, her hair unwashed and eyes red-rimmed after a breakup. How could he possibly consider *that* classy?

"Whatever," she muttered.

"You're not really annoyed with me," he said with the confidence of a longtime friend. "You should come over for Game of Thrones later. It's been a while since we watched season two."

She bit her lip. "Much as I'd like to, I'm busy today. I'm seeing Bex about a workout plan and I'm falling behind on my thesis. Maybe we could do something in a couple of days?"

"You're on. Hey, what do you say we have a public outing? Get Jack's attention. Make him jealous."

She rolled her eyes. "You're being ridiculous. He's not interested in me." Pain pinched at her chest even as she tried to tell herself she didn't care. "Anyway, I'm not the type to play silly jealousy games, so drop it, okay?"

"Fine," he grumbled. "It would just be nice if one of us were seeing some action."

Inwardly, she sighed. She couldn't disagree with that. "You're more likely to get action than me, hot librarian."

***

Bex studied Brooke from above, mirth dancing in her eyes. "Brooke doing a sit-up. That's something I never thought I'd see."

Brooke groaned midway through and collapsed onto the floor. She plucked at her tank top, which was plastered to her chest, and tried to let her skin breathe. Everything was sweaty, even her hair.

"Heeeelp," she pleaded. "I have zero core strength." She tried to get up, but her legs wobbled, tired from the walk earlier. "Okay, make that zero strength anywhere."

Bex chuckled and helped her to her feet. "What else is new? And why the sudden interest in an exercise plan?"

Brooke lowered herself, bit by bit, onto a seat and swung around to face her friend. "Have I said you look great today?"

To be fair, Bex always looked good. It was the perk of having a flawless bronze complexion, a fit body and lustrous black hair. Even when she was worn out after a full day of work and single-mothering, she possessed a radiance other women could only dream of.

"Don't change the subject. You're up to something, I can smell it. Spill the beans."

"I think what you smell is sweat. Maybe a little dirt, too."

Bex crossed her arms. "I'm a mum, Brooke. Don't think you can play coy with me."

Brooke took a breath. She needed to just blurt it out. In theory, the more often she said it, the easier it would become. "I want to go to Mount Everest Base Camp."

She waited for Bex to laugh, or for her brow to furrow in concern as Kat's had, but instead she hummed deep in her throat and said, "Good for you, girlfriend. That's awesome."

Brooke stared. "You don't think I'm deluding myself?"

"Hell, no." She held a hand up for a high five, and Brooke obliged. Their palms smacked together loudly. "I think that's a kickass plan and I'm totally on board."

Relief made Brooke giddy, and her heart felt like it had expanded so much it pressed against the inside of her ribcage. She grabbed Bex's hand and squeezed. "Thank you."

Bex smiled, her lips curving mischievously. "Hey, don't thank me yet. Thank me when I get your cute tush to Nepal."

Brooke's eyes watered, ready to spill over, and she blinked. She hadn't realized how much it meant to have someone accept her dream without hesitation. "I could kiss you, Rebecca Cane."

"Please do. It would be the closest I've gotten to sex in years."

"And the moment is over." They both laughed. "What do I need to do?" Brooke asked, turning serious.

"First, you need to make sure your health is the best it possibly can be. Listen to your body—it will know when you're pushing too hard. But," she cautioned, "you do need to push to a certain extent."

"Right, got it. Push a moderate amount."

"Just like Goldilocks." When Brooke looked at her quizzically, she explained, "We were reading *Goldilocks and the Three Bears* last night. Anyway, the point is, it will be hard work. Are you up for the challenge?"

"Yes." She'd never been more sure of anything in her life.

"Then that's all I need to know." Bex's fingers drummed on the desktop as she thought. "Come by the gym next week and I'll do some tests to see what your baseline fitness is."

"Bad," Brooke answered. "It's very bad."

Bex shrugged. "You've got to start somewhere. I'll put together some ideas for a workout regime, but I'll need to do a little research first." Her grin widened. "I'm glad you called me."

"Me too. And I'm glad Jack suggested it."

Bex's eyes narrowed, dark and glinting. "Did he? I didn't think the two of you had much to do with each other."

"Oh, we don't," Brooke said quickly, her voice telltale high. "He's just helping me a little."

"Jack Farrelly doesn't 'just help' people. He isn't exactly a social butterfly."

Brooke's cheeks heated more the longer Bex watched her without blinking. "Maybe he's turning over a new leaf."

"I wouldn't be so sure about that. Be careful with him, babe."

"Don't worry. We won't end up stranded on a mountain-side somewhere."

"That's not what I meant."

"*Mummy!*" a little girl shrieked.

Bex shot to her feet. "I've got to go. Drop by the gym, okay?"

Jack slung one leg over the edge of his sea kayak and cold water sloshed his feet as he found the sandy ground and stood. He dragged the kayak onto a dry section of beach and grabbed the towel he'd left with his shoes, wiping the moisture from his legs, and the sweat and dried salt from his face. His pocket buzzed and he ignored it, tipping back his water bottle and draining it in a few mouthfuls. Being out on the ocean could dehydrate a man something wicked.

His phone buzzed again, and he answered. "Hi."

"Hey there." The voice was female. Young and perky. Brooke.

Pleasure suffused him, and he refused to examine the reason why. "Hey, yourself."

Not a good idea to flirt, jackass. She's a bad match for you. Anyway, Kyle wants her.

Yet here she was, on the phone with him—not Kyle.

"I talked to Bex like you suggested," she told him, apparently unfazed when he didn't ask how she was or offer up any other pleasantries. "I'm going to see her later in the week to get an exercise plan, and she's really positive about it." She sounded upbeat and excited. Jack grinned despite himself. "Thanks so much for mentioning her, she really motivated me. I'm going to nail this exercise thing."

Spoken like someone who'd never seen the inside of a gym. He couldn't help but admire the way she kept bouncing back, each time more optimistic than the last. The limitations she was working within would put many people off, but not her. She was talking a million miles an hour and ready to take on the world.

Perhaps Brooke Griffiths—he'd learned her last name from Tione—had more stickability, or outright stubbornness, than he'd given her credit for. She wouldn't be easily swayed, and damned if that wasn't an attractive trait in a woman.

"What will you start with?"

She laughed, and he loved the sound of it, easy and care-free. The laugh of a person unburdened by life's difficulties. *But she's not*, he reminded himself. She'd had heart surgery, for crying out loud. It couldn't have been an easy road to healing, but she still found it within herself to laugh like she'd never known hardship. Shit, she'd been through more than him and was only a fraction as cynical.

"Truthfully, I'm not sure," she said. "I tried to work on my core today and that was a dismal failure."

I'd like to work on your core.

"I doubt my legs are any better, based on the way they feel after walking to the waterfall, and I can't remember the last time I used my arms for anything more arduous than gardening, so it'll be equally challenging wherever I decide to start."

"You should ease into it." Listen to him, dispensing advice left, right, and center. Shouldn't he be trying to talk her down so she wouldn't be disappointed if she failed? But his traitorous mouth wasn't done yet. "I'm not working tomorrow. How would you like to come for a short hike?"

He heard a quick intake of breath. This was the part where she should turn him down, for both their sakes. Surely she couldn't actually want to spend time with him. He'd acted like a jerk toward her, and he wasn't a great catch on his best day. If he hadn't already known that, Claudia had sure as hell hammered the message home.

"He's just so gauche," she'd confessed to her friend on the night he'd discovered how she'd made a mockery of him in front of hundreds of thousands of people. "But the project is coming along nicely. Notice the haircut? Next, I'll work on getting him clean-shaven, and then focus on his clothes." She'd giggled. "How much plaid can one man own? But he has potential. I just need to bust through a few layers of country. You'll see. I'm going to work a freaking miracle."

He'd confronted her immediately after to ask what she'd been talking about, and the answer had made him sick.

"Seriously?" Brooke's question jolted him out of the memory. "That would be amazing. I'd love to. Are you sure?"

No. "Yes."

"Thank you so much. I can't wait."

"I'll pick you up at ten." He hung up and stared at the phone, utterly baffled. He'd lost all ability to resist as far as she was concerned. Muttering an oath, he powered the phone off so he didn't do anything else stupid. Then he sank to the ground with a groan and rested his forehead on his knees. He needed to get a grip. However much he genuinely liked Brooke, his heart had to stay out of it.

If he gave in to his attraction, she could well become Claudia 2.0, and he didn't know if his self-confidence could survive that. He'd be better to stick with women he knew he was on a level footing with, both socially and physically. Besides, he wasn't built for a normal, civilized life, and Brooke wasn't built for the wild. This had disaster written all over it. But regardless of everything, a little compartment in a corner of his heart looked forward to seeing her, and it refused to be subdued.

9

———

Laying out the last of her supplies on the bed, Brooke examined them one final time.

Water bottle? Check.

Snacks? Check.

Electrolyte powder? Check.

Inhaler? Check.

Antihistamines? Check.

Emergency kit? Check.

Never mind that the likelihood of them getting stranded was near zero, she wanted to be prepared. She hefted up the new hiking boots she'd purchased with Kat's help and ran her thumb over the tread. It was chunky and rubbery. The boots weighed a ton, but they would provide good ankle support and improve her stability on uneven or slippery surfaces—or so the salesman had said.

She'd already sunscreened, and now she packed the bottle of lotion into her backpack along with the other supplies. From a shopping bag on the floor she pulled out her collection of new activewear and debated which to go for. A t-shirt rather than a tank top, she decided, because she didn't want the backpack straps to rub on her bare shoulders, and shorts rather than yoga pants because it was a warm day.

When she pulled on her thick new hiking socks, a cluster of butterflies took up residence in her stomach. She was actually doing this. Going hiking with Jack Farrelly. Her teenage self never would have believed it. This was the kind of thing she and Olivia had dreamed of while they lay side by side in matching hospital beds.

Adventure? Check.

Hot guy? Check.

If she thought about it, this outing was almost like a date. Just the two of them, communing with nature.

Not a date, she told herself. *He's not interested in you.*

She checked the time. Another twenty minutes until he was due to arrive, and she'd already packed and unpacked three times. Lacing her boots, she battled with the complicated crossover system, and then sat at her computer and tried to focus on the paragraph she'd been writing about women artists in the early twentieth century. The cursor blinked at her, and she scowled at it. Maybe she should check her bag one last time...

No. Don't be silly. Everything is there.

She shoved away from the desk, stood, and strode out of the room. There was no point forcing herself to concentrate when she knew she wouldn't accomplish anything. In the garden, she found Pixie snoozing in the sun and scooped the Chihuahua up, tucking her under one arm. Then she headed to Tione's cabin and released Bella, Trevor, and Zee from confinement. They bounded out, ears flopping, tails waggling, and she giggled.

"Bring them back when you're done," Tione called, accustomed to her borrowing his pets from time to time.

Pixie squirmed in her grasp, and she set her down so the tiny dog could join her friends. Trevor broke away and roared across the garden, kicking up lumps of dirt and grass. He stopped just short of the foyer door and whined.

"Trev, here boy!"

With much less enthusiasm, he loped back, his doggy lips flapping each time he hit the ground. Brooke patted his furry body all over, and he wagged his tail with enough force to send Pixie flying when she got in the way.

"You great big lump," she said affectionately. "You wanted to destroy another one of Tina's paintings, didn't you?"

Trevor seemed to enjoy the scent of wet paint. That, and shredding paper. The pooch was a lovable goof, but a destructive one. Leaving his side, Brooke searched for one of Zee's chew toys, finding it near the stairs to the cabin. She picked it up just as Zee spotted her and leapt, grabbing the other end between her teeth. The two of them wrestled over it until Brooke won, and tossed the toy as far as she could, both Zee and Bella taking off after it. Bella, who was lighter on her feet, reached it first.

Pixie yapped, demanding attention. Brooke patted her, then wandered over to one of the flower beds. Pixie followed, twining between her feet as she walked. When she bent to check the garden for weeds, Pixie leaned on her thigh and shivered.

"Good girl, Pix."

"You ready to go?" A voice from the foyer caught her attention. Glancing up, heat pooled where it ought not to at the sight of Jack in a dark t-shirt and shorts, a cap shading his gorgeous face.

"Yeah." She brushed herself off. "Just give me a moment to corral the troops." Yelling for Trevor, she herded Bella and Zee back into the cabin. When all four dogs were safely inside, she paced over to Jack and smiled. "Hi."

"Good morning," he replied. Was it her imagination, or

did his hooded gaze skim over her as she approached, and darken as though he liked what he saw?

"I'll grab my bag." She went to her room, slung the backpack over her shoulder, and glanced at her reflection, then locked the door before joining him outside, slightly out of breath because she'd been afraid he might vanish if she took too long.

"Thank you for this," she said as they hopped into his four-wheel drive and shut the doors. "I've been looking forward to it all night. I could hardly sleep."

"No problem." His tone was gruff.

"Where are we going? Will it take long to get there? How far is the hike?"

All he said was, "It's a surprise."

"Okay, I like surprises. Were you going anyway, or is this trip because of me?"

He leveled her with a wry smile. "Anyone ever said you ask a lot of questions?"

She laughed. "Is that supposed to put me off? Because if so, you need to work on your delivery. It wasn't nearly grumpy enough."

His lips twitched. Good. She prided herself on her ability to lighten the mood.

"Just an observation," he said.

"Yes, it's one that a few people have made." Bouncing in the seat, she watched the scenery fly past. He'd taken a back exit out of town, one of the ones that went into the hills rather than around to the state highway. "I'm sorry to say, you're not terribly original."

"I was never the quickest kid in school. I guess some things don't change."

She preferred to think that many things could indeed change. "Where did you go to school?"

"Auckland."

"You were a city boy?" She couldn't fathom that.

"Nah, never like the other boys in my year, and we moved to a place in the country near Taupo when I was fourteen. That's when I discovered a love for the great outdoors."

"Huh. I just figured you'd grown up on a farm and gone hunting with your dad since you were five, that kind of thing."

"Miles off. My dad was a real townie. We only moved after he and Mum separated."

"I'm sorry to hear that."

He lifted one shoulder. "It happens. I still keep in touch with them both, but it turns out that when you take Mum out of the equation, I don't have much in common with Dad."

"Parent troubles. I can relate." She sighed. "Mine are crazy overprotective, which I totally understand, considering how sick I was when I was little, but I've grown up now and they can't see that. It makes it hard for us to have conversations on a level footing. Especially when they're supplementing my scholarship to help cover my study and living expenses until I graduate." Something she was eternally grateful for.

"You're their little girl," he said softly.

"I *was* their little girl," she corrected. "I'll always be their daughter, but I'm not a child anymore."

He shook his head. "You're fighting a losing battle there. Your parents will always see you as their child. I know mine do."

That made her feel a little better. She'd assumed the way her parents helicoptered around her said more about her than them, but perhaps she'd been wrong. "Thanks. You know, you're sweeter than I thought you were."

He briefly met her gaze. "Don't go getting the wrong idea, Brooke. I'm not a big softie."

She wasn't sure she believed him. "Are we nearly there?"

"Nearly," he answered, with exaggerated patience. "Another few minutes."

As Jack pulled onto the gravel road that led deeper into the national park, Brooke continued to natter from the passenger seat. She'd moved on from asking questions and was telling him, in detail, about the biography she'd read of Sir Edmund Hillary, the first man to summit Mt. Everest, along with Sherpa Tenzing Norgay. He was amazed both that one girl could talk so much, and that she was practically vibrating with energy when, supposedly, she was still in recovery.

He glanced over at her discreetly. The woman beside him was most decidedly not sickly. Her cheeks were peachy pink, her eyes bright, and her excitement reminded him of Shane's kids on the last day of school. Fucking adorable. And while he'd been determined to get this trip out of the way as quickly as possible, he was enjoying her company. Yeah, she talked a lot, but she was knowledgeable and damned cute with her upturned nose and sweet voice. Her enthusiasm was endearing, if a little misplaced.

Hopefully the constant stream of conversation would dry up when they began walking. When he and Claudia had hiked together, she'd spent the whole time complaining about how bad sunscreen and bug repellent were for her pores, and if they'd happened upon beautiful scenery, she was more interested in finding the best and most flattering angles for photographs than anything else. Her mind was always on how she could manipulate a situation to advance her influencer career, and while he'd met few women as self-motivated as she was, her antics had ruined his quiet appreciation of their surroundings. Hiking—technology-free, the way he preferred—just hadn't been for her. And, apparently, neither was he.

They arrived in a parking area at the end of the gravel road and found it empty. Just the way he liked it. "We're here."

"Fantastic." Brooke unclipped her belt, threw the door open and leapt out. "I can't wait to get started." She grabbed her backpack from the back seat, took a swig of water and puffed on her inhaler.

"Are you okay?" he asked.

"Yeah, just being careful."

He hoped so, because while he could easily carry her down, there wasn't a lot he could do if she were to have a severe asthma attack, other than cross his fingers and pray.

She hurried to the beginning of the track and read aloud from the sign. "Amber Saddle, three hours return." She looked back to him. "You think I can manage three hours?"

"I do. It's far less steep than what you did the other day, and there's only the two of us, so we can stop any time you need a break." He didn't mind pausing every two minutes if that was what she needed, as long as he was able to enjoy the serenity that came with being in nature. She nodded, and stood to the side, waiting for him to lead the way. Hoisting his bag up, he gestured for her to go first.

"You're the one who knows where we're going," she said.

"There's a track," he pointed out. "If you get lost here, you might have bigger problems with getting to Everest than your health and fitness."

"Smart-ass," she muttered. "You should take the lead. I'll be slower, and I don't want to get in your way."

"The fact you'll be slower is exactly why you should go

first," he said. "When you're hiking, the slowest person should always set the pace so they don't get left behind."

Plus, if she were in front, he could keep an eye on her and make sure nothing was wrong, because he wasn't one hundred percent sure she'd tell him. As an added benefit, he could watch her pert butt as they walked uphill.

"Okay. You make the rules." Her tone was dubious. "But don't say I didn't warn you."

She started along the track, and he waited a respectable distance before following. It was best not to tailgate anyone in case branches disturbed by one person flicked back and walloped another in the face. He expected her to ask more questions or keep up her stream of dialogue, which seemed to need very little input from him, but she fell quiet as soon as they were beneath the canopy of the trees.

Despite her silence, she was anything but still. She tipped her head back and stared through the foliage, then gazed between the beech trees, at one point stopping to watch a wasp collect honeydew. Even when the wasp buzzed toward her and she had to leap out of its way, she didn't say a word, just stared until it was gone from view, and then continued on. If he hadn't been able to see her, or hear her breathing—which grew labored as the path became steeper —he wouldn't have known she was there.

Fortunately, she seemed to have taken his comment about resting when she needed it to heart, and paused frequently to catch her breath. The first time she did, he instructed her to remain standing and face downhill so her legs didn't become stiff. She complied without arguing, and they hadn't exchanged more than a few words. It was disconcerting.

"Are you okay?" he finally asked when they neared the top of the saddle.

She mopped a hand over her forehead and grinned. "Couldn't be better."

"Good. I was concerned, you haven't said much."

"I'm trying to take everything in. I'm not here for the sound of my own voice." She scrunched her nose. "I can hear that anywhere."

He couldn't believe his ears. "Wow," he said, as though to himself. "Is this what love feels like?"

She laughed but her expression shuttered, and disappointment settled like a weight in his gut. Of course she wouldn't want him joking about something like that. Not when she was pretty, perky, and beloved by many, and he was a cranky old man by comparison.

She slid her backpack off and sipped from her water bottle. Her throat rippled and he swallowed, trying to ignore the untimely tightening in his pants. A flash of color darted across his vision and then a fantail, or *piwakawaka*, as the Māori called them, landed near her feet.

Her entire body stiffened and her eyes locked on it, twice their usual size. "Oh. My. God," she breathed. "What do I do?"

"Don't move," he murmured, "or you'll scare it away. Just stay very still."

Contrary to his advice, she edged toward her backpack.

"What are you doing?" he asked.

"I want my camera."

He rolled his eyes, annoyed with himself for being surprised. She was a blogger, after all, and apparently the need to document everything was something bloggers and Instagrammers had in common. "Stop."

"But—"

"My phone is in my pocket. You can use that."

"Oh." She smiled, and slowly extended her hand. The fantail hopped from one spot to another but didn't fly away.

He inched his hand into his pocket and retrieved his phone, offering it to her. She bent in a smooth motion and aimed the camera. Just as she snapped, the fantail cocked its head and took flight, landing on a branch above them. She took another photo, her cheeks glowing, an enormous grin stretching from ear to ear. She went onto her tiptoes, watching the little bird flit along the branch.

"I can't believe it," she whispered. "It's so cute. I've never seen one so close."

The bird flew off, and she whirled around. The excitement in her expression took his breath away. Okay, so maybe he'd misjudged her. She'd appreciated the magic of that fantail as much as he did, and the whole trip was worth it to see her delicate features flushed with happiness, and to know that in an indirect way, he was the cause of it. She handed the phone back, passing by him so closely that he could have bent and kissed her. He wanted so badly to know whether her lips tasted like the peaches they reminded him of. For a moment, their gazes locked and he could have sworn she wanted the kiss just as much as he did, but then she blinked, and the spell was broken.

10

———

Privileged. That's what she was. So insanely privileged to be here, surrounded by the wonder of nature and the breathtaking scenery. Nothing could bring her down. Not the burn in her thighs or the sting of blisters on her heels or the tightness in her chest. The forest was lush, green, and so very *alive*. She could sense the forest animals around her. Once, she thought she caught sight of a deer in the distance, but it could have been a trick of the light.

Jack's footfalls behind her were light, and at times she forgot he was even there. She shook her head. So much for worrying she'd be too self-conscious to enjoy herself. Except for when the fantail landed, they hadn't exchanged a word, but she felt oddly connected to him.

Up ahead, light shone brighter through the trees. The track steepened and Brooke paused to rest before starting up the slope. A park sign declared they were ten minutes from Amber Saddle. Those ten minutes were by far the most difficult, but finally the ground flattened to a low point between two hills, with a brilliant view over Haven Bay and to the ocean beyond.

"Oh my God," she breathed.

"Stunning, isn't it?"

She crossed to where the land began to dip on the other side of the saddle and shielded her eyes while she scanned the horizon, tracing the contours of the land, down to the edge of town. She noted cars, like ants, winding their way along roads, and a scattering of dots on the beach that might be people. The expanse of the Tasman Sea glittered in the high noon sunlight.

"It's beautiful." She couldn't tear her eyes away. "I've never seen anything like it."

She'd seen views during her lifetime that left her awestruck, but none had affected her as greatly as this, and she wondered if that was because she'd worked so hard to get to this point. It was totally worth the raw patches on her feet.

Dropping her bag, she opened pockets until she found her camera, then snapped a photo. It could never capture everything she felt in that moment, but at least it would be something to share with her readers. Then she backed up and gestured for Jack to stand in front of her.

He shook his head. "Nah, photos aren't really my thing."

"Pretty please," she cajoled. "Just one."

He didn't move. "I can't compare to all that. I'd be getting in the way."

She laugh-snorted. "Oh, please. A handsome man and a gorgeous backdrop. You're a perfect combo."

One side of his mouth hitched up. "You think I'm handsome?"

Her heart pitter-pattered erratically. That cocky half-grin was way too potent for her peace of mind. "You're all right."

The grin widened. "That's not what you were saying a moment ago."

She rolled her eyes. "Just get in the picture, Farrelly."

"On two conditions. You're in it too, and it doesn't go on your blog."

"Okay, a private selfie it is."

He joined her, their heads ducked so close to each other that she could feel a charge zapping between them, and when he shifted, the air moved around her, too. With clumsy fingers, she took a photo, then made a show of hurrying to her bag for her drink, to put space between them. She sank onto the ground, readjusting her position when a twig jabbed her in the ass, and gazed over the forest and the bay that sprawled out before them. The summer sun beat down on her back and everything was shades of blue and green and yellow. She could happily stay there forever.

"Ready to head back?" Jack asked, standing over her.

She turned to face him, squinting into the sun. She should probably invest in some sunglasses. "Can we just stay a few more minutes?"

He smiled, and for once, the expression looked natural on him. Not like it had fought its way to the surface, which seemed to be his default. Come to think of it, basking in the sun and surrounded by trees for miles, he was the most relaxed she'd ever seen him.

"Sure," he agreed. "Let me know when you're ready to go. I'm in no hurry."

THE HIKE BACK to the parking lot passed in much the same fashion as the walk to Amber Saddle, with Brooke taking the lead, stopping when she wanted to look at something or simply rest her legs. Jack followed behind, admiring her more with each step. She was filled with the same wide-eyed fascination she had been all day. It hadn't faded an ounce.

Nothing had gone like he'd expected it to, and to his absolute astonishment, it had turned into the best day he'd had in ages.

He'd even been willing to be photographed for her. Photos were usually a dealbreaker these days. He'd posed for a million with Claudia, but it had never been enough. Brooke was different, so he made an exception. She was enthusiastic and chatty at times, but quiet when it mattered, and constantly in high spirits. He wished he could channel a little of her positivity and excitement for himself. When they got to his four-wheel drive, he unloaded his backpack while she yanked off her boots and socks, then wriggled her toes and sighed. Her feet were white, but spotted with angry pink and red splotches. A lead ball sank in his gut.

"Holy hell, are they blisters?" he demanded.

She leaned forward and studied them, her expression strangely satisfied. "Yep."

When he came closer, he could see that several of them had already lost the top layer of skin. "Why didn't you say anything? That must have hurt like fuck."

She shrugged. "They're new boots, so I figured this would happen. Nothing anyone could do about it, so there wasn't any point in complaining. Do you know, it's the first time I've had blisters like this? Cool, huh?"

"No," he grumped. "Not cool. You should have told me. I could have put Vaseline or salve on them."

"Jack," she said with a smile. "Chill out. They sting, but you're talking to a girl who had open-heart surgery when she was ten. These barely register on my pain scale."

Chill out? He couldn't recall the last time anyone had told him to chill out. He was chill as an ice cream in summer, but something about this girl got under his skin. And seriously? Open-heart surgery when she was ten? His own heart ached at the thought. No child should have to endure something like that.

"At least let me put salve on them now," he groused.

"Okay," she said. "If you don't mind touching my gross feet."

"I'm sure I've smelled worse." He found the salve in his first aid kit and, with gentle touches, applied a thin layer to each of her blisters. She didn't flinch or make a noise, though it must have hurt. She just watched him with those big, curious eyes. The whole thing was too intimate for his liking. "Do you wear contacts?" he asked, to break the tension.

"Sometimes." She cocked her head. "I thought they weren't noticeable."

"They aren't, but I remember seeing you in glasses once before. How bad is your vision?"

She smiled, visibly amused. "Pretty bad. Without these contacts, I wouldn't be able to tell you from any other person-sized blob."

"'Course you could," he replied, without thinking. "I'd be the handsomest blob."

Her cheeks flushed scarlet, and he regretted the quip immediately. He shouldn't be flirting with her.

"All blobs are equal in my eyes."

Well, that put him in his place.

"There." He smeared salve over the last blister. "You're good to go."

She hobbled away and climbed into the passenger seat. "I don't suppose you'd let me drive."

He huffed a laugh. "Not today."

Not *ever*. He valued his vehicle enough to know that letting an inexperienced person behind the controls was a bad idea.

"Too bad." She sounded disappointed, and he ignored the urge to make it up to her.

They drove back to Sanctuary with less conversation than they'd had coming in the opposite direction. Once or twice, he glanced over just in time to see Brooke's chin dip and her eyes flutter. Then she'd lift her head and blink sleepily. She was struggling to stay awake, and it was completely endearing. Or at least, it would have been, if he hadn't felt a niggle of anxiety over whether he'd pushed her too far.

"We didn't overdo it, did we?" he asked.

"Not at all." She smiled at him, eyes unfocused. "I'm tired, but in a good way. I need a solid ten hours of sleep and then I'll be fine."

"I can't even remember the last time I slept for that long." He crunched into the parking lot at Sanctuary and stopped outside the lodge. Brooke flopped out of her seat and collected her bag. He followed. He needed to talk business with Kat and re-evaluate how things were going.

"You're coming in?" she asked.

"Yeah, gotta catch up with Kat."

They entered together and, just inside the door, Brooke turned and launched herself at him. She caught him off guard and he stumbled back a step, his arms closing around her automatically. She'd pressed herself right up against him and he was shocked to feel a tightening in his pants and realize his body was reacting to all the soft, womanly good-ness suddenly rubbing over it. His jaw clenched and he willed himself not to get a hard-on. But damn, she felt right in his arms, and she smelled faintly of earth and sweat, but not in an unpleasant way.

"Thank you," she murmured into his chest. "Today was amazing. I had the best time."

Not a date, he reminded himself. *It would not be appropriate to cop a feel, or steal a kiss.*

Instead, he patted her back as he imagined a brother might, and cleared his throat. She stepped away, blushing again. Did she not know how appealing that made her?

"No problem," he said gruffly.

Remember, jackass, you don't deserve her gratitude.

"Get some rest and we'll talk tomorrow."

She nodded. "Bye, Jack."

He watched as she hurried off, almost tripping over something invisible on the floor. He shook his head. Only her.

"That seems like it went well."

For the first time, he noticed Kat lingering in the doorway between the dining hall and the foyer. How long had she been standing there? Had she witnessed the world's most awkward hug?

"Yeah, I guess so," he replied, hedging his bets. "She handled the hike better than I thought she would."

Kat straightened and crossed the room. "I know she doesn't look it since she's so little and cute, but she's a tough chick. Has a steel backbone and the stubbornness of a bull."

He scrubbed a hand over his stubble. "Yeah, I'm starting to see that."

Kat grinned in a way that made him nervous, clapped him on the shoulder, and said, "Don't worry if you can't fully see it yet. You will before long."

11

———

Brooke hesitated on the threshold of The Hideaway the next morning. She'd been inside the gym-slash-art-studio many times before, but only to visit Bex, not as a customer. She'd often watched people on the gym equipment, or lifting weights in the corner, but made sure they never caught her looking. Most of the people who frequented The Hideaway were fit—the women lean and toned, not soft and pale like her. And the men... She sighed dreamily. Watching the men was no hardship at all.

Yet here she was. About to join them. Feeling excited but totally unprepared.

"You all right there?"

Jumping in surprise, she released the door handle like it was sizzling hot, and turned to face a stocky blond guy who was patiently waiting to enter. She blushed ferociously and stammered an apology.

"No worries," he said. "Is this your first time?"

"Yeah," she admitted. "I'm a bit nervous. Okay, make that really nervous. I'm so out of shape."

"You'll be fine," he said, smiling. "Just relax and have fun."

Relax and have fun. She could do that.

"Thanks." She grabbed the handle again and let herself in. Her new friend followed. "Are you visiting town?" she asked as they climbed the stairs. Perhaps it was just her, but having the gym located at the top of a flight of stairs seemed unnecessarily cruel. Especially when her legs ached from yesterday.

"Yeah, I'm here until the end of February, teaching some kiddies how to surf."

She nodded. "With Logan?"

"That's right. And you?"

"Oh, I'm a local."

"But you've never been to the gym before?"

She paused at the top of the stairs and pushed her hair back off her face to look down at him. "I haven't been in the best of health." She held out her hand. "I'm Brooke."

"Riley," he said. "I'll be around if you need a hand with anything."

"Thanks. That's sweet of you." After opening the door, she beelined to Bex, her chin tucked down because she had the odd sensation that people were judging her. Ridiculous, when she'd never felt that way when she'd visited before. It was all in her head.

"Hi, Bex." She greeted her friend with an anxious smile. "I'm here, and ready to go."

Bex took one look at her, threw back her head, and laughed. "Calm down, Brookie. You're not marching to your doom." Coming around behind her, Bex dug her thumbs into the tense muscles of Brooke's upper back.

Brooke moaned. "That's so good."

"You sound positively pornographic." But she didn't stop kneading.

"Yeah, Bex, give it to me more," Brooke teased.

Bex spun her around and raised a brow. "You talk like

that and these knuckleheads won't let you leave until they've tried to get into your pants."

Brooke rolled her eyes. "Whatever." She doubted the hot gym guys would look twice at her. "I'm a bit sore from a hike Jack and I did yesterday, but I'll try not to let it slow me down."

"Where does it hurt?" Bex asked, evaluating her.

"Legs, back, feet." She nibbled on her lip. "I may or may not have worn brand new boots and gotten a few blisters."

Shaking her head, Bex murmured "Nincompoop" affectionately. "We'll need to warm you up first, and hopefully your muscles loosen up a bit once that happens. There's not much I can do about your feet, but let me know if it gets too painful and we'll stop, okay?"

"Okay." Brooke snapped the elastic band off her wrist and tied her hair back. Butterflies danced in her stomach, but thanks to Bex, they were of the excited variety rather than the terrified type. "So, where am I starting?"

Bex walked to three treadmills lined up by the window that overlooked the square. "Five minutes jogging, just to limber up. Set the pace at six miles per hour and adjust it if you need to, but try not to walk."

"Okay," Brooke agreed. "I can do that."

"If for any reason you need to stop immediately, hit the big red button."

Brooke nodded, even as she knew she would *not* hit the big red button. Would. *Not.* For any reason. Bex wandered off. Scanning the buttons, Brooke found the one that read "Quick Start". The belt started moving. She waited until she'd gotten a feel for the speed, then stepped onto it, pacing quickly so she didn't fall off or trip. The screen said she was moving at two miles per hour, so she hit an up arrow and the speed climbed. She started jogging, and by the time she reached six miles per hour, as Bex had recommended, she was panting and struggling to move her legs fast enough to stay in place.

Glancing at the timer, she saw fifty seconds had passed. Dear God, this was the warmup?

Everest Base Camp, she reminded herself, and refused to wave the white flag. Finally, the five minutes were up and she slid off the end, bracing her hands on her thighs and sucking in deep breaths.

Someone patted her on the back. Looking over her shoulder, she saw Riley smiling down at her. "You're doing good," he said. "Keep it up."

"Thanks," she wheezed, and reached into her pocket for her inhaler as she headed over to a machine that looked like a torture device. When she'd eased the ache in her lungs, she waved and caught Bex's attention. "What next?"

Bex consulted her tablet. "Leg presses. They help strengthen your hamstrings, which will be important when you're carrying a heavy bag uphill."

"Mmhmm," Brooke said, like she knew what hamstrings were, then followed Bex to an exercise machine with a seat facing a metal plate. At least she'd be sitting down. How bad could it be? The diagram beside the machine showed a person with the balls of their feet pressed to the plate. She assumed it was connected to the stack of weights beside the seat. She sat, put her feet on the plate and tried to push. It didn't budge an inch.

"It might be easier if it weren't set to a two hundred pounds," Bex remarked, her lips twitching.

"Oh, yeah," Brooke said, feeling like a fool. "How do I change it?"

"Use the peg to your right and slot it into the number you want to lift." She scanned Brooke's body critically, no doubt noting the lack of muscle mass. "For you, I'd start with thirty pounds and increase if that's too easy."

Brooke moved the peg and tried again, this time with more success.

"Good," Bex said. "Now do a set of ten. If you're not struggling by the end, increase up to the next weight bracket. I want you to do forty total, got it?"

Brooke did as she was told. Her thighs burned, but it was a good burn. Under Bex's instruction, she learned how to use several other machines, and how to properly do crunches and other abdominal exercises. By the time she finished, everything ached, but she was also totally exhilarated and felt like she could leap high enough to reach the ceiling.

She skipped over to Riley and his friend, who were spotting each other for bench pressing. "Spotting," she'd learned, was when people buddied up to make sure they were safe when doing heavy weights or risky exercises. She'd also discovered that she'd been completely wrong to assume gym buffs would look down on her.

"I did it," she exclaimed. "One day down, about two hundred to go."

Riley's friend finished with the bar, and together he and Riley placed it on the rack, then Riley high-fived her.

"Will we see you back here tomorrow?" he asked.

"Tomorrow or the next day," she replied. "Depends when I can walk again. Thanks for being so encouraging."

"My pleasure," Riley said. "See you round, Brooke."

She left the guys and danced to the far end of The Hideaway, where Bex's easel was positioned in front of the window on the ocean-view side of the building. Her friend was sketching, and Brooke assumed she'd fill the lines in with paint later.

"That was awesome," she said. "Once I got over my nerves. Thanks so much. I actually feel like this is real now. I could get to Everest." She squealed a little. "I just need to do this every day for the next eight months."

"And build on it," Bex reminded her.

"That too." She hugged her friend. "You're the best. I love you."

"Yeah, yeah," Bex muttered, returning her hug. "Ease up before your new friends' eyes bug out of their heads."

"I'll come again soon," Brooke promised, backing off. "Kiss your beautiful little girl for me."

"AND THAT CONCLUDES our ocean wildlife tour," Jack said as he docked his boat and stepped onto the wooden jetty. Assisting each member of the tour group onto dry land, he suppressed a grin when one of the older ladies groped his bicep. Days like today, he didn't mind being eye candy for a cougar. The sun was shining, a warm ocean breeze stirred the air, the water was calm, and the dolphins had put on a great show, zipping around and under the boat, and surfacing frequently to watch the tour with interest. All in all, the morning couldn't have gone better. He gazed out over the shimmering expanse of blue-green. It was peaceful and still, but hid a thriving aquatic ecosystem.

"Thank you, that was life-changing," one of the younger women said to him. "I've never seen anything like it."

"I'm glad you enjoyed yourself," he replied, and waved as she left. Then he finished with the boat and wandered off the jetty, whistling to himself. He stopped at Sailor's Retreat, the seafood restaurant, and the proprietor bundled up a package of fish and chips to go.

Seagulls circled as he ate on the beach, hoping for crumbs, and he was in such good spirits that he tossed a few handfuls of chips into the sand—enough to ensure all of the birds got something, although they still squawked and squabbled.

He crumpled up the wrapping, tossed it in a recycling bin at the pavilion, then drove to Sanctuary, where he'd planned an early-afternoon kayaking session. Going straight to the shed where Kat stored the water sports equipment, he inspected the eight open-topped ocean kayaks stacked against one wall. They seemed to be in good order, so he began carrying them out to the empty stretch of beach opposite the lodge. He'd moved two, and had started on the third, when he heard voices behind him.

"Jack! Excuse me, Jack!"

Uh-oh, he knew that voice. *Betty.*

"Pay attention to your elders, Jack Farrelly."

He cringed. And that was Mavis. Laying down the kayak, he looked over at them and had to shield his eyes against the sun. "Ladies, lovely day we're having, isn't it?"

"Word is you're helping Brooke prepare for a hiking trip to Nepal," Mavis said, ignoring him. "Is it true?"

He put his hands on his hips and studied them. Mavis wore her pit bull expression, which meant that shit was about to go down. "It is."

"You'd better be serious about it," she warned.

"Yes," Betty added, "because Brooke is a lovely girl, but she's had a bad run of it and she doesn't need anyone flaking out on her."

"Me? Flake out? I think you've got the wrong end of the stick. I'm not the flakey type." If someone was going to flake out in this scenario, it would be Brooke. He could tough his way through anything, but she was soft—although he couldn't deny she had a high pain tolerance and a radiant smile.

Mavis grumbled, "Keep it that way."

"Yes, ma'am." He saluted. Betty covered her mouth and

giggled, her white curls bouncing. Mavis glared, her fore-head a collection of dubious crinkles.

"You're too cheeky for your own good," Betty said. "Don't you agree, Mavis?"

Mavis's eyes narrowed. "Impertinent, is more like it."

He'd been called worse, but he got the feeling they weren't done here. The ladies shifted from one foot to the other and glanced at each other like they had something to say, but were both hoping the other would do it.

"What's on your mind?" he asked.

"Do you intend to accompany her to Nepal?" It was Mavis who asked the question.

Go with her? To the Himalayas?

The possibility had never occurred to him. To be fair, he'd also never imagined she'd make it that far, try as she might. At least, not this year. If by some miracle she did, would he consider joining her? He turned the idea over in his mind. It was exactly the sort of trip he'd love to be a part of, and it would be a once-in-a-lifetime experience. He was certainly fit enough, and he had the right gear.

It's not going to happen.

He shouldn't get caught up planning something when it would go nowhere.

Betty and Mavis looked at him expectantly.

He cleared his throat. "If she doesn't get to Everest, it won't be because of anything I did or didn't do." It was a cop-out, and they all knew it. He changed the subject, because the alternative was to sweat beneath the combined weight of their stares until he agreed to something he didn't want to. "Are you two kayaking with me this afternoon?"

"Not today," Betty said, looking disappointed. "My back and shoulder are too stiff."

"That's a shame."

Thank God for small mercies.

He continued dragging the kayak over to join the others. When he headed back for the next one, Betty and Mavis had continued their stroll up the beach. He finished setting up and headed to the lodge, where a small group awaited him. Brooke's eager face smiled from amongst them, and he couldn't suppress an answering grin.

He whistled to gain the group's attention. "We'll be kayaking off the beach today, so let's all head down there. Grab some sunscreen or a hat if you need to."

He waited for the first people to pass him and fell into step with Brooke. "You don't have to come if you're tired," he told her. "I'll talk to you after."

She raised her chin, the movement oddly imperious, and a memory tickled at the back of his mind but he couldn't quite place it. "I'm not missing out on sea kayaking."

"It's unlikely to do you much good as training."

"Maybe not, but it's an experience I want to have."

He could see he wasn't going to win this debate without making a big deal of something that didn't warrant it, so he didn't argue further. "How are you after yesterday?"

"Good," she said. "A little sore, and I had a really deep sleep, but otherwise I seem to be fine."

"Your feet?" he asked gruffly, remembering how painful they'd looked. All those blisters on her soft white skin.

She pulled a face. "They sting a bit, but I've had worse."

He'd bet his left nut that they hurt more than she was letting on, but if she wanted to downplay it, that was her business, provided it didn't interfere with her performance today. They reached the kayaks and he did a quick head count. Everyone on his list was accounted for.

"Everybody grab a kayak," he instructed, and waited while they did so. "Are any of you new to kayaking?"

Brooke raised her hand, and he shook his head. Seriously, how had this girl not done anything when she lived in a place surrounded by wilderness and water?

"Okay." He lifted the oar. "You want to keep this centered and dip the curved part into the water like so." He demonstrated the correct movement. "Then rotate it slightly to do the same with the other side. Not too deep. You want it just below the surface, enough that it works your arms when you pull it back. Got it?"

She nodded, chewing on her lower lip, and frowning faintly. "Think so."

"Let's go, then. Stick close to me."

The group of them hauled the kayaks into the shallows and he laughed when Brooke stumbled trying to get in and would have flipped if the water were deep enough.

"Take it slowly," he said. "One foot at a time so you don't overbalance."

On the second attempt, she made it in. Then she reached for the oar and mimicked the motions he'd shown her moments earlier, although hers were short and jerky.

"Smooth movements," he coached her. "And try to keep them even on each side, unless you want to turn."

She took direction well, and before long, the group had paddled past the breakers into the gently rolling ocean. He stayed in the lead, heading toward a collection of rock pinnacles just offshore. He'd paddled around them before and knew they were an excellent place for beginners to explore.

A strange choking noise made him stop. He glanced over his shoulder just in time to see Brooke heave the contents of her stomach over the side of her kayak. Straightening, she wiped her mouth, her complexion pasty. He swore. Had she lied earlier when she said she was fine? Had he pushed her too far again?

"Sorry," she moaned. "I get motion sickness."

Of course she did. "Is there anything I can do to help?"

She shook her head, then groaned. "I'll be fine, once I've thrown up a couple of times."

"We'll have to ply you with chocolate when we get back," one of the other women said. "I have a stash in my car."

"If I can stomach it."

They continued paddling, and Brooke vomited another three times before they reached the pinnacles. By this point, Jack felt like tossing up his own lunch because the sound of her retching had really gotten to him. They circled the pinnacles once, then he suggested they head back, suspecting that Brooke regretted joining them but had too much pride to ask to return to shore.

He felt for her, he truly did, but this afternoon had only served to emphasize how much she wasn't designed for his lifestyle. He needed to shut down his out of control attraction to her, and the little part of his heart that sped up when she smiled.

She came alongside him. "I wanted to tell you, I went to the gym this morning. It went really well. Much better than I expected. I can't wait to go back."

He chuckled.

"What?" she demanded, a sheen of sweat on her forehead.

"You've been pretty ill for the last half hour, and you still have the energy to be enthusiastic about the gym," he explained. "That's a lot of dedication to the cause."

She shrugged, as much as one could while holding an oar. "Dedication is my middle name."

"So it's not 'stubborn-as-a-mule'?"

Digging the end of the oar into the water, she flicked it up, spraying him with salty water. Spluttering, he wiped his eyes and stared at her in astonishment.

She giggled. "You deserved that."

He stopped paddling and splashed her, dousing her upper body so that water dripped from the ends of her hair and ran down the sides of her neck. "Bring it on, baby girl."

Brooke's jaw dropped, but he could tell she wasn't really mad. Then she smiled with a mischievous glimmer in her eyes. "Oh, it's *on.*"

12

———

BROOKE'S BODY burned like a thousand tiny elves were stabbing her with flaming pitchforks. She tried to move, and everything seized up. Was this what dying felt like? She opened her eyes to blackness. Holy hell, had she gone blind?

Her chest constricted in panic and she flailed about, realizing she was face down in bed. She stilled, then with a massive effort, rolled onto her back and blinked up at the ceiling until her vision cleared. It was daylight. A drilling pain buzzed behind her right eye, and her arms were like lead weights at her sides. She'd only just woken, but she felt like she'd gone three rounds in the ring with a bulldozer and could sleep for another eight hours. She'd overdone it again. Jack would have a field day with this.

He can't know.

She'd have to hide it. Once she'd summoned enough willpower to move, she eased into a seated position, her limbs creaking from exertion. Her hair flopped over her forehead and she rubbed her cheek, her fingers running over creases from the sheets. She must look a fright.

Grabbing her cell phone, she checked the time. After

twelve. She'd slept half the day away. Her stomach gurgled, reminding her that she hadn't eaten since yesterday evening. Compared to the discomfort in her muscles, the hunger was nothing. She slid her feet to the floor and carefully transferred her weight to them. Her legs trembled, but she managed to totter into the bathroom, bend at the waist until she was low enough to put the plug in the bathtub and turn the faucet on. She shook a generous portion of Epsom salts into the water, and poured a splash of eucalyptus essential oil in after. Selecting the biggest, softest towel and her favorite body lotion, she left them on the vanity for later. When the tub was full, she bundled her hair atop her head and sank into the water up to her neck.

For a long while, she soaked, allowing the tension in her muscles to seep away. When everything had loosened and the pain had dulled, she used her thumbs to rub the lactic acid out of her thighs, calves, upper arms, and shoulders. It hurt like hell and she had to grit her teeth to get through it, but by the time she'd finished the massage, and cleaned, dried, and moisturized herself, then swallowed a couple of painkillers, she felt human.

Next, she donned her new sunglasses—both to prevent the headache from worsening and to hide her bloodshot eyes—and wolfed down a cooked lunch in the dining hall, ducking her head to avoid Tione when he looked her way. He was a smart guy. If he came over, he'd be onto her in twenty seconds, and the last thing she needed was a lecture on her limitations. As if she weren't already aware of them. Murmuring a quick thanks to any divine beings, she was grateful Bex hadn't listened when she'd argued she didn't need a rest day between gym visits. If she'd had to go in today, she'd probably have faked illness to get out of it. Not that much faking would have been involved.

Making a concerted effort to walk like someone who

didn't wish her nerve endings were numb, she returned to her room for her laptop and took it to the communal lounge. Settling into a well-padded armchair, she opened the chapter of her thesis she was currently working on. Once she got stuck in, she didn't move until her leg cramped and she needed to stretch. She'd settled back into her chair and typed another few sentences when Kat came through the door and waved at her.

"Hey, girl," Brooke said. "Long time, no see." It had been all of twenty-four hours.

"It's been an age," Kat replied, her lips twisting wryly. She sat on the arm of the chair. "You look like you've been through the wringer."

Brooke sighed and glanced away. She should have known her best friend would see right through her. "I may have overdone the exercise yesterday."

"You've got to take care of yourself," Kat chided.

"I know." She truly did. But being patient wasn't easy. "Please don't tell Jack."

Kat's brows flew up. "Why not? You did promise to be open and honest with him."

Brooke clasped her fingers together and made puppy-dog eyes from behind her glasses. "Pretty please, Kitty-Kat. I'll do better next time; it's just hard figuring out the right level to push myself without going too far. And I don't want to give him any reason to drop me, or not take me seriously."

Sitting on the arm of the chair and slinging her legs over Brooke's lap, Kat asked, "Are you sure that's all it is?"

Brooke's heart stuttered. "W-what do you mean?"

Kat watched her with dark eyes that saw too much. "Are you sure it's not because you have a thing for Jack and want to impress him?"

Suddenly, Brooke became fascinated by a pattern on the chair. "That's not it at all."

"Oh, really?" She sounded amused now. "Then why won't you look me in the eye?"

Brooke growled in frustration and looked up. "Okay, I admit it. But what do you want from me? He's hot."

Kat smirked. "I knew it."

"What gave me away?"

"Couldn't say for sure. I just picked up on a vibe you were sending out. I'm your friend, so I'm in tune with stuff like that."

Brooke's stomach sank. "Do you think he knows?"

"Doubt it. He's not the most observant guy, and you're not obvious about it. It's just obvious to me."

"Phew!" She really hoped she hadn't given herself away, because how humiliating would that be? Especially when they'd kissed in the past and it had been so unmemorable he'd literally forgotten her. Not that she was bitter or anything.

On top of that, she thought maybe—just maybe—he was starting to see her as a fun, capable person. Why else would he have engaged in an intense water fight with her that had them both in fits of laughter? She recalled the way his brown eyes had turned to liquid gold in the sunlight and couldn't help but smile. He'd had fun with her, she just knew it.

"I actually came to see if you could help me out at reception for a while," Kat said. "Are you too busy, or can you spare an hour or so?"

Brooke saved her document and closed it. "For you, I can spare the time."

Kat moved from the arm of the chair and Brooke got up and hobbled toward reception, resolving to listen more closely to her body the next time she went to the gym—and not to pile on everything at once. Just because she wanted to be superwoman didn't mean it would happen instantly.

Progress took time, and from now on, she was balancing her gym and outdoor sessions more carefully.

13

Jack was in a special kind of hell.

All he'd wanted was to check on Brooke's progress at the gym. Yet here he was, spying on her like a creep, watching her slender body in those tight exercise clothes as she climbed on the stair climber. From behind her, where he was squatting with a weight bar on his shoulders, he had an excellent view of her perfect ass and the beads of sweat forming on the exposed skin of her upper back.

He swallowed. Damn, he ought to be ashamed of himself for thinking what he was, but she was a hell of a sexy woman and the devil on his shoulder pointed out the way her tank top plastered to the curve of her hips. When she tipped her head back to catch her breath, she looked like she'd exerted herself in a far more suggestive way than walking up imaginary stairs.

He forced himself to look away. If he spent too much time ogling her, Bex would probably kick him out. She had a zero tolerance rule when it came to harassment. Flirting was fine, as long as it was mutual and didn't cross any lines. God knew how she judged that, but she seemed to have a perv-o-meter in her head that was disconcertingly accurate. He glanced around at the other people who'd chosen to spend their valuable Sunday morning at the gym. One young man kept chugging a dirty brown protein shake, and Hugh MacAllister, the town council representative, was on a cycle.

Finishing his set of squats, Jack dropped the bar onto a rack just as Brooke stepped off the stair climber and headed to the free weight area. She smiled and said hi before settling onto a mat and stretching. He replied in kind and fought the urge to strike up a conversation. They hadn't talked since he'd taken her on a walk along the beach a few days earlier. While they'd followed the meandering trail through the dunes on the more isolated west end of the beach, it had dawned on him how much he enjoyed her company. She was fun, chatty, and cute as hell. He'd found himself dreading the day she realized she'd bitten off more than she could chew, and that scared him.

Wiping his forehead with a sweat towel, he went to the bench press, and tried to play it casual while she hesitantly added tiny plates to the end of a bar, wrapped a bit of foam around the center, and juggled it onto her shoulders. Watching her in his peripheral vision, Jack slid onto his back. She did a squat, then launched the bar into the air above her head. It came down on the back of her neck a little too hard and she dropped it, scrambling to get out of the way as it crashed to the floor. Blood rushed to her cheeks and she removed the weights from the end of the bar and lifted it gingerly back onto her shoulders. Jack glanced around the room, wondering if he should offer to help, and noticed that Protein Shake Guy was also keeping an eye on her, although with a little less concern and a little more interest.

She tried again, her tongue sticking out of the corner of her mouth in concentration, which for some insane reason, he found adorable. It really shouldn't be. If she messed up, she could bite her tongue off. This time, she managed eight reps before dropping the bar. He could tell that she'd been taught the correct form, but she wasn't quite getting it right.

He bench pressed for ten reps, his arms straining more with each one. When he sat up, Brooke wasn't alone anymore. Protein Shake Guy had left his spot and was standing behind her, guiding her into position, his hands skimming over her ribcage, waist, and hips. He wasn't being inappropriate—quite—but Jack's teeth ground together when the guy drew back and glanced at her butt before giving her the all clear. Jack looked around at Bex, who was also watching Brooke and her new friend, but she was relaxed, her perv-o-meter apparently malfunctioning.

Brooke did a single rep, and the guy murmured something, then touched her shoulder. Her cheeks were flushed, whether from the exercise or something else, Jack couldn't tell. He stacked more weights onto his bar and began another set, grunting with each thrust. At the end of this set, Brooke and Protein Shake Guy were conversing. She was smiling and nodding, but not in a flirtatious way. More like she wasn't picking up on the horny vibes coming from her companion.

Was she actually that clueless? Or was she playing it up?

He didn't want to know.

After another set, the guy gave her a thumbs up and returned to his routine. Jack unloaded the bench press, selected the heaviest dumbbells he could lift, and perched on the edge of a seat, curling them up until his biceps strained with the effort. He noticed Brooke glance in his direction. Once. Twice. A third time. Her tongue flicked out and wet her lips. Stifling a groan, he pumped the iron harder. She continued stealing peeks at him as she started doing weighted rows, angling her body toward his. Feral satisfaction tightened his gut. She liked what she saw. The way her lips parted and her eyes darkened gave her away. And he was only human. He wanted to puff his chest out and flex every muscle he had for her to admire.

By the time he finished his workout, his arms were killing him, but he had zero regrets. Sometimes a man had to sacrifice his comfort for the cause. As he put the equipment he'd used back in place, Bex crossed to him, a smirk twisting her pretty face.

"You done being macho now?" she asked.

"Never," he replied. "I'm always macho."

She grinned. "Speaking of never, I've never seen you do so many bicep curls."

"What do you want from me?" he teased, knowing she'd put two and two together.

"I— Never mind." With that, she turned and sauntered away.

A moment later, Brooke appeared at his side. "What was that about?"

He shrugged. "No idea."

"So," she said, leaning on the wall beside him. "Did you approve of what you saw?"

He answered without thinking. "Do you mean your progress, or your flirting?"

She straightened and folded her arms over her chest, her expression one of outrage. "Excuse me? What I meant, you ass, was my ability level and work ethic, which is what I'd assumed you were here to assess, since you've been watching me nonstop." Her eyes narrowed. "Or have I got it wrong? Were you just ogling me?"

Guilty as charged.

But damn, he'd put his foot in his mouth and he needed to set it right. "I'm sorry, I was out of line. You're right, that's why I was here, and you've got a long way to go, but you're doing well."

She narrowed her eyes, but her righteous anger diffused. "Well. Thank you for being honest. Next time you want to check up on me, don't feel like you have to sneak around behind my back to find out when I'll be here. I'm more than happy to tell you."

Now it was his turn to be embarrassed. Yeah, he'd sweet-talked Bex into finding out Brooke's schedule, but how was he to know she wouldn't take offense?

"All right. Agreed."

"Okay then. Glad that's all sorted."

Without saying goodbye, she strode away. When the exit swung shut behind her, he grabbed his towel and water bottle and hurried after her. He caught her in the stairwell.

"Brooke, wait!"

She reached the bottom and pivoted to face him, hands on hips. "Yeah?"

She was still riled up, like an angry hedgehog, her bristles standing on end. The chatty, sweet Brooke he'd been getting to know was nowhere to be seen. Apparently he'd upset her more than he'd thought. He swallowed, hoping what he was about to say wouldn't make it worse.

"For what it's worth, I'm sorry. Seeing that guy flirt with you drove me crazy."

Her jaw went slack, and she sucked her peachy lips into her mouth, then released them. He stared, entranced. "But he was going about everything all wrong. A real man would have just kissed you." He proceeded to do just that, cupping her sweaty face in his hands and claiming her lips. They were softer than he'd thought possible, and tasted fruity and a little salty. At first, she was stiff beneath him, but then her lips parted and she let out a happy sigh.

He froze. He'd heard that exact sound before. He'd recognize it anywhere. And judging by the expression on her face when he slowly backed away from her, she knew it.

14

Brooke sensed the exact moment Jack *finally* remembered they'd kissed before. He froze, then drew back, staring at her with shock. His hands fell to his sides. She didn't know what the proper etiquette was for this situation, so she kept quiet and waited to see what he'd do or say.

"*Fuck.*" He grabbed her hand and tugged her toward the exit.

She resisted, not about to let him drag her off without an explanation. "Where are we going?"

"My place."

Relaxing, she allowed him to pull her outside and across the courtyard to his store. The woman behind the counter started to greet him, but trailed off when she got a good look at his face. She glanced at Brooke. "Miss, are you okay?"

Jack growled. "She's fine, Erica."

Erica looked to Brooke for confirmation.

"I'm all right," Brooke said, hoping it was the truth. She had no idea what to expect once Jack got her alone, but she didn't think ravishing her was part of his plan, more's the pity.

At the far end of the shop, he opened a door labeled

"Staff Only" and escorted her through it. As soon as the door clicked shut behind them, he spun to face her, eyes bulging, nostrils flared.

"So, *Khaleesi*," he spat. "Were you ever planning to let me in on your little secret?"

Brooke's jaw dropped, and just like that, she was flaming mad. Her hands tightened into fists, but she forced them open, planted her palms on his chest and shoved. Not hard enough to knock him over, but enough to push him back a step. She advanced on him, forgetting in her fury that he had several inches and fifty pounds on her.

"*Excuse me*?" she demanded. "You've got some nerve, jackass. I never tricked you, or was anything less than honest. I wasn't wearing a mask at that party. If you didn't recognize me, that's on you."

He didn't give any ground, and was so close to her that their chests nearly touched. His was heaving with emotion, his mouth set in a harsh, unyielding line, but he glanced to the side, as though unsure of himself for the first time since he'd made the connection between her and the girl from the party.

"It must have been obvious I didn't remember," he said. "You could have told me at any point, but you chose not to. That's deceptive."

Resisting the urge to cave in beneath the weight of her humiliation, Brooke held her head high. She wouldn't let him see her shame. "What, exactly, did you want me to say?" she demanded. "'Hi, I'm the girl who's so forgettable that a guy can make out with me for fifteen minutes and not even pick my face out of a crowd afterward.' Would that about do it?"

"I... uh..." A dozen different emotions flickered over his face, and she could see when he began to realize how poorly his actions reflected on him. All of a sudden, he was on the back foot when he'd considered himself the only injured party moments earlier.

Yeah, that's right. You'd better back down.

"Yes?" she asked, not about to let him off the hook.

Had she thought she'd moved past this over the last couple of weeks? She'd been deluding herself.

"It wasn't about you," he grumbled, eyes downcast, decidedly uncomfortable.

"I'm sorry?" She laughed, but the sound was humorless. She'd bypassed embarrassed and gone straight to furious. "It sounded like you just said that it wasn't personal when you kissed the ever-loving hell out of me and then never called and didn't recognize me later. Tell me, how is that not about me?"

He raised his eyes to meet hers and swallowed, his throat rippling. When he spoke again, his tone was quiet. Conciliatory. "I'd seen my ex earlier that day. I just wanted to forget everything for a while." He shrugged one massive shoulder, like it didn't really matter, but every word was a stab in her gut. "I figured you were an out-of-towner who was up for anything and that we'd never see each other again."

The humiliation she'd staved off hit her with the force of a battering ram, and the backs of her eyes burned. It truly hadn't been about her. She'd just been the nearest available woman to serve as an outlet for his pain. Had he been imagining his ex as their tongues tangled and they ran their hands under each other's clothing? The thought made her stomach rebel and she spun away and retched. Luckily, nothing came out.

He was at her side in an instant, his hand on her shoulder. "Are you all right?"

She shook him off, angry at herself for showing any weakness. "Fine."

"Are you sure? I can—"

She batted him away. "I said I'm fine!"

"Okay." He clearly didn't believe her, but he stepped back. "Once again, I'm sorry. I wasn't thinking straight that day, and I acted like an asshole."

She shook her head slowly from one side to the other. He still didn't get it. At least, not all of it. He may have had the decency to apologize—not that doing so made anything better—but he didn't understand why she was so upset.

"Jack, do you know how many times we met before that party?"

The confused crinkle of his brow was answer enough. She wrapped her arms around her waist to hold herself together.

"Three times," she told him. "We'd been introduced to each other three times before that day. When we were at that party and you kept calling me Khaleesi, I thought you were just being cute. That you knew who I was. It wasn't until the day you came to Sanctuary that I realized you were clueless." She unwrapped her arms, clasped her hands together and studied them. "You didn't even remember my name."

I'M A GRADE A ASSHOLE.

Jack watched Brooke's lower lip quiver as it sank in, for the first time, exactly how much of a jerk he'd been. Prior to this, he hadn't been proud of his behavior at the New Year's Eve party, but he'd suppressed any twinges of remorse by reminding himself that his Khaleesi had been a tourist out for a good time, and he'd certainly given her that. Although not as much as he'd have liked to, because they were interrupted before they could get to the good stuff.

That said, he had tried to hunt her down to pick up

where they'd left off, but she'd been long gone. It was probably just as well. With how fucked up he'd been after seeing Claudia, he probably wouldn't have hesitated to take her to bed, which made him an even bigger bastard. What kind of guy used an innocent woman to work off his anger?

Jesus, he'd messed up, and this sweet, beautiful—fuming—woman had paid the price. And *what* a woman. He felt like he'd never seen her properly, and now she was coalescing in front of him. Brooke—Khaleesi—one and the same, merging together in his mind. The passionate, mischievous woman from the party overlaid the sweet, determined Brooke he was coming to know. But despite all the time they'd spent together, had he ever really *seen* her? Or had he seen what he expected to see? Because his Khaleesi had fire, and he'd been too damned blind to recognize that same quality in Brooke.

"I'm really goddamned sorry." It wasn't enough, but he couldn't think what else to say.

"Oh, you're sorry?" Her eyes flashed and her lips twisted. "I guess that's all right then. You can do or say whatever you like, as long as you're sorry. That's how it works, right?"

There she was. His Khaleesi, in all her righteous fury. How had he ever overlooked her? Crossing his arms, he stood solid. He could take whatever she needed to throw at him.

"I've been a shitty person to you," he said. "I wish I could take it back, but what's done is done." He recalled that first session at Sanctuary. The way he'd asked her name like the world's biggest dickhead. She must have been seething. "Why didn't you say anything the day we went to the cave?"

She huffed. "I love how you keep putting the responsibility for this fuck-up on me."

He winced, both at the sound of the curse word out of

her mouth, and the accusation. That certainly wasn't what he'd meant to do. At least, not this time.

"Sorry. That came out wrong. I just meant, you must have been furious, but you didn't say a word. Other people would have ripped my throat out for less."

She sucked in a deep breath and let it out slowly. Some of the tension in her spine dissipated. "Yelling might have made me feel better in the short term, but it would have been embarrassing and I'd have burned my bridges in terms of learning from you." She shifted from one foot to the other. "Getting to Everest Base Camp means more to me than the temporary satisfaction I would have gotten from acting like a spoiled child. It's a promise I'm fulfilling to an old friend, one who isn't around to do it for herself. On top of that, I'm proving something to every person who doesn't think they can live their dreams. So I sucked up my pride. It was a small price to pay, in the scheme of things."

Whoa.

She was bringing him to his knees. Her mission was in honor of a friend who'd passed? How did he not know that? And how had he gotten her so horribly wrong? He squeezed his eyes shut and swore. He had a lot of ground to make up. He'd categorized Brooke in a way that suited him, and it hadn't been fair. A woman who could put aside her pride and self-righteous anger for the sake of achieving a nearly unattainable goal was one who demanded the utmost respect. Comparing her and Claudia hadn't been fair. All it had done was reinforce his prejudices.

His throat felt thick, and his arms were heavy at his side. "I think we can agree I've been an asshole, but I'd really like to make it up to you. Can I buy you dinner tonight?"

To his surprise, he desperately wanted her to agree. He'd liked spending time with her, and now that he knew she was hiding such passion behind her deceptively serene exterior, he wanted to get to know her better. He could scarcely breathe as she studied his face, indecision flickering over her features.

"Not tonight," she said finally. "I'm tired, and I have a lot of work to do on my thesis. My next chapter is due to my supervisor soon."

Disappointment slumped his shoulders. He couldn't argue with that, not without being more of a jerk. "Maybe some other time?"

She shrugged, but didn't meet his eyes. "Maybe." Turning, she started toward the exit. His arm rose to stop her of his own accord, but he cut the movement short before she noticed. In the doorway, she paused. "It's nothing personal. I'll see you tomorrow at Sanctuary." Then she was gone.

Nothing personal, his ass. He'd blown any shot he had with her.

15

———

Brooke v. World: Monday 18 February

I've been visiting the gym for a week now, and everything is going according to plan. More or less. I've suffered some minor setbacks, but I really believe I can do this. I'll keep you updated on my progress.

I'd love to hear what your goals are. Comment below and let me know. We can all provide support for each other, because you know what? You can do this. Our only limitations are the ones we impose on ourselves.

Much love XX

Brooke

As Brooke proofread an essay she'd written about female impressionists, the Darth Vader ringtone she'd assigned to Jack broke her concentration. She debated whether to answer. After yesterday, she didn't particularly want to speak to him, but she'd be seeing him later today, so she bit the bullet and lifted the phone to her ear.

"Hi." She'd rather have opened with, "What do you want?" or "Leave me to die of shame in peace," but that wouldn't be conducive to having an adult conversation, and she wanted to be able to say she'd taken the high road.

He cleared his throat. "Hey, Brooke. How are you doing?"

"Never better." Okay, so maybe she was feeling a tad snarky.

"Good." He cleared his throat again, sounding even less comfortable than he had in the back room of his shop yesterday. "I'll be over an hour early this afternoon. Can we talk?"

Picking at the fraying hem of her shorts, she asked, "About what?"

"Your plan to get to Everest."

"Oh." Relief cut sharp. "Yeah, sure thing. I'll be in my room or the lounge. If you can't find me, just call."

"Thanks." He sighed, as if a load had been lifted from his mind. "I'll see you soon."

WHEN HE ARRIVED, she was in her bedroom. She'd considered heading to the lounge for neutral ground, but had decided she'd rather keep their conversation private. If anyone overheard them, the gossip would be all over Haven Bay within an hour, so while Brooke would rather not be in a room that contained both Jack and a bed, here she was. She'd just have to remember to keep a healthy amount of space between them. It was strange how the thought of being near him flustered her more than it had before they'd kissed at the gym, even though they'd gone further at the New Year's Eve party. She supposed it might be because they now knew each other on a deeper level—and he'd actually been aware of who he was kissing, which had to mean something. Didn't it? Or was it only the presence of another man that had driven him to kiss her—some kind of weird macho competitiveness?

When he knocked, she counted to five before going to the door. She didn't want to seem too eager.

"Jack," she said, cracking it open. Damn, had no one informed her hormones that he was in the bad books?

"Brooke, hi." He scraped a hand through dark hair, which stood up in untidy tufts, like he'd just rolled out of bed after a night of tossing and turning. Was it bad that she was secretly delighted to think he'd slept like crap? She had, too, and only partly because she was angry with him. The rest had everything to do with that kiss.

She opened the door wider and pointed to her desk chair. "Come in. Have a seat."

She closed the door behind them and sat cross-legged on her bed, leaning against the wall. She didn't speak. Call her vindictive, but she wasn't going to do him any favors by making this easy for him.

He rubbed a hand down his pants leg. "I want to apologize for everything. I can give you a list of things I'm sorry about if it makes you feel better, but let's just say it's long."

She nodded. She'd be gracious. For now. "Thank you."

He tugged at the collar of his shirt, as if it were too tight. "If your goal of getting to Everest Base Camp means enough that you'll put all of this behind you, then I can do the same. I wasn't taking you as seriously as I should have done because I had reservations about your ability and commitment, but now I'm all in." He paused. "If you want me to be."

Her wariness faded a tiny bit. Okay, so maybe he was trying to bribe her for forgiveness, but if it meant she had his wholehearted support, perhaps it would be worth the tradeoff. After all, it wasn't as though he really wanted to be anything more than her training buddy, right? He hadn't suddenly developed feelings for her, or been overwhelmed by passion because he'd learned the truth. He was still him, and she was still her. He'd kissed her in the heat of the moment, and she ought not to read too much into it. The ensuing dinner invitation was damage control, and nothing else. It wouldn't do for her to start getting romantic thoughts about him. He was her trainer. And she could keep a respectful distance and forget the past if he was willing to commit to helping her.

"Yes, I do."

"Great." He cracked a grin. Hell, it was sexy. Her innards fizzed in response. *No, do not go getting butterflies over Jack Farrelly.* "Here's the big news. There's a mud run obstacle course in Te Awa Tui next month." Te Awa Tui was a neighboring town, a little bigger than Haven Bay. "That can be your first test. It has several different challenges. An army crawl, a river crossing, a wall climb, a net climb, and a few other things that change every year. If you finish that, I reckon you're more than ready for your first multi-day hike."

"Wait. Hold on a moment." She needed to get her head around this. She couldn't believe how quickly things were happening. "What about the list you gave me? Do I keep working on that?"

He shrugged. "It can't hurt. All of those exercises will be useful, but to be honest, I gave you the list to scare some sense into you." He grimaced. "Item number seventeen on the list of things I'm sorry for."

His confession was like a blow to her gut, but she hid it before he could see. She should be used to being discounted, but it stung every time, like a festering scab that people kept prodding.

When she didn't say anything, he continued, "Your main focus should be on the mud run. Bex will be able to adapt your program to get you there, and I'll help where I can, too. Then, if you finish, I'll take you hiking. I know some great tracks for newbies and you can buy a backpack and test it out, break your boots in properly, and really get the full experience."

She rubbed her temples, doing her best to take this in stride. "You and me, hiking together?" she clarified. "For more than one day? And all I have to do is finish this muddy obstacle course thing?" She wasn't sure what she thought of sharing a tent or a hut with him. Not after everything that had happened. But she could treat him like any other man. She *would*.

If only she could convince herself.

He nodded. "That's right, but it'll be harder than you might think."

Harder, but totally doable for someone as persistent as her. Her chest lightened. If she gritted her teeth and made it through this test, she'd not only prove to Jack that she was worth his time, she'd prove to *everyone* that she was just as capable as them.

"I'm in, one hundred percent." They could figure out the sleeping arrangements later. Anyway, making that kind of progress would be worth a little discomfort.

He laughed, throwing his head back. "That's my girl."

His casual statement gave her heart stupid ideas. She tried to contain it, but the silly organ wanted to beat out of her chest. She wasn't *his* girl. He didn't mean it that way. Did he?

Why did she even care? He was still a bastard.

"So, this is going to be strictly a professional relationship," she said, needing to clarify the boundaries so she didn't start envisioning a future they would never have. "I promise I'll take the training seriously and listen to instructions."

He chuckled again. "You think you can manage that?"

"Of course I can," she snapped indignantly.

"Glad to hear it. And hey, here's another thought." He leaned forward, muscular forearms resting on his thighs. She refused to let her gaze linger on those gorgeous limbs. "Why don't you look for a sponsor? Someone to cover the cost of travel and equipment?"

She blinked at him, bemused. "You think someone would be willing to sponsor me?"

"Hell, yeah."

She loved his tone. Full of confidence.

"It's an inspirational story, and a great publicity opportunity. Especially since you have a successful blog."

Still, she was skeptical. "I'm not so sure about that."

He reached over and laid a hand on her knee. The heat from his touch diffused throughout her entire body, turning her muscles languid.

"Brooke, look at it from a potential sponsor's point of view. You're a smart, enthusiastic woman, with a face the camera would love. You've had it a little rough, but you're not letting that keep you down, and your motivation is pure gold. People will love it."

"Um, thanks." She couldn't take her eyes off him. He'd entranced her with his intensity.

"And you know what else?" he continued. "If you find a sponsor who'll cover my costs, I'll go with you."

Her heart stuttered. "Oh my God, really? All the way to Everest?"

He squeezed her knee. "All the way."

She squealed and threw her arms around him, hardly able to believe it. He'd do that for *her*? Training was one thing, but to go all the way there... it was a whole other level. Since Olivia had died, she'd assumed she'd be making the trip alone. But now, she might not have to. How special was that?

"That would be amazing." She could explode from

excitement-overload. With extreme difficulty, she managed not to kiss him. He returned her hug, then released her, and she drew in a breath. He smelled good. Like pine needles.

"Does this mean I'm forgiven?" he asked.

She wrapped her arms around herself. She really ought not to hand out forgiveness so easily. He'd hurt her, insulted her, and generally been an ass. She should hold out for longer, just to punish him. But this was *Jack*. She'd never been able to resist him, even when wanting him filled her with shame and self-doubt. And the gesture he'd made was huge. It showed he believed in her, and that was rare.

Finally, she nodded. "I suppose I can forgive you."

He smiled, the expression almost tender. "Thank God for that."

JACK LOVED the feeling of Brooke in his arms a little too much and had to remind himself the hug didn't mean anything. She was excited, nothing more. And goddamn, it felt good to be responsible for her wide grin and cheerful chatter as she talked about the upcoming trip and the plans she was making. He watched her lips move and tried to focus on what she was saying, but the sun streamed through the window and turned the darker streaks of her hair to spun gold. With her glasses magnifying those gemstone eyes, she hypnotized him.

A line formed between her brows and he wanted to smooth it out with his thumb. How had he not realized she was his Khaleesi when her eyes were that singular shade of blue? Had a layer of makeup and mascara really made her look so different? Or, once again, had he just seen what he wanted to see?

"Jack," she said. "Are you listening to me?"

He blinked, clearing his head. "Sorry, what was that?"

She rolled those wonderful eyes. "Never mind. I'll explain later."

He nodded, then checked his watch. "Hey, I've got to go soon. You should come. I'll be taking some of the fitter guests rock climbing. It will be a good chance for you to learn." Plus he'd enjoy her company. He wasn't ready to say goodbye to her yet.

She flashed her white teeth. "Sounds like fun. Just let me change and I'll be there."

Stifling a groan at the thought of her stripping out of her jeans and t-shirt, he adjusted his position to hide his growing erection. He'd love to stay and help. To see what she had on beneath. Learning she was his mystery woman had only fueled his lust for her. But she wasn't inviting him, and he wasn't a creep, so he nodded.

"I'll get a drink. Come find me when you're done."

He headed out before he could change his mind. In the dining hall, he poured himself an instant coffee, then wandered onto the back lawn, where Tione was throwing a tennis ball for his dogs. Trevor, the bull mastiff, tripped over a patch of uneven ground and plowed through one of the flowerbeds, flattening a row of purple pansies. Jack winced. Betty would have Tione's head when she found out. Bella zipped alongside him and snatched the ball up before Trevor could recover. Zee, the rescue pup, bounded beside her, and Pixie trotted at the rear.

"Hey, Tee," Jack said, jerking his chin in greeting.

"*Kia ora,*" Tione called back. He took the ball from Bella, who'd returned it to him, and lobbed it in the other direction. The dogs took off, except for Trevor, who paused to shake himself off. Tione turned to Jack. "Saw you go into Brooke's room earlier. Is that the reason you've got a big-ass grin and look pretty pleased with yourself?"

Jack shrugged and fought the urge to look away so his friend didn't see his cheeks redden. "She's a nice girl. I like talking to her. Nothing wrong with that."

Tione's tattooed arms crossed over his chest. "She's one of the good ones." His expression darkened. "Don't play with her feelings. If you upset her, you'll answer to me."

Jacked gave a strangled laugh. "Is that so?"

He nodded. "Just thought it was fair that I warn you."

"Consider me warned. But honestly, man, I doubt anything will happen, and if it does, she scares me more than you do. She really let me have it yesterday." Tione would punch him out and consider the job done, while another verbal bashing from Brooke would deliver more lasting damage.

Tione's lips twisted into a smug smile. "Bet you deserved it."

"Too right, I did. Won't let it happen again."

The door to the garden opened and he smiled as the subject of their conversation emerged, looking fresh and pretty. "You good to go?"

"I sure am. Who else is coming?"

Jack checked his watch. "Not sure. Give it five minutes and we'll find out. I let the Bridge Club know that today's outing would be beyond their ability."

Brooke snorted, and clapped a hand over her mouth. "They must have loved that."

He melted on the inside. God, she was adorable. His new mission in life was to hear that snort-laugh again. "Mavis was prepared to go three rounds to prove me wrong."

"I'm not surprised. She could probably take you."

He clucked his tongue. "Cheeky, cheeky."

"That's how I roll."

He liked that she could laugh at herself. Claudia had

never been able to, and if he'd ever poked fun at her, she'd taken it personally.

"Yeah, yeah. Calm down, MacGyver." He turned back to Tione as she walked to his side and found his friend staring at him with narrowed eyes and a pursed mouth.

"Catch." Tione tossed a tennis ball his way.

Luckily, Jack's reflexes were good and he caught it. The dogs raced toward him, and he lobbed the ball to Brooke, calling her name. She fumbled with it, her eyes widening as the ball dropped to the ground and the dogs flew at it. She snatched it up and at the same instant, Zee leapt and gifted her with slobbery lick to the side of her face.

Jack and Tione roared with laughter as she furiously wiped her cheek with the hem of her shirt. "Ew, Zee!"

Zee panted, her tongue lolling out the side of her mouth, then bounced up on her hindquarters and tried to nudge the ball from Brooke's hand.

"You little monster," she grumped, holding it above her head. She turned to Tione, swung her arm back, and arced the ball in his direction. It hit the dirt well short of him and rolled into a rosebush. "Oops, my bad."

Tione held his hands up. "I'm not getting that."

While Brooke searched the bush, a pair of lean brunettes exited the foyer and headed straight for Jack.

"Hi," the taller of the two said, speaking with an Australian accent. "Are you the guy who runs the outdoor adventure sessions?"

"That's me." He offered a hand. "I'm Jack."

She clasped his hand, her grip firm. "I'm Savannah, and this is my sister, Willow."

"Nice to meet you. We'll be doing a beginner's rock climbing lesson today. Are you coming along?"

Savannah nodded. "Yeah, we've done a little rock

climbing before, but not in New Zealand, so we're keen to join. You're here three times a week, right?"

"Yes, but I mix it up so we don't do the same thing each time."

"Great!" Her amber eyes lit up. "Then I'd say you'll be seeing more of us over the next few days."

A moment later, a Chinese couple joined them. Jack greeted them, then waited a few more minutes, but no one else turned up. He directed the group around to his four-wheel drive, which was parked on the other side of the building, and told them to squish in. The Chinese couple squeezed in the back with Willow, while Savannah took the front seat, and Brooke—with far more glee than warranted—agreed to sit on the trailer until they reached their destination, which was only a few hundred meters down the road. Jack crossed his fingers that Sterling wouldn't see, or he'd be read the riot act. He was supposed to be abiding by a new-and-improved health and safety plan. Having not yet fully familiarized himself with it, he couldn't be certain, but having a woman on the trailer seemed like a no-no. He took it easy as they trundled away, then pulled onto a side road, traveling until they reached a collection of rocky outcrops.

"Here we are."

Savannah peered out through the windshield. "The rocks look much the same as the ones back home."

"Probably fewer creepy-crawlies that want to kill you," he replied. A knock on his window drew his attention to Brooke, who was staring in with flushed cheeks and shining eyes.

"Ohmygod," she said all in one breath as he wound the window down. "I want to go everywhere in trailers from now on. That was such fun."

He put a finger to his lips. "Don't tell everyone, or you'll get me in trouble."

She mimed zipping her mouth. "Don't worry. I'm like a vault when I want to be."

Everyone unloaded, and he handed each person a helmet and harness, watching while they adjusted the straps—some more successfully than others. When Brooke looked like she was wrestling an anaconda, he came closer to assist. A mistake. Instantly, he could smell whatever body spray she'd applied prior to leaving the lodge, and became hyper aware of the way her breasts rose and fell with each breath. Her tank top fitted too well for his peace of mind, and she looked soft and touchable.

His fingers fumbled with the harness straps and his knuckles nudged her stomach, which reflexively retracted. He longed to turn his hand over and caress her delicate skin, then kiss her as he had at the gym yesterday. But kissing wasn't part of their deal, and it wouldn't be professional, so he released her as soon as the harness had been fitted correctly.

He tried to clear his head because he needed to be on his A-game, but she kept infiltrating his awareness. Everywhere he turned, he heard her infectious laugh, saw her smile, or nearly perished of a heart attack because she slipped while climbing. She was secured from above and wouldn't fall, so his panic made no sense, yet he couldn't turn it off.

For Christ's sake, he even found it sexy when she mulishly set her jaw and insisted on making a fourth attempt to scale the cliff despite the fact that attempts one through three had been dismal failures and her arms were trembling from overuse. She muttered under her breath, referencing Star Wars on more than one occasion—something about how Luke Skywalker had made climbing look easy—but beneath it all, he caught glimpses of the vulnerability she didn't want the world to see, and that's what really undid him. He wanted to gather her in his arms and protect her, but he knew she wasn't the kind of girl who would welcome that, so he channeled his newfound energy into getting her as high up the damn cliff as he could.

When she hugged everyone in the group, a smile stamped on her face as they packed up, he was pleased as hell that he'd gotten over himself and offered her what it took to make her happy.

16

———

Brooke v. World: Tuesday 19 February

Hi all. I hope you're healthy today, and less sore than me. I learned to rock climb yesterday (badly!—see terrible photo below) and I was grateful for every minute because it's something I never thought I'd be able to do. That said, my arms ache like crazy. It's not easy trying to build muscle—something to remember if you're on the road to recovery, like me. Be patient and take it day by day. Celebrate the small wins. They're worth it, and so are you.

In other news, Jack made a really wild suggestion yesterday. He believes I could find a sponsor to help me get to Everest Base Camp. I'd never have thought of it—who would be interested in sponsoring little old me?—but maybe I should give it a go. What do you think?

Brooke XX

SWEAT PLASTERED Brooke's shirt to her body beneath a ten-pound weight vest as she walked at an incline on the tread-mill at the gym. She reached for her water bottle, her nonex-istent pecs complaining at the movement, and slugged back a few mouthfuls before returning it to the holder, wiping perspiration from her forehead.

A ringing phone cut through Florence and the Machine, who were playing on her headphones. She wasn't expecting a call, and the number was unknown so she let it go to voicemail and finished her workout. When her legs were nearly as shaky as her arms, she got off, unplugged her headphones, and listened to the message. A man's voice filled her ears.

"I'm calling for Brooke Griffiths. I hope this is the right number. I had my P.A. track you down. My name is Andrew Walters, and my daughter, Sarah, follows you online. She's a massive fan, and she showed me your post from earlier today. I'd like to talk to you about a sponsorship. My number is 027-475-3298. Call me anytime. If I don't answer, leave a message and I'll get back to you soon. This is a priority for me."

A click sounded and the message ended.

"Oh. My. God." Brooke spun in a circle, waving her hands in the air. "Bex, get over here!"

Her friend looked up from where she was sketching on a canvas by the window. "What is it?"

"Gah." Brooke raced over to her, discovering newfound energy, and thrust the phone forward. "Listen to this."

She watched Bex's face while the message played, a smile gradually easing across her features. When it ended, Bex grabbed her and hugged her tight. "Congratulations! When are you going to call him back? You should do it now. Seriously, call him now, Brookie."

Brooke's stomach somersaulted. "What do I say? I've never done this before. What if I mess it up?" She was blathering, but she couldn't seem to help it. "I haven't done anything to earn a sponsorship. What if—"

"No." Bex pressed a finger to Brooke's lips, smooshing

them shut. "No more 'what ifs.' You're a kickass woman and you haven't been given a damn thing you didn't earn, so you call that man back and negotiate like the boss bitch I know you are."

Thank God for girlfriends. "You're the best."

"And don't you forget it." She made a "hurry up" gesture and Brooke selected his number from her call log, holding her breath while the phone rang, a cowardly part of her soul hoping she could leave a message and sort out the whole sponsorship without talking to anyone. No such luck. Andrew Walters came on the line almost immediately.

"Hello?"

"Hi," Brooke said, wincing at her falsetto tone. "Andrew? This is Brooke. Brooke Griffiths. I'm returning your call."

Could she be any less professional?

"Brooke," he said. "I'm glad you called me back."

Her shoulders sagged with relief. Maybe it was silly, but she'd feared it was all a misunderstanding. There were a lot of Brookes in the world. Probably several of whom had blogs.

"My daughter, Sarah, is thirteen," he continued. "She has a heart condition that keeps her inside most of the time, but she reads your blog every day and you inspire her. Seeing someone who's been through the same things as her, but who is getting out there and experiencing life, gives her hope that one day she'll be able to do the same."

Tears welled in Brooke's eyes and she sniffled. Bex mouthed, "Are you okay?"

She nodded and swiped her towel across her face. She'd always hoped she was helping people, but hearing the words... she'd never imagined how good that would feel.

"Thank you. I'm so glad to hear that."

"I think it's important for you to know," he told her. "I want to make sure money doesn't hold you back from accomplishing your goals, because you've got the hopes of girls like Sarah riding on your shoulders. Easing the financial burden is the least I can do. My law firm, Howard & Walters, will gladly cover any travel costs, to a reasonable degree. We can discuss the details later."

"That sounds wonderful, thank you so much." If this was a dream, she prayed it would never end. "Are you really sure?"

Why had she asked that?

"I'm one hundred percent certain."

Oh, my God. She was going to Everest. She was going to *Everest.*

She squealed.

She whooped.

She laughed, tears streaming down her cheeks.

"Is this actually happening?" she whispered, to no one in particular.

"It's happening," Andrew said. "I'm completely serious."

She calmly laid the phone down, did a happy dance, her limbs flailing wildly, then picked it back up, took a deep breath and said, "Thank you. You have no idea how much this means to me."

He chuckled. "I have a better idea than most. You're very welcome, Brooke. I'm grateful to you. Without you blazing the trail and showing her what's possible, Sarah wouldn't be in a good place right now. So as your sponsor, I'm officially telling you that you're not allowed to give up. You need to do this, for her sake as much as your own."

"I will," she agreed, sobering. "Unless my body gives out on me, I'll get there."

"Good. That's what I want to hear."

Bex gave her two thumbs up, and a broad grin. Brooke slung an arm around her and squeezed, keeping the phone to her ear with her other hand. "I'm doing everything I can to improve my fitness," she told Andrew. "I'm also signing up for a mud run challenge in a month's time to test my progress."

"Have you considered inviting your followers to come and watch you?" he asked.

"No, I haven't." She considered it now. What would it feel like to have people in the audience who were pinning their hopes and dreams on her, like she was some kind of symbol? She swallowed. The prospect terrified her. She'd be carrying the weight of her readers' expectations. She supposed it might motivate her. If they traveled to watch, she couldn't fail. Couldn't let them down.

"You know what?" she said slowly. "That's a brilliant idea. I'll issue an invitation tonight."

"Great. Sarah and I will come, and I insist on taking you out for dinner afterward to celebrate and discuss the terms of the sponsorship. She's dying to meet you."

A dozen knots tightened in Brooke's stomach. She hoped the girl wouldn't be disappointed. Brooke wasn't a gorgeous Instagram celebrity or a fierce athlete. She was just a girl stumbling through life, trying to find her way.

"I'd love to meet her, too."

"Then it's sorted. You post the details online, and we'll be there. Take care, Brooke."

"Bye." The call ended and she stared at her phone, dazed. Had that really happened?

"I'm so happy for you," Bex said. "And yes, that really happened."

She must have spoken out loud. Then something else struck her. "I have to tell Jack."

She shoved her gym gear into her bag, slung it over her shoulder and raced down the stairs, where she nearly crashed into a man coming the other way. She scooted around him and dashed across the square to Seafaring

Adventures. When she'd covered half the distance, she spotted him, the sunlight gleaming off his dark hair, a hand on one hip, his t-shirt pulled tight across his chest. He saw her coming, but didn't wave, and that was her first inkling something was off.

When he shifted, the glare from the sun blinded her and she had to squint, then she came to an abrupt halt. Standing beside him, so close that only a sliver of space separated their bodies, was a tanned, athletic brunette. Brooke's brain stopped functioning, and she stared.

Then, as rapidly as her mind had fallen silent, a million questions popped into it.

Was Jack on a *date*?

Was this his *girlfriend*?

If so, why had he kissed Brooke—not once, but twice?

Perhaps they weren't dating, but something about the way they held themselves, their bodies angling toward each other, made her think they'd been intimate before. Was this an ex-girlfriend? Ex-lover? She was exactly his type. Fit, bronzed, everything Brooke wasn't. She'd bet the unknown woman didn't talk too much or spend months planning her outfit for sci-fi conventions.

"Hey, Brooke," Jack said, smiling in a way that didn't reach his eyes. "What's up?"

Her smile wavered, and she did her best to mask it, but his companion's expression became pinched. "I, uh, think I found a sponsor. For Everest."

"That's great. Well done, you!" His fake smile stretched wider, and though the expression sat awkwardly on his face, it made him so handsome it hurt to look at him.

He's with another woman.

Had she thought she could be friends with him and nothing more? Yeah, she'd been kidding herself. It seemed he'd always make her heart beat a little more rapidly.

"Thanks," she said, but the excitement she'd felt moments earlier had deflated faster than a balloon with a hole in it. "I just got off the phone with him. His daughter reads my blog, and she saw my post earlier this morning..." She trailed off as the woman scanned her from head to toe, her lips twisting in a dismissive smirk.

Suddenly, Brooke was all too aware of her red face, unflattering t-shirt, and the helmet of blonde hair plastered to her scalp. Next to the perfectly made up woman who looped an arm through Jack's, she must look a fright. She had never been one to compare her attractiveness to others, but given such a superb example of womanhood, it was impossible not to. And clearly, the brunette wanted her to leave.

"It's all coming together," he said. "Good for you."

She nodded, afraid to speak past the lump in her throat. He gave her a questioning look. She managed to choke out a brief farewell, then turned on her heel and bolted, heading for Sanctuary.

What had given her the stupid idea that Jack might view her as anything other than a mistake? She shouldn't be upset to see him with another woman. She was the one who'd insisted they keep their relationship professional. But damn, it stung.

Blinking back hot tears, she picked up her pace. She needed to shut herself in her bedroom, have a hot shower, and forget everything about Jack Farrelly except the fact he could help her accomplish her mission. That's all that really mattered.

If only she could believe it.

17

"WELL, THAT WAS WEIRD," Jack said, watching Brooke retreat. One minute she'd been racing across the courtyard toward him, wearing the biggest smile he'd ever seen—while he wondered what he'd done to deserve being sandwiched between the woman he was currently interested in and one he'd previously slept with—and the next, her face had turned splotchy and she'd careened away.

"That wasn't like her at all," he mused out loud. "Usually, when she's in a mood like that, it's all you can do to get a word in edgewise."

Though puzzled by her abrupt about-face, he couldn't deny being relieved over not having to introduce her to Hannah. Having the two of them in one place had made him uncomfortable. He'd had a casual relationship with Hannah while they were classmates at the polytechnic. She was the type of woman he'd always imagined ending up with, but it had never been serious between them.

"You're welcome," Hannah said, tossing her hair over her shoulder and winking.

He frowned. "What do you mean?"

She released the arm she'd latched onto and moved

away from him. "It's obvious that girl has a mad crush on you." She shrugged one shoulder and added, "It was also obvious from your body language that you don't feel the same way, so I put my resting bitch face to good use."

What the hell?

His shock must have shown on his face because she folded her arms and scowled. "Don't look at me like that. If the poor girl doesn't have a chance with you, it's nicer to let her know straight up."

His fingers curled into fists, and he replayed the entire interlude in his head. How had he missed the subtext? The two women had held an entire unspoken conversation, while he'd stood by like a dimwit. Heat flushed the back of his neck in recalling Brooke's wide eyes and open mouth as she'd stammered a goodbye and run. His stomach plummeted to the soles of his shoes. She'd been upset, and once again, he was responsible.

"Uh-oh," Hannah said. "Maybe I misread the situation."

"You think?" He hated the thought of Brooke hurting because of him. He wanted to go after her, gather her in his arms and promise there was nothing going on between him and Hannah. But why? He owed her nothing. He just... Well, shit. Suffice it to say, the mad crush was mutual.

"*Jack.*" Hannah's tone had grown impatient. "If you're interested in her, you shot yourself in the damn foot, because you weren't giving out those vibes, and if I picked up on it, you can bet she did, too."

He didn't answer, dozens of thoughts tumbling around in his brain, knocking against each other. He didn't know what to do, and for him, that was bloody unsettling. Maybe it was best to leave things as they were. He and Brooke were so different that any relationship between them probably wouldn't last, but shouldn't he explore the possibilities before making that decision?

Growling, he stomped into his shop, Hannah on his heels. He didn't want to have this conversation in public. Hell, he didn't want to have this conversation, full stop. Once inside, he sat on the sofa his tour groups typically waited on and gestured for Hannah to join him. When she did, he started talking.

"I like Brooke," he told her, trying not to take his frustration out on her just because he'd had to talk more about his feelings in the last few weeks than he had in years. "She's cute and funny, but I don't know if I *should* like her, you know?"

Hannah shook her head. "You lost me."

"We're really different people. If I ask her out, who knows how long we'll last?" He looked at the wall, the floor, anything but the woman beside him. If any of his friends heard him now, he'd never live it down. "But I can't just flip a switch and stop liking her. It doesn't work that way."

Hannah made a disapproving sound in the back of her throat. "You're my friend, so I'm going to be blunt with you. You're acting like a tool. You can't just string this girl along because you're not sure if you want to be with her. Do you even know how insulting that is? Make it clear, one way or the other. You're either into her, or you're not. It's that simple."

Nothing was that simple, but Hannah had a point. It wasn't fair to Brooke for him to keep flicking between hot and cold. The thought of her shutting him out of her life left a sour taste in his mouth. Closing his eyes, he imagined seeing Brooke stroll past his shop with another man's arm around her. A pinching, searing pain started in his gut, and he wanted to rip the imaginary man's arm from its socket.

"You're right," he said. "Thanks for not going easy on me."

She smacked his shoulder. "No problem. Now, stop being a dumbass and go get your girl."

He shot to his feet. "Erica!"

His assistant's head jerked up, as though she hadn't been eavesdropping during the entire exchange. "Yes?"

"Do I have any bookings this afternoon?"

She checked the calendar on her computer. "You've got a wildlife cruise at four."

Four. That was hours away. He had plenty of time. "Thanks. You're in charge now."

She nodded, and he stuffed his wallet and keys into his pocket and took off. Brooke had a head start on him, but she'd been on foot and his four-wheel drive was parked nearby, so he hopped behind the wheel and went after her.

"Brooke!" a man's voice called.

Brooke lengthened her stride. If it was Jack, she desperately didn't want to see him, nor was she feeling particularly social. Unfortunately, her legs were like jelly from her workout and didn't want to obey.

"Brooke," he called again. She winced. It *was* Jack, damn it. A four-wheel drive pulled alongside her, and the passenger window lowered. "Brooke, wait. Can we talk?"

For God's sake, couldn't she at least outrun her humiliation? Was that too much to ask?

Huffing, she slowed and glanced around, as though only just hearing him. "Oh, hey, Jack."

Good girl, play it cool. No feelings were hurt. You're running because exercise is good. Nothing more.

He slowed to a crawl, matching her pace, and kept his eyes on her rather than the road, which couldn't possibly be safe. "Can you stop for a minute?" he asked. "We need to talk."

"No, we don't," she said, lifting her chin. If he wanted to explain, he needn't. The situation had been totally self-explanatory, and she had no desire to hear the 'let her down easy' speech he no doubt had planned. "Why would we need to talk?"

His eyes darted to the road ahead of him, which fortunately was empty, then flicked back. "I know how that situation in the square looked, but I'm not dating Hannah. We... she..." He sighed. "Will you please stop?"

"Fine." She moved off the road, hands on hips, and waited for him to pull onto the shoulder and get out. In that time, she tried to check her ego. She was acting like a brat, as if he'd done something wrong, when he hadn't. He owed her nothing, and it wasn't his problem that her unruly heart wanted him.

When he came around to face her, she said, "You don't owe me an explanation. It's okay if you are seeing her. I'm sorry I was weird about the whole thing. It just took me by surprise."

Especially since they'd locked lips only a couple of days earlier. But then, they'd done that once before and he'd promptly forgotten her, so clearly his kisses didn't mean much. She was worth more than that.

"Maybe I don't owe you an explanation, but I'd like to give one anyway. Hannah and I used to see each other, years and years ago, before I moved to the bay. I ran into her in town half an hour ago and we chatted. It was completely innocent."

"That's not how it looked to me," she said, dubious. "Are you sure Hannah knows there's nothing between you anymore?"

He nodded, but looked pained. "She got the wrong end

of the stick. She thought I needed saving from you, so she stepped in.”

She laughed. Of all the ridiculous things she’d ever heard, that topped the list. “That’s crazy.”

He rolled his shoulders forward. “Yeah, but it came from a good place.” Stepping closer, he reached for her hand. She let him take it, hyper conscious of how damp and clammy it was.

His touch stoked a fire deep within her. One that had nothing to do with anger and everything to do with desire.

“Seriously, I’m not interested in her.” His eyes slid to the side. “I probably should be, but I’m not. You’re the only one I seem to want.”

Ouch. Why did it hurt so much to hear that? Knowing he wanted her should be gratifying, but learning that a guy liked her against his better judgment wasn’t exactly flattering. She’d known all along she wasn’t his type, but it was rude of him to come out and say it.

“I’m so sorry,” she snapped, tearing her hand away. “That must be terribly inconvenient for you. Little old me and my black magic sorcery getting in the way of your romance with someone who’s actually your type.”

He swore. “That’s not what I meant.” He fisted his hands in his hair and tugged. She hoped it stung. “I’m explaining this all wrong.”

Was there a way he could possibly have explained it right?

“Life tip, Jack. Don’t pull a Mr. Darcy on the next woman you’re interested in. Modern women don’t appreciate being told you only like them because your dick is overruling your brain any more than Lizzie Bennet did.”

Her reference went right over his head and he blinked in confusion, but seemed to focus in on the pertinent bit of information. “Don’t put words into my mouth, Brooke. My brain likes you just fine, but I didn't expect to feel this way about you. You're different from the other women I've been with."

Different.

She closed her eyes and turned away so he wouldn't see how badly that word flayed her. What was it about her that was so defective no one would just fall happily in love with her? Was it that she lacked an air of vibrancy? Or was it her preference for Star Trek over Love Island, and gaming over shopping, that marked her as someone to befriend rather than date?

"I get it," she said, her shoulders slumping. "You didn't have to chase me down, but I guess I should thank you for trying to explain." Though she still wasn't sure gratitude was in order. She wiped her palms on her tank top, itching to resume her walk back to Sanctuary, where she planned to lock herself in her room for the afternoon. Perhaps with a bottle of cider and the BBC series of *Pride and Prejudice*—the entertainment equivalent of fluffy socks and a chocolate bar.

He grabbed her elbow. "No," he said slowly. "I don't think you do get it."

Then he spun her around and planted a kiss on her. It was driven by frustration, she knew that, but he tasted of oranges and smelled like man. She inhaled, greedy for the scent of him, and he took advantage of that to press forward, aligning his body with hers. His tongue darted out, the tip touching her lips. She sighed and opened for him. His tongue explored the inside of her mouth with confident strokes. Her mind whirled and spun, unable to figure out which way was up. Her world became a pinpoint of sensation that centered on her mouth, and the wicked things his tongue was doing to her.

And not only his tongue.

His hands slid along her sides, one dropping down her

spine, his strong fingers flexing into her bottom, and the other rising to cup her breast. Her own arms banded around him, pressing tight to his lower back and holding him to her. Heat pooled at the junction of her thighs and she rocked into him.

Wait—what was she doing?

She was sweaty and gross, locking lips with the hottest man in Haven Bay. That didn't seem like a recipe for success. She stiffened, but Jack pulled his lips from hers and buried his face in the crook of her shoulder, his stubble rubbing her sensitized skin, making her shiver in pleasure. His lips brushed along the length of her neck, and he dropped a kiss in the hollow above her collarbone, then another below her ear.

She sighed. "Oh, my God."

"I can't get enough of you," he murmured into her skin. "The way you taste, the way you smell, the way you make that sexy fucking noise like you want me to strip you bare and lick you out." He inhaled deeply. "Like nothing else matters."

She whimpered, her underwear growing damp. She remembered how he liked to talk dirty. How he'd made her wet and aching with nothing more than his words at that blasted New Year's Eve party. He'd slipped his hand inside her skirt and rubbed her with a finesse her only other lover had never had. She wanted him to do the same now.

But they were in public. Anyone could come along. Two minutes ago, she'd been sick of the sight of him, but now she was greedy for more. More of the wonderful things he was doing with his hand on her breast, more of the scrape of his facial hair over her softest parts. More of his kisses. She grabbed his chin and directed his lips back to hers, taking the initiative this time and sampling him like he was a platter of her favorite sweets. Like he was Captain Kirk and Luke Skywalker rolled into one.

"More," she moaned. "I want more."

"I'll give you more, sweetheart. I'll give you so fucking much you won't be able to take it. You feel me?" A hot, hard rod throbbed against her core, and the last of her doubts evaporated. Jack was as wild for her as she was for him, squeezing her ass, nuzzling her jaw, rubbing his thumb over the outside of her sports bra, which was frustratingly thick. "That hard cock is all for you, Brooke. No one else." He gave a long, low groan as she squirmed and pushed closer. "It hurts for you. Wants to be inside of you." He released her body and cupped her face, tilting it up to look at him, to see his eyes blazing with raw want. "Will you let me make you feel good?" he asked. "Will you let me take you back to your room and do what I want?"

18

Jack was barely aware of the filthy words spilling from his mouth. All he knew was that his hands were on Brooke and there was a good chance he'd carry out an arrestable offense if he didn't get her somewhere private in the next two minutes. He was drunk on the taste, smell, and feel of her, as though his suppressed passion had accumulated behind floodgates until it was a raging torrent he could scarcely control.

When her muscles turned rigid and she drew back, eyes wide with something that resembled panic, his insides chilled. *Shit*. He'd gotten carried away. Gone too far, too fast, and left her behind on the journey. Just because he was ready to fall into bed didn't mean she was. He loosened his hold on her and backed away until a foot of air separated them.

"Forget I said anything. If it's too soon, I don't want to rush you."

"Wait." She caught his forearm, sucked her kiss-swollen lips inward, then took a deep breath. "There's no way in hell I can forget what you just said to me, and I don't want to."

She glanced down, her eyelashes fluttering, hiding her vibrant blue eyes. "I want everything you said."

Scarlet blazed across her cheeks, and he wondered how much redder she'd get if he made her repeat exactly what she'd like him to do to her. He was eager to find out, but maybe another time. She was still shy with him, and he didn't want to push her too far beyond her comfort zone.

"It's just that I'm gross and sweaty, and you're all..." She motioned up and down his body. "Clean and sexy."

He grinned. *Clean and sexy?* Hello, Miss Adorable.

"I don't care if you're sweaty," he told her. "I'll happily lick you all over, but if it makes you feel better, we could shower."

"*Together?*" she squeaked, the scarlet extending down her throat to the neckline of her shirt. He watched it, fascinated, and wondered how far it extended. Did she blush with her entire body?

Damn, he deserved a sainthood for resisting her this long. His mind filled with memories of his Khaleesi at that fateful party. Of the way she'd been boneless in his embrace, her rounded bottom in his lap, her blonde hair spilling over her shoulders as she threw her head back and let him kiss and suck his way up her neck. He'd left marks, and that had only turned him on more. Unfortunately, the only relief he'd found had been later, at home, with his hand. He hadn't taken things further with her, partly because they'd been interrupted and partly because he'd felt like an ass for being with her when his heart was wounded from running into Claudia.

Brooke still hadn't spoken. Maybe she'd started thinking properly and realized she wanted nothing more to do with him. He backed away another step.

"Okay," she said, raising her chin. "You and me, in the

shower, then the bed." Her eyes narrowed. "And no running away when the job is half done, understand?"

Hot relief cascaded through him. She wasn't turning him away. She wanted him as much as he wanted her. He saluted. "Yes, ma'am."

She laughed and shook her head, muttering "ma'am" under her breath. He took her hand and yanked her into his four-wheel drive, then hurried around to the driver's side and threw it into gear, the wheels spinning as he took off. The drive was short, but he couldn't stop grinning, the sides of his mouth tugging up of their own volition every time he tried to relax them. He'd finally been honest, and look where it had gotten him. Hannah was right, he'd been acting like a tool, but not any longer. He parked at Sanctuary, then reached over and curved a palm around Brooke's cheek, drawing her in for a kiss.

"You're sure?" he asked when their mouths parted.

She nodded, her eyes cloudy with desire. "Yes, but..." She hesitated. "Let's be low key about this, okay?"

He frowned. "How do you mean?"

"I mean, I have to live here, so I'd prefer the other guests and staff don't have anything to gossip about."

"Ah." He ignored a twinge of hurt at the thought she didn't want anyone to know about them. She had every right to privacy, and she was the one who had to stay here while he'd return home to an empty house, where there wasn't even a potted plant to judge him. "Got it."

"Jack..."

He unbuckled his seatbelt. He didn't need to hear whatever conciliatory words she had to offer. "Come on. I want to get you undressed."

She sighed, and met him at the front of the vehicle. They entered the lodge together. The foyer was empty, but Betty was sitting in the garden, gazing in. Jack nodded to her, and

Brooke waved. Then she turned her face into her shoulder and muffled a giggle.

"I feel like she knows exactly what we're doing."

He huffed in amusement. "She probably does. She was young, once."

When they reached the hall, they both sped up, Brooke already reaching into her bag for the key. She inserted it into the lock with trembling fingers and turned the handle, then closed the door behind them. This time, he didn't bother to scan the textbooks on her desk or study the mural on her wall. He crossed the room in long strides, yanked the curtains closed, then gathered her against his body, groaning in pleasure from the contact.

"You're so fucking soft," he murmured, lowering his head to nuzzle her. Most of his sexual partners had been firm and athletic. He'd always thought he preferred women that way, but there was something heady and addictive about the silkiness of her lower belly as he ran his thumbs along the skin above the waistband of her shorts.

"Need to shower," she said, drawing him through the door into the en suite. He went willingly, without releasing her. She had an open-plan bathroom, with a tiled floor and a shower head attached to one wall. She started the stream of water, then melted into his arms. He dropped kisses on her lips, cheeks, eyelids, then turned her head to the side so he could access the length of her neck. It was white and smooth and so fucking perfect. He latched onto the point where her pulse beat, and sucked. She moaned, sounding deep and contented.

Just like that, he was hard again.

He grabbed the hem of her shirt, but before he could pull it over her head, her hands flew down to stop him.

"Um," she said, licking those delicious peach lips, her hands still confounding his efforts to get her naked. She swallowed, and he watched her throat work. "The thing is, I'm not built like a fitness model." She met his eyes. "And I have a scar from surgery." She lifted her shoulders ever so slightly and dropped them. "Just thought I should warn you."

"Brooke, it makes no difference to me if you have green alien skin beneath this shirt. I'm still gonna want you."

"Okay, then."

She didn't believe him? He'd just have to prove it.

"Can I?" he asked, tugging on the hem. She raised her arms and let him remove her shirt. He did so gently, easing it over her head, and stood back to look at her. Pale, flat stomach—soft, like the rest of her. The scar she'd been so worried about was a thin pink line running down her sternum, several inches long, the center of her bra passing over it. He touched a fingertip to the scar and traced it from bottom to top. He'd known about her heart surgery, but for some reason it had only ever been a distant concept. Here was the proof of a very real procedure. Her chest had been opened up for a life-and-death operation, and his own heart wrenched at the thought of what she'd been through. She was a survivor. A warrior.

"It's hideous," she muttered.

Tenderness surged within him. "It's part of you," he replied. "And it's beautiful, because it means you're still here, with me. You made it through."

Her gaze flew up to his. "Kiss me, Jack."

<hr>

THE WAY he looked at her... God, his admiration was a potent aphrodisiac. Brooke locked her hands behind his head and dragged him down for a long, thorough kiss, trying to convey through her actions how much his words meant to her. Jack wasn't a shallow boy, he was a man—one she wanted with every fiber of her being.

"Wow," he said, as their lips separated. "We gotta get you into that shower, or I'm taking you right fucking now, sweaty or not."

She laughed and wrestled her sports bra off, then pulled the tie out of her hair and tugged off her shorts and underwear, not giving him a chance to ogle her before she stepped under the spray. But as the water soaked her hair and ran in rivulets down her back, over her breasts, and to the floor, she kept her attention focused on him, not wanting to miss a moment of the show as he performed a similarly hurried striptease.

His hard stomach rippled as he took his shirt off, and dark hair dusted his chest, with another arrow of hair disappearing into the waistband of his jeans. His shoulders were broad and bulky, his nipples little brown nubs. She swallowed as her eyes tracked lower. There was a bulge beneath the fly of his jeans. An impressively-sized bulge. One she wanted bare as soon as possible. He caught her gaze and one side of his mouth quirked up in a cocky smirk. He undid the zipper agonizingly slowly, and a groan of frustration tore from her throat.

His chocolate eyes darkened. "Patience," he teased.

"I've been patient enough," she grumbled. "Hurry up. The sooner we get clean, the sooner we both get what we want."

He laughed, stepping out of his jeans. "You know, the shower doesn't have to be a means to an end. You might enjoy it more than you think."

She swallowed. Did he mean sex in the shower? Yeah, she knew some people did that, but had never thought anyone would want her so much that they couldn't wait ten minutes until they were somewhere more comfortable.

Shower sex was for people so carried away by lust that they didn't notice how awkward it was.

"Uh-uh," she said. "I doubt it."

His smile faded. "Then I guess I'd better persuade you otherwise."

With a smooth motion, he removed his underwear and stalked toward her, his thick erection bobbing with each step. If she had been wearing panties, they would have been soaked, and not just from the shower. She squeezed her thighs together, trying to contain herself, but she couldn't take her eyes off him. He was all man. His strong legs were corded with muscle, and at their apex was a thatch of dark hair with his dick jutting proudly from it. The visual overwhelmed her. She whimpered, and automatically, his entire drool-worthy body tensed.

"You like what you see?" he demanded.

"It's all right," she said, her voice husky.

One eyebrow leapt up. "Just all right?" He stepped closer, crowding her, but not quite touching. "I think you like me better than 'all right.'"

She swayed toward him, initiating contact. Her slick skin slid against his, the sensation divine. Her eyelids fluttered closed. "Okay," she admitted. "I like it a whole lot."

He growled in satisfaction, and his arms went around her, fingers sinking into her ass to drag her closer. "That's what I thought."

He tilted her face up as he lowered his, and their lips met halfway. The kiss consumed them. She was aware of nothing but the texture of his lips, and the exquisite press of his erection to the part of her that seemed to have become the new center of her nervous system. His hands smoothed up her sides, and came around to cup her face. They felt large and rough against her skin, and she shivered. He was turning her into nothing but a puddle of endorphins.

Who knew kissing could be so good?

Then he drew away. She tried to clutch him closer, but he gently disengaged and reached for the soap.

"You wanted to be clean, remember?" His voice was so low, she felt it as much as heard it.

"I changed my mind."

He shook his head. "I'll clean you."

Oh, hell. Did he actually mean...?

Rubbing the bar of soap between his hands, he worked up a lather, then set his palms to her shoulders and spread the soap over them with gliding movements. She bit her lip, determined not to moan. He was toying with her. Trying to drive her crazy. But she could handle it.

His hands journeyed down to her breasts, where he proceeded to do a very thorough job of cleaning her. His outdoorsman hands were dark against her pale breasts, and the contrast excited her. He rubbed his thumbs over the tips, then continued downward, splaying his hands over her belly, making her a writhing mass of sensation.

His lips touched her ear. "You feel clean yet?"

She fisted her hands and shook her head. She never wanted this slippery, sensual exploration to end. "No," she whispered. "I think you missed a spot."

His fingers twitched, and that was the only sign her words had affected him. His questing hands slid lower, and she gasped as one wedged between her tightly clenched thighs, his fingers delving into the folds of her sex. She shot upright and grabbed his shoulders.

"Shh," he soothed. "Easy, Brooke. I've got you."

His fingers began to rub rhythmically against her, and she rocked into his palm, burying her face in his shoulder. He crooked a finger, and she almost exploded from pleasure.

He groaned, and it rumbled through his chest. "You're so

fucking hot. And so wet. This is all for me, isn't it? You're so needy for me."

She didn't answer. She didn't need to. It was self-evident. But then he pulled his hand away and peeled himself off her.

"Come back," she said.

He chuckled, the sound deep and dirty. "You're a bossy wee thing, aren't you? I like it."

She wanted to roll her eyes, but didn't have the presence of mind. Instead, she let him guide her out of the stream of water and pin her to the wall. She thought he was preparing to demonstrate how amazing shower sex could be, but then he dropped a single kiss on her lips and sank to his knees.

"What are you...?"

He gripped her thighs and his tongue darted forward.

"*Oh, God.*"

Her legs were boneless. If not for his support, she'd have ended up on the ground. She tried to hold herself up on the tiled wall, but her muscles wouldn't cooperate. Instead, she gripped his shoulders as he feasted on her. She'd never felt anything like it. Her other lover had never gone down on her, and she'd assumed all men found the act distasteful. But Jack was uttering filthy things and lapping at her like she was a delicacy. Thanks to him, she was riding the edge of orgasm. She focused on his face. His eyes were closed, his brow furrowed in concentration. Suddenly, the flat of his tongue padded her clit. Hard. She shuddered, and struggled to keep her eyes open. She didn't want to miss a moment of this.

"Mmmmm," he murmured against her, his eyes opening and locking with hers. "I can taste how bad you want me."

Oh, fuck. Had she thought it was erotic before? Hearing him say that, his dark eyes blazing into hers, she had to bite her lip so she didn't cry out loud enough to bring the whole lodge running.

"I do," she said, low and sure. She'd never talked dirty in her life, but she had the urge to repay everything he was giving her with more of the same. "I want you so bad. I want you inside me." She swallowed, hoping he couldn't see her nerves. "I want you to fuck me. Right here."

He started to stand. "Hell, yes."

"But first, *I* want to taste *you*."

His jaw went slack. "I'm, uh—" he cleared his throat "—not sure that's such a great idea."

"Oh, but I am."

He hesitated, though she could tell from the way he eyed her mouth that he wanted it.

"I'll stop the moment you say the word."

At that, his lips twisted into a wry smile. "I think that's my line."

He raised himself the rest of the way up and leaned over to tangle his tongue with hers. She never wanted the kiss to end, but she tore her mouth from his, loving the way his gaze followed her and his chest rose and fell rapidly as she lowered herself to the floor.

He was ruddy and engorged, a pulsing vein running the length of his erection, from his balls to the ridged head. She stroked the vein with the pad of her thumb, then touched the very tip, spreading a bead of pre-cum with her fingertip. His hips thrust forward, pressing him into her palm.

"Suck it," he ordered.

She dropped her hands to her sides and looked up at him. "Say please."

His eyes burned down into hers. "*Please*," he growled. "Suck me, Brooke."

Ooh. She'd never have thought being ordered around would turn her on, but it did. Perhaps because she realized she was the one with the real power here. He might be telling her what to do, but he was desperate for her. She could leave him hanging, and he'd be frustrated and horny with no outlet.

But that wasn't fun.

Experimentally, she licked him like an ice cream. He tasted salty, and was hot and heavy in her mouth. She closed around him and sucked. He rocked forward. Her eyes widened in surprise as he lodged more firmly in her mouth, but she didn't move back. His fists tightened, his forearms cording with muscle. She used one hand to anchor herself to him, and stroked his shaft while she unleashed the full force of her enthusiasm with her mouth. Licking, sucking, kissing, swirling. A series of nonsensical noises spilled from his lips. Half-words, curses, sounds of encouragement. Then, all of a sudden, his hands were on her shoulders, pushing her away.

"Fuck, fuck, *fuck*. No more, sweetheart, or I'm done for."

His eyes could have been mistaken for black, and every muscle in his body was popping, his jaw clenched. Brooke's mouth went dry. *She'd* done that to him. *She'd* pushed him to the edge of his control, and *she* was the reason he was aching for release. The thought made her legs so shaky she couldn't stand. She reached for him, trying to take him in her hand.

He evaded her. "Play time is over. It's my turn now." He inhaled deeply, his nostrils flaring as he breathed out. Then he cracked his neck, seeming to find his equilibrium. "Serious question. Do you give a shit if we mess up your bed?"

She shook her head and whispered, "No."

"Good." He grinned, and it was absolutely feral. She wanted to jump his bones, if only her legs had the strength.

But then he turned off the shower, bent, slipped an arm behind her thighs, and scooped her up.

She gasped. "What are you doing?"

Mischief flickered in his expression. "Looked like you were having trouble moving."

She sputtered. That... that... presumptuous, *sexy* jerk.

He opened the door to her room, and steam billowed out. He carried her to the bed, and she held onto his neck, amazed that he could hold her up so easily. And to think, she'd been proud she could walk in a ten-pound weight vest. Jeez, she had a long way to go before she was at his level.

He dropped her in the center and immediately covered her body with his own, then raised himself up on one elbow, creating space between their bodies. She stretched up to kiss him. The kiss wasn't languid, it was all-consuming. Unmistakably a prelude to more.

She couldn't think, could only feel. Being this near to Jack was like nothing she'd ever experienced. She was ready to crawl out of her skin. No one had ever made her feel like this. Not just physically, but emotionally. It was like he couldn't get enough of her. Like he was an addict and she was his next fix. It was heady. Wonderful.

His hand slipped between them and found her sex. "Mmm," he rasped. "So hot and wet. You want me now, baby?"

"I want you," she breathed.

"Thank fucking God."

He withdrew from her, and she bit her lip, watching his ass muscles flex as he retrieved a condom from his wallet. He rolled it on and settled over her again, pressing into her in a single motion. She cried out as he filled her, stretching her to the limit. She'd been slick, and he entered easily, but it had been a *really* long time since she'd been with anyone, and the invasion felt a little unfamiliar.

"*Shit*," he cursed. "You okay?"

"I'm good," she gasped. "So good. But go slow for a bit, please."

He did as she asked, giving her a moment to adjust, then sliding back into her in a long, smooth thrust. Her heart thumped so rapidly she feared he'd notice and stop, but after the third glorious thrust, it started to slow, and by the fifth, she was moaning and trying to get closer.

"You're so fucking tight," he muttered between kisses. "You haven't had a man take care of you for a long time, have you honey?"

She squeezed her eyes shut, not wanting to admit exactly how long it had been. "No, I haven't."

He hooked an arm around one of her legs and drew it up, opening her wider, pounding into her in the best possible way, driving her higher, into a crescendo of passion, again and again and *again*.

"Tell me how it feels."

"Feels so good." She was barely aware of speaking, let alone what the words were. "Feels like I can hardly take it anymore. Feels like I'm gonna go crazy if I don't come soon. *Please*, Jack, I'm so close. So close."

"I know you are, baby." His voice was gravelly. "I'm right with you."

Her eyes flew open as his mouth contorted in a grimace, the lines of his neck deeply pronounced. The sight of him, that big, strong man, craving relief but desperate to get her there first, was all it took to send her crashing headlong into orgasm, shuddering and trembling and calling his name.

"Thank fuck," he grunted. "Keep coming, baby, I got you." And then he muffled a litany of swearwords in the crook of her shoulder as he finally allowed himself to claim his own pleasure.

19

———

Whoa.

Jack felt wrung out. Wonderfully, blissfully spent. Rising up on his elbows, he dropped a kiss on the tip of Brooke's nose. Her lips curved up at the edges, and he smiled back. He hadn't expected this when he chased after her earlier, but he had no regrets.

"Wow," he said, kissing her once more, then rolling off to lie on his back beside her, their shoulders touching. "That was really fucking amazing."

She giggle-snorted, then hid her face in her palms. "Better than when Luke blew up the death star."

A laugh burst from his chest. Damn, it felt good to laugh with a woman, and to enjoy himself without worrying whether she was judging him and finding him wanting. Brooke *definitely* hadn't found anything lacking when it came to his performance in bed, he was certain of it.

"No matter how many layers I peel back, I'm just going to find more nerd, aren't I?"

"Yep," she said proudly. "All the way to the core, and I'm not sorry for it."

"Nor should you be."

They lay side by side in companionable silence. He reached between them and gripped her hand, thinking once again about how he'd gotten her all wrong. Thank God she was patient enough to give him a chance—although he got the feeling he wouldn't get another.

Somewhere on the floor, his phone vibrated. He glanced at the clock. His afternoon cruise would depart in an hour. He needed to get going. Sitting up, he squeezed Brooke's hand, then released it.

"I have a cruise. I've got to go."

Her face fell, and he belatedly realized his words sounded like a brush-off. Jeez, it had been too damn long since he'd been in a relationship. He was messing it all up.

"You should come over to my place later," he said, pleased when her smile returned. "If you want to, I mean." He hesitated, then decided to go all in. "If you're comfortable with it, you should bring an overnight bag." He kissed her again, then lingered, nuzzling the side of her neck. "I'd love for you to stay."

Indecision flickered in her clear blue eyes, but then she nodded. "I'll be there, and I'll bring dinner."

"I can't wait."

COULD this afternoon get any better?

Brooke grinned at the ceiling as the door closed behind Jack. Her entire body tingled from the marvelous things he'd done to her. Dear God, the man knew how to use his hands. And his *mouth*. Sitting up, she fanned herself. Was it hot in here, or was it just her?

She stood on wobbly legs and teetered over to find a bra, panties, and her most flattering summer dress. The one that made her skin look radiant rather than washed out. Then she opened the curtains, unlatched the window, and breathed in a lungful of fresh air.

Life was good. She'd had her mind blown in the most sensual of ways, she was feeling stronger than ever, and someone was willing to pay for her to go to Everest. Sighing contentedly, she crossed to the mirror and smiled at her reflection, wanting to see if the effects of the day were visible. It might be her imagination, but she thought she glowed. She grabbed a tube of pink lip gloss from her purse and swiped it on. Even better.

She slipped on a pair of sandals and strolled out into the hallway, where she came face to face with Kat, who was heading up the hall, carrying a wrench.

"*Kia ora*," Kat said, stopping. "Something good happened. You're grinning like you won the lotto. Does it have anything to do with the fact you had Jack alone in your room?"

Brooke blinked, wondering how she'd known. "*Betty*."

Kat nodded. "Betty sees all, and what she sees, she shares. So?"

Glancing furtively around to make sure Betty wasn't in earshot, Brooke tugged Kat into her room, lowered her voice and said, "I'm only telling you this because you're my best friend. No one else needs to know." She wasn't sure if she and Jack were an item now, and she wanted to have that conversation with him before anything got churned through the rumor mill. "We had sex. It was epic. Ah-maz-ing." She sighed rapturously at the memory. "That man... the things he can do..."

Kat held up her hands as if to ward her off. "Please spare me the details, chick. There are some things I don't need to know about my friends. But I'm happy that you're happy."

"I *am* happy," she agreed. "It's been a wonderful day. Earlier, I was at the gym, and I got a call from this guy whose daughter reads my blog. He wants to sponsor my trip to Everest."

"*Tino pai!* That's amazing." They high-fived. "And don't think I didn't notice how you mentioned the gym, all casual-like." She beamed at Brooke. "Everything is really coming together for you."

"I know. I can hardly believe it."

"So, when are you seeing Jack again?"

"He invited me over tonight. To stay."

Kat's jaw dropped an inch. "That's very un-Jack. He must really like you."

Brooke's stomach fluttered, like kittens with pitter-pattering little paws were scampering around in it. She fought the urge to pump her fist or wave her arms above her head in victory.

"You think?"

Kat's jaw snapped shut and she grinned. "Yeah, I do. Who wouldn't love you? You're a great person. And tonight, you should go over there and be a total hussy. Enjoy yourself. You've earned a bit of fun."

"You know what? I think I will." It was a pity it was so late in the day or she'd have made a trip to the next town over to stock up on gorgeous lingerie. Her current supply was pretty limited. As in, she owned one thong and a couple of bras that used to be nice. Truth was, she hadn't been with a guy since her first year of university—the year she'd actually been well enough to spend on campus, away from her hovering parents.

"I've got to go fix the sink in Mrs. Tanner's room," Kat said. "But I want a full report tomorrow."

"You got it, Kitty-Kat." They left the room together, and parted ways. Brooke waved to her friend and went to make a mocha. Tione wasn't in the kitchen, which was just as well because she didn't think he'd approve of her sleeping with

Jack, and Betty was bound to have told him by now. Drink made, she traced her steps back and sat at her bedroom desk, where she opened her blog and typed a new entry.

*B*ROOKE *v. World: Tuesday 19 February Part 2*

Thank you, you absolutely brilliant people! I now have a sponsor for my trip to Everest Base Camp because of your support and generosity. A special thank you to Sarah. You're a princess among women.

I'm also thrilled to be able to invite you to watch me compete in a mud run event on the 9th of March—the first real test of my fitness. I'm nervous and excited at the same time. I'm afraid I'll let you down, but I really believe I can do this. I'd love it if you could be there to cheer me on. I'm doing this for all of you.

I'll include the details below this post. For those of you who can't make it, I've decided to wear a GoPro, so you can watch my progress in real time, streaming directly onto the website.

Stay healthy.

Brooke XX

U SING the camera incorporated into her laptop, she snapped a photo of herself smiling, inserted it into the post, and added the when and where of the mud run. Then, her heart in her throat, she pushed "publish" and prayed she wouldn't screw this up.

I'M DONE *for the day and heading home. See you soon?*

Jack sent the text to Brooke, smiling to himself. It was nice to have someone who cared when he was finished with work. Made him feel less alone. But damn, his afternoon tour had lasted for an eternity. Usually, he enjoyed spending time on the water, but today all he'd been able to think of was getting back to Brooke. He wanted to learn how she liked to be kissed and touched, hear more about her life, and ask some of the questions he was dying to have answered.

Why had she moved here?

What were her family like?

What made her tick?

A reply popped up two minutes later. *Great! I'll finish this section of my thesis and come over. What's your address?*

He sent it to her, a touch disappointed that he'd have to wait. Strange how he'd occupied the same town as her for years and never yearned for her, but now that he knew the way she sighed when he kissed her, he craved her the same way he craved the outdoors. With a desperate, achy longing.

He drove home, showered, dressed, and was pouring himself a beer when he noticed the dirty laundry discarded on the floor. Not ideal when he had a woman coming over. Scouting through the house, he scooped up every item of clothing he could find and stuffed as many of them as he could in the washing machine. He piled the rest in the hamper, then shut the laundry door. That done, he opened every window in the house and hoped a healthy breeze would clear any staleness away.

Looking around, he realized with dismay what a disaster area his place was. How had it gotten this bad? Beer cans, glasses, and empty plates littered the floor, and the trash cans were overflowing. With a curse, he carried the trash out to the wheelie bin, stacked the plates and glasses in the dishwasher, and stashed the beer cans in the recycling bin.

But still, the floor needed vacuuming.

And his bedroom...

He peeked around the bedroom door and cringed. The

bed was a mess and his cabinets were dusty. Sighing, he rested his forehead on the wall. He couldn't tidy everything. He needed to prioritize. If he made a couple of rooms presentable, he could keep Brooke out of the others. Mind made up, he walked through the house and closed every door except for the ones leading to the kitchen, living room, bathroom, and main bedroom.

Then he started cleaning in earnest, whipping off the bedsheets and replacing them with fresh ones, taking care to straighten the blankets rather than tossing them on haphazardly. He grabbed a rag from the laundry cupboard and wiped down the cabinets. In the kitchen, he threw away everything that looked rotten or moldy, and sterilized the counter. Then he ran a vacuum over the floor and the sofa cushions. Finally, he slumped in an armchair, satisfied that his house no longer resembled a scene from one of those "renters gone mad" reality TV shows.

He'd been resting for less than two minutes when the doorbell rang. Hastening over, he opened it and grinned down at Brooke, who was standing on his doorstep with a newspaper-wrapped package tucked under her arm and her glasses perched on the bridge of her nose.

"Hey, there," he said, bending to kiss her cheek.

"Hi," she said, looking up at him through her lashes almost shyly. "I hope you like chocolate donuts. I got two to go along with the chips."

"Love 'em," he told her, wanting to erase the hint of tension from her posture. "Come on in." He started toward the living area, gesturing for her to follow. "Can I get you a beer?"

She laughed. "No, but water would be good, thanks."

He glanced over his shoulder. "Don't tell me you don't like beer."

"Eh." She waved a hand from side to side. "It's okay, but I

prefer sweeter drinks."

Why didn't that surprise him? Maybe because she was so sweet herself.

"Thanks for bringing dinner. Do you want a plate?"

"Nah, I'm happy to eat with my fingers like a savage."

He left her in the living room, filled a glass of water, tucked a beer under his arm, and grabbed the ketchup from the fridge.

"Here you go," he said, coming back and handing her the drink.

"Thanks."

"No worries."

She unwrapped the bundle of chips and donuts and laid them on the coffee table. He squeezed ketchup onto the open paper and dunked a chip into it.

"How'd the work on your thesis go?"

"All right." She chose one of the donuts and bit into it, chocolate oozing from the sides. "Mm," she moaned, her mouth full. "That's good."

The sound messed with his equilibrium. Lust arrowed downward. He wanted her again. Damn, he was in trouble where she was concerned.

He cleared his throat. "What's it about?"

"The overarching theme is female artists and the influence they had on art at different periods of time."

"Sounds interesting." He started in on his own donut.

She rolled her eyes. "You can say it. It sounds far too boring and tame for you. That's okay. I love art and art history, but I mostly chose to major in it because it was something I could do by distance learning. My first year of study was actually in mechatronics engineering. I was accepted into the second year courses, but by that time I wasn't well enough to attend classes so I had to change direction, and here I am."

Jack grinned. "I'm glad you're here."

Her eyes softened. "Me too."

There was a spot of chocolate above her lip. He reached over and wiped it off with his thumb. Her eyes fluttered closed and she hummed, then they snapped open again, a flush staining her cheeks.

"So that's me," she said, a little louder than necessary. "A crash course in the last few years of Brooke. Now, tell me. Who is Jack Farrelly and how did he come to be here?"

She was nervous, he realized. Nervous, and trying not to show it. It warmed him to think that she wanted this dinner to go well just as much as he did. But his past wasn't much to talk about. Not compared to hers.

"It's a boring story."

"Somehow, I doubt it." She finished the donut and licked cinnamon sugar from her fingers, her pink tongue darting out from between her lips.

He grabbed a chip and shifted to conceal his growing erection. "Do you really want to hear it?"

"Yeah," she said. "I want to know what made you You, you know?" She giggled. "I just said 'you' way too many times, didn't I?"

He held his fingers an inch apart. "Just a little." He considered her question. There was no way to tell his story without mentioning Claudia, but it wasn't good form to prattle on about ex-girlfriends, so he decided to keep it as brief as possible. "You already know the basics. I messed around for a while after high school, working odd jobs, then once I had my head on straight, I did an outdoor education course in Auckland. Planned to leave as soon as I was finished, but then I met my ex and ended up staying for a couple of years." Which had been a constant source of tension between him and Claudia, because he'd resented her for keeping him in the city, and she wouldn't hear of moving away. "When we broke up, I came here and set up my own business. I knew Logan—we studied together—and he let me room with him until I was back on my feet."

She nodded. "Seems like everything worked out for you."

He shrugged. Yeah, he could see how it looked that way, on the face of things. But something was *missing*. Something he was beginning to think might look a lot like Brooke.

"I could say the same for you, *Dr.* Griffiths."

She laughed. "I don't get to call myself 'Doctor' until I've stood in front of a panel of experts and defended my thesis. That's a way off yet."

"You'll rock their socks off."

"I don't think I'd go that far, but I have faith in myself."

A thought occurred to him. "You always do, don't you?"

Not once had he seen her waver. Not while she'd been dead on her feet, and not even when her feet were raw and blistered.

She popped a chip in her mouth and looked uncomfortable. When she'd finished chewing, she swallowed and said, "I guess I've never seen the point in doubting myself. Enough other people do that already. In my experience, if I'm patient, persistent, and work hard, everything is possible. It just takes time." She ate another chip, gazing at a stain on the tabletop. "Even if I wanted to run a marathon one day, I know I could do it. It might take years of grueling training, but eventually I'd get there."

"That's amazing." He'd never been more attracted to any woman than he was to her in that instant. Her attitude was sexy as hell. "Are you still hungry?"

She cocked her head. "I think I'm good for now. What did you have in mind?"

He wiped his hands on a napkin and winked. "Come to the bedroom and find out."

20

—————

"You mean we're going to be old-fashioned and start in the bedroom this time?" Brooke asked as she laid her glasses down, took the hand Jack offered and followed him to one of the only open doors in the house. Either he really liked to compartmentalize, or the place was as much of a pigsty as any single man's, and he was trying to hide it to make a good impression. Strangely, she found that prospect hopelessly endearing. "What did I do to deserve this treatment?"

He drew her inside and pinned her between him and the wall, with scarcely enough room to breathe. She'd seen his eyes darken with arousal moments earlier, but didn't know what had caused it.

"You're just so damn sexy," he said in that raspy tone she was beginning to recognize as his horny voice. "Your body is sexy." He nuzzled the side of her neck. "Your mind is sexy," he continued, his lips moving against her skin, sending shivers dancing down her spine. "And your attitude is the sexiest thing of all."

"My attitude?" This, she had to hear.

He scooted closer, if such a thing were possible, and she could feel the hard length of him through the clothes

184

separating them. His proximity muddled her mind. She wasn't used to men like him. Ones who were virile, rough around the edges, and accustomed to taking what they wanted.

The guy she'd lost her virginity to had been sheltered during his teenage years, like her. They'd never been more than friends, but they'd made a pact to be each other's first if no one else came along in the initial semester of university. No one had, for either of them. Sex with him had been okay. They'd both been totally inexperienced, but it could have been worse. He'd been gentle and attentive, and they'd stayed friends afterward.

Nothing about what Jack was doing to her could be called friendly.

"Your whole 'I can do anything' talk. It really inspired me." He imbued the word "inspired" with innuendo.

A sense of power surged through her. For the first time since she'd arrived, she had the reins. They were on a more level playing field. Or maybe it had never been anything but, except in her mind.

"Oh, you like that?" She bit her lip and closed her eyes. "I can fly to the moon if I want. No, wait. I can take a spaceship to Mars. I can trek across Antarctica. Sail around the world. How's that for inspiring?"

He chuckled, and the vibrations traveled through her body, then he gripped her hips and lifted. Her eyes flew open and she wrapped her legs around his waist instinctively. His palms smoothed around the underside of her bottom.

"I'm feeling *very* inspired."

So was she. She rubbed herself against him and sighed. "I like it when you're inspired."

Resting her head on his shoulder, she rocked into him, loving the way he hissed and swore at the contact.

"*Fuuuuck yes.* Just like that, baby. Let me feel your sweet spot."

Every nerve ending tingled. Every part of her was inflamed and battling to get closer to him. Closer still. It would never be enough.

He smelled like citrus. She kissed up and down the length of his neck and breathed him in. God, his scent was good. Addictive. She wanted to find the source and roll around in it. He carried her to the bed and sat. She straddled his lap, her knees on the duvet, and raised herself up, taking his face between her palms and kissing him like she had all the time in the world. She tasted him, caressed his tongue with her own, drank him up like he was her favorite cocktail. He groaned and yanked her more firmly on top of him, grinding into her, pressing up with his hips to feel more of her.

They were wearing too many clothes. Brooke stripped off her shirt and Jack raised his arms so she could do the same for him, then he reached around and flicked her bra open. Cupping a breast in each hand, he buried his face between them.

"Mmm," he hummed, gently squeezing their fullness. "Love these."

"Glad you approve." She was aiming for sarcasm, but fell short.

Her hands skimmed up his sides, learning the feel of him, the bumps of his muscles and bones, and the tiny scars that spotted his skin, souvenirs of past adventures. His muscular arms banded around her, pulling her tight to his chest, and the friction between their lower bodies increased. She shifted. It still wasn't enough.

"Get naked," she ordered.

He drew back, wearing a cocky smirk. One that said he

was fully capable of delivering on the promise he was making with his hands and lips. "Bossy."

She grinned lopsidedly. "We've established that. Now, *please* Jack, will you get naked?"

His hands went to her hips and he lifted her—wowzers, the man was strong—then he dumped her on the bed beside him. She scrambled up and glared as he moved away. His eyes widened innocently, and her own narrowed. But he did as she'd asked, sliding his jeans down past his ankles. After that, she doubted she'd be able to remember her own name.

"That's right, baby. Lick your lips."

Her tongue paused in the corner of her mouth. She hadn't even noticed she was doing it. He watched her, eyelids heavy, irises only a thin band around his dilated pupils.

"Your turn, sweetheart."

She hastened to do his bidding. When she'd discarded all of her clothing, she guided him backward until the bed hit the backs of his knees, then pushed him down and straddled him the same way she had earlier, except this time, nothing separated the slick glide of his hard shaft from her wet heat. They both sighed at the contact. He took her chin between his thumb and forefinger and claimed her mouth. The kiss was raw and messy. Exactly what she needed. She sank into it, aware of the sensations swamping her body as they touched each other with greedy hands, but oblivious to the details of everything except what they were doing with their mouths.

As need spurred her on, settling hot and heavy in her lower abdomen, she realized she was almost riding him. If he slipped his hand between them and she lifted up—

"Gotta get inside you, baby," Jack panted in her ear, his

thoughts flying along the same trajectory as hers. "Condoms in the drawer beside the bed."

With a groan of reluctance, she drew away from him and sifted through the top drawer until she found a foil packet. She ripped it open and unrolled it over his length with shaky fingers. Then, with confidence she didn't feel, she spread her legs and lowered herself onto him. The blunt head of his erection speared into her, the pressure almost too much, but she bore down on him and after an initial tightness, her arousal eased the way.

"*Shiiiit*," he groaned. "You're so perfect. I'm never gonna get enough of you."

He thrust up into her, burying himself deeper, and she cried out. She wanted to believe what he said, but it was early days. Who knew what would happen? All she knew for sure was that she could die from the sheer bliss of the way he stretched her body. She slid off him a little way, and back down, then did it again. Again. Slowly finding her rhythm.

"Oh!" she cried.

He'd latched on to one of her nipples, worrying it with his teeth. She buried her fingers in his hair and clutched him tight. He eased back and came at her again, his tongue lathing a languid path around her areola. First one, then the other. He moved with the laziness of a cat, as if she weren't bucking on his lap like a wannabe stripper. His brows were furrowed in concentration. All of that focus. All of that intensity. All channeled at *her*.

But still, it wasn't enough. She wanted him to be as weak and desperate and needy as her. She stopped moving, and waited until he raised his head and met her eyes. Then she unfurled her legs so they encased his sides and leaned back, resting her weight on her palms. In a smooth, purposeful movement, she slid along the length of him until only the tip was left inside her. Then she inched back, moving excruciatingly slowly, clenching her core muscles to grip him as tightly as possible.

His eyes rolled back in his head and his hips jerked. "*Damn*. I love how you move." He wrapped his arms around her and flipped her beneath him. "Enough play," he growled. "I want to hear you scream." But then he clambered off her.

She whimpered at the loss of him. "What are you doing?"

He dragged her to the end of the bed, leaned over and caressed the side of her cheek. "I'm gonna fuck you like you've never been fucked before."

The tender touch was at odds with the harsh words, and it took her a moment to make sense of them. By that time, he'd already notched into her entrance, risen up, and slammed down into her. A torrent of pleasure ripped through her. Her first instinct was to close her eyes, but Jack was brutally beautiful above her, lean muscles outlined by light and shadow, and she didn't want to miss a second of it.

He pounded into her again, the unfamiliar angle helping him reach depths no one else ever had. She watched, spellbound, as his powerful thighs bunched, and he moved inside her. He swore, beads of sweat rolling down the sides of his neck. This was a man on the verge of becoming undone, and she sensed that he'd undo her, too.

His dark eyes locked on hers and his lips peeled back from his teeth. His hand came between them and pressed, sending her into a shuddering, moaning, mindless oblivion. He tensed and threw his head back. The lines of his body could have been carved from granite, but he pulsed in release deep within her.

Finally, he sank to his knees and rested his head on her belly. "You wanna see something?"

He'd made the suggestion on a whim, but he meant it. He'd shared wonderful sex with Brooke, and now he wanted to share something potentially even more meaningful.

She laughed weakly. "If you show me anything else, I'm not sure I'll survive." She held up a finger, indicating he should wait. "Hang on, give me a moment. I'll rally."

He grinned, pleased to discover she was the type of person who could have fun in the aftermath of sex. He'd been accused before of being too flippant, but he never intended for that to be the case. Humor was simply an easy, uncomplicated method of communication.

"It's nothing like that," he assured her, and kissed her pouting lips. "You'll love it. There's this place I like to go in the bush over the other side of the creek."

At that, she perked up. "I'm in. Let's go. What are we waiting for?"

She picked herself up off the bed and pulled her clothes back on. He watched, partly amazed and partly amused. He wasn't sure his legs could hold his weight, but she seemed to be fully recovered. How was she so damned resilient?

"What?" she asked, self-consciously.

"You're beautiful," he said. It seemed easier than admitting he was waiting for his bones to solidify.

She blushed. "Thanks."

Shy. He had never applied the descriptor to her before, but at the moment, it seemed to fit. She had no qualms riding him buck naked, but she was shy afterward. Tenderness welled within him.

He shuffled down the bed and tested his legs. They seemed able to hold him, so he disposed of the condom, strode over to her, cupped her face, and kissed her. She blinked, her eyes dazed and unfocused.

"Hey," he murmured.

She smiled softly. "Hi."

"I like you," he said. "And I want to show you one of my favorite places in the whole world. Is that all right with you?"

"Yes." This time, she stretched onto her toes and initiated the kiss, her palms resting on the flat of his chest. He fancied she'd be able to feel his heartbeat, and that filled him with a sense of rightness.

"You'll need a sweater," he told her. "Did you bring one, or do you need to borrow one of mine?"

Her blush deepened. "Borrow one, please."

He fished a dark hoodie out of a drawer and tossed it to her. She pulled it over her head and it fell to mid-thigh, the sleeves hanging past the bottom of her fingers. With her mess of blonde hair and oversized clothes, she was freaking adorable. How had he ever resisted her?

He dressed and led her to the kitchen, where he pocketed two chocolate bars and grabbed a water bottle. He paused. "Have you got your inhaler with you?"

She nodded. "Always do."

"Good." He breathed a sigh of relief. He'd almost forgotten her health issues. Hopefully he hadn't pushed her too hard earlier. "Come with me."

They left the house and got into his four-wheel drive. He drove across town and parked on the residential side of the footbridge at the end of Elizabeth Street. On the far side, a grassy picnic area extended to the nature reserve, where a number of paths entered the trees. He carried his water bottle in one hand. They crossed the bridge side by side in a peaceful silence. No one was around, it was growing dark, and neither of them felt the need to speak.

He guided her to one of the trails and had to release her hand because it was only wide enough for one person.

Twigs snapped beneath their feet as they made the short trek to the first park bench.

"We veer off the track here," he told her. "It's only a couple of hundred meters into the bush. Are you up for that?"

She grinned, white teeth flashing in the dim light. "Hell yeah, I am."

That's my girl.

He led the way, holding branches aside so she could pass unhindered. Eventually they arrived at the back of the rock overhang.

"Is this it?" She sounded disappointed.

He didn't say anything, just took her hand and edged around the overhang until they faced the part that jutted out. It was too short for either of them to see under. He lowered himself to the ground and sat, legs sprawled before him, then tugged her hand. "Trust me."

She dropped into his lap, her back pressed into his chest, and tilted her head. He knew the moment she caught sight of the underside of the overhang.

"Wow," she breathed. "That's magical."

He followed her gaze. Above their heads, dozens of glow worms hung from the mossy rock ceiling, shining white in the dying light of the day. The first time he'd stumbled onto this spot, he'd wondered if he was drunk or if one of his friends had slipped him a hallucinogen. It was too much like the faerie glens he'd seen in his niece's picture books.

He looped his arms around her, hands resting on her belly. She hadn't taken her eyes off the glow worms, and her expression held all the awe he'd hoped to see.

"Are they always here?" The question was hushed, as though she feared she'd frighten them away if she spoke too loudly. Ridiculous, but cute.

"They have been since I discovered them a couple of months ago, but long term, I have no idea."

"How is it that everyone in town doesn't know about this place?"

He laughed, and kissed her cheek. "How many people climb under a rock overhang?"

"Fair point."

They settled into a comfortable quiet. Brooke made no move to leave, and he was perfectly happy to snuggle her beneath the glow worms all night if she wanted. The scent of damp earth and moss permeated the air, and he inhaled deeply. He couldn't remember feeling so content to just exist with another person. It was the same sensation that overcame him when he was alone with nature. Usually having someone nearby would interfere with his enjoyment, but not this time. And that, more than anything, told him all he needed to know about being with Brooke Griffiths.

21

THE NEXT FORTNIGHT passed in a string of dates, gym sessions, outdoor activities, study, and lovemaking. Brooke stayed with Jack most nights and returned to Sanctuary in the mornings. Some days she joined his tour groups, and he seemed to like her accompanying him. Her confidence in their budding relationship grew. As she spent more time with him, he became more of an equal rather than a hero to admire from a distance.

Unfortunately, however much she was enjoying herself, the upcoming physical test loomed in the back of her mind, refusing to allow her to relax completely. So far, twenty of her blog readers had promised to be there in person to support her. A further fifty, both national and international, had RSVP'd to the livestream. In short, there were at least seventy reasons why she couldn't fail. And so, a week and a half before the big day, she was at The Hideaway at an abominable hour of the morning, wearing a ten-pound weight vest and firing up a treadmill.

There were many places she'd rather be. In bed with Jack. Sipping a latte at Café Oasis. Walking along the beach.

But here she was, with Bex by her side to give her a kick up the ass if needed.

"You can do this," Bex said. "Seven miles, with a ten percent incline. No stopping. Are you ready?"

"Totally." Brooke embraced the fear fluttering in her chest like a hummingbird's wings. That fear would drive her to keep pushing through. She stepped onto the moving belt and wobbled until she fell into a rhythm. Her arms pumped and her thighs started to burn.

"I'm going to leave you," Bex said. "But I'll be nearby. Don't take a break unless you absolutely have to." She hesitated, then added, "Let me know if you're struggling, okay?"

"Okay." She would *not* struggle. If she couldn't succeed today, she'd have no hope at the mud run. Failure wasn't an option.

Time passed. Enough of it that her legs would've been crying if they had tear ducts. She didn't so much as slow the pace. Unless her knees ceased functioning, she'd maintain this painful speed, so help her God. Before much longer, her legs numbed and her breathing grew labored. Without pausing, she huffed her inhaler and rinsed her mouth, swallowing the bitter water. She plugged her headphones into her ears and selected a playlist of angry girl music, turning the volume up loud.

Finally, *finally*, the counter ticked over seven miles, and she hit the big red "Off" button. Stumbling to the floor, she shrugged out of the weight vest and closed her eyes.

Bex appeared at her side. "You did it!"

Adrenaline drove her back to her feet. "I did."

Everything felt weak and shaky, but her heart was soaring. She could have danced a jig, then strapped on a backpack and headed into the mountains right then and there. She high-fived her friend.

"*We* did it. Thank you so much, I couldn't have done it without you." She gave a Cheshire cat grin that stretched from one ear to the other and bared lots of teeth. "I can't believe I just did that. If you'd told me six months ago that I'd be able to walk seven miles uphill, carrying extra weight, I'd have laughed in your face. This is life-changing." Tears welled in her eyes, and she let them fall. She didn't care who saw. "I'm in your debt, Bex. Like, a million times over."

Bex laughed, her eyes flashing with the same excitement Brooke felt. "This is all you, girlfriend. I gave you the tools you needed, but you put in the hard yards. I'm proud of you." They hugged fiercely. "Did you tell that man of yours what you were doing this morning?"

"No," she admitted. "I didn't want to jinx myself."

"You will tell him though, right? He'll be thrilled for you."

"Give me two minutes to catch my breath, then I'm heading straight to his place." She waggled her eyebrows. "I'm sure he'll help me celebrate appropriately."

JACK ROLLED onto the pillow Brooke had slept on and inhaled the floral scent of her shampoo on the fabric. She'd left a couple of hours ago, but he wasn't due at work until ten and was reveling in the chance to sleep in. He wriggled further into the mountain of blankets, murmuring in contentment. The only thing that could improve his mood was having Brooke tucked into the crook of his arms.

A distant banging disrupted his peace. He buried his head beneath the pillow and tried to tune it out. The banging stopped, and he was drifting on the edge of a dream when it sounded again, far closer. Blinking, he lifted his head an inch from the mattress. Was someone at his bedroom door?

"Go away," he grumbled.

"You don't really mean that."

Brooke's voice broke infiltrated his cocoon of warmth, and he sat up, rubbing his eyes. "You're back?"

She entered the room fully and gave him a toothier grin than he'd ever seen from her before she'd had a coffee. "I just walked seven miles on an incline, wearing a weight vest." She announced it as proudly as if she'd single-handedly won New Zealand the Bledisloe Cup. And no wonder. This was a massive achievement for her.

"That's fucking awesome, Brooke." He jerked his head. "Come here."

She did, wearing that shy smile he adored. He tilted his face up and she bent over to kiss him. Then, before she could react, he yanked her onto the bed. She squeaked in surprise and rolled, taking him with her, and landed with her palms splayed over his chest, her body sprawled along the length of his.

"Ugh, I've just been exercising," she protested. "I'm disgusting."

He kissed her nose. "You could never be disgusting. How come you didn't tell me what you were up to this morning? I would've come and supported you."

She fidgeted, and stared at something to the side of his head. "You know I appreciate you having my back, but I needed to do this on my own."

He frowned, not liking that thought. "You know I wouldn't ever give you a hard time if you came up short, don't you?"

"Of course. I just..." She sighed. "I think I needed to prove something to myself."

Squeezing her tight, he kissed her cheek. "Fair enough. I won't question that."

"Thanks."

He kissed her sweaty forehead, his mind wandering to the hiking equipment he'd already bought for her because he had no doubt she'd succeed at the upcoming mud run. She was working her ass off. The weekend after it was done, he planned to whisk her away. He'd chosen a track he'd done several times because he wanted to be familiar with the terrain, but he was eager to watch her expressive face as she took in the scenery. It would be like seeing it through fresh eyes.

"Here's an idea," he said. "Why don't you have a shower while I make breakfast?"

She looked down at him dubiously. "Dare I ask what?"

"Snails and bush grubs."

She winced, and he grinned in response. "Pays not to ask. Just trust me."

"Fine. I can do that." He could hear the shrug in her voice. She rolled off him and he mourned the loss of her body. "I need to update my blog, but I can do that once you've gone to work."

"It's no trouble if you want to do it now. You don't have to keep me entertained." In fact, he wouldn't mind seeing her blog for himself. It struck him as odd that it was responsible for the sponsorship, but he had yet to get a glimpse of it. He couldn't even look it up himself because he didn't know what it was called. He could ask Kat, but that seemed too intrusive. Brooke would tell him herself when the time was right. It probably hadn't occurred to her that he'd be interested. She didn't know about Claudia, and her Insta-famous project to transform him from bushman-boyfriend to suave man-candy, so there was no reason for her to understand his caution toward social media.

"I know," she said. "But I want to. I'll do it later; it's no big deal." She shed clothes as she headed to the bedroom door, and cast a coy glance over her shoulder. "Sure you don't want to join me?"

No. No he wasn't. She exited the room, and he stumbled after her. "Hey, wait up!"

22

SHE WAS GOING to be sick. Brooke clapped a hand over her mouth and ran to the toilet in the en suite off her bedroom, dry retching into it. Her stomach revolted. There was nothing inside of it to throw up, but it roiled and seethed nonetheless. A hand landed on her lower back, rubbing circles through her shirt.

"You're okay. You've got this. You're going to kick the mud run's ass tomorrow."

"There are going to be so many people watching," she whispered.

"They're coming to support you," Jack assured her. "They've got your back."

She straightened and looked him in the eye. "But what if I fail?"

"You won't." He sounded confident in her when she was anything but. "Even if everything goes to hell, I'll still be here for you."

At that, she turned and retched into the toilet again. Because yeah, she'd come to believe that he truly did care for her, and that they were equals in a lot of ways, but how long would he stay around if he decided she could never be the partner he took on two-week hiking adventures to the middle of nowhere? What if she let him down? Let Olivia down? Let *all* the people who were pinning their hopes on her down? She wasn't just doing this for herself, and that added to the pressure.

While she'd always known that her blog readers were actually out there in the world, living their lives, they'd seemed abstract until now. She'd be meeting many of them in person. She couldn't blow this. If she did, dozens of people who'd grown up like her might lose faith. Stepping around Jack, she turned on the faucet and splashed cold water on her face with shaking hands, then she exhaled and looked herself in the eye. She had to believe she could do this, or it was all over.

"That's it," he encouraged her. "Get your game face on."

She tried to smile at him. "You know you didn't have to skip poker night to hang out with me. I'm not going to be much fun. I'll just be sitting around, stewing about the race."

"It's not a race," he reminded her. "You're not trying to win, just finish."

In her mind, finishing equaled winning. Giving up equaled losing. Even if it wasn't a race, it was still a win-lose situation.

"I know. My point is, I'm probably just going to drink hot chocolate and binge watch Doctor Who."

He cringed. "Make it Game of Thrones and I'll join you."

She shrugged. "If you insist."

God knew she could use something to keep her mind off things, and hey, maybe they could reminisce about their first kiss, when she'd been dressed as Khaleesi. Perhaps it had been long enough by now that they could look back and laugh. She certainly felt like they'd come leaps and bounds in their relationship from where they'd been a few weeks ago.

"I do," he confirmed. "I'm here, and I'm ready for blood, gore and nudity."

"All right then. You get the show set up, I'll figure out dinner." Not that she thought she'd be able to eat much. Nevertheless, it was sweet of him to want to keep her company tonight. Despite her nerves, she smiled all the way to the kitchen.

"Oh, shoot!"

Jack glanced over at Brooke, who was tying her shoelaces. "What's up?"

They were at the rugby field in Te Awa Tui, where a couple of hundred people were preparing for the mud run, which would begin in an hour and a half. At the far end of the field, a colorful start line had been erected. The runners and their support teams were being kept separate from viewers at this point, but they'd seen Brooke's contingent of fans arrive earlier.

"I forgot Kyle's GoPro for the livestream. It's plugged into my laptop back at Sanctuary." She made a sound of distress. "I have to register soon. I can't go back for it, but I hate to let my viewers down."

"You stay here. I'll get it," Jack said, checking the time. "I should make it back before eleven." He grasped her by the shoulders. "Will you be okay without me?"

She nodded, looking fierce and determined, although the color had drained from her face. "I'll be totally fine." Stretching onto her toes, she kissed him. Her lips were cool and clammy. "Thanks so much."

"No worries." He caressed the side of her neck, reluctant to go, but he knew Bex and Kat would be here soon. "I really don't want to leave you, but I'd better not waste any time."

She waved him away. "I'll see you soon."

He jogged to his four-wheel drive and fired up the engine. The trip back to Haven Bay took twenty-five minutes, even driving as fast as he could without risking getting pulled over by the police. At Sanctuary, he parked near the door, then let himself into Brooke's room and found the GoPro exactly where she'd said it would be. He snatched it from the desk, tugged the cord out of the laptop, and was about to turn away when the screen lit up. He paused as a photograph of Brooke at the gym caught his eye.

Resting his palm on the edge of the desk, he leaned over to read the screen. It was her blog. The web domain made him laugh. *www.BrookeVersusWorld.com.* He laid down the GoPro and scrolled to read her latest post.

It's not snooping, he told himself as guilt settled heavy in his stomach. *She puts this out there for everyone to see.*

Never mind the fact that if she wanted him to read it, she would have shown him. This blog was at least partially responsible for her journey, which meant it was relevant to him. He had a right to know what it was about. Especially given how Claudia made a mockery of him online for weeks while he was completely in the dark.

He scanned the last entry and smiled. The writing sounded so much like her that she could have been standing at his shoulder, whispering in his ear. His phone vibrated in his pocket, reminding him that he was on a deadline. He glanced at the time. Staying for a few extra minutes wouldn't hurt. He pulled out her chair and sat. Then, out of morbid curiosity and a hint of fear, he used the search function and entered his name.

The search returned seventeen matches, which meant she'd mentioned him a lot. He hit the key that transported him to the first time she'd used his name, and his heart sank. He scanned the words, growing colder inside with each sentence he read. By the time he reached their first encounter at Sanctuary, his heart felt like a lump of ice.

Brooke v. World: *Monday 3 February (evening)*

You might be wondering why I'm posting twice in one day. Today has taken a nosedive and I really just need your support. You remember how I finally got up the guts to kiss Jack at the New Year's Eve party and then he didn't call? It turns out, he doesn't remember me. How freaking humiliating is that?

He and I shared a toe-curling make out session—the best of my life—and it was apparently so unmemorable that he doesn't even recall my name.

Please tell me there are men out there who would appreciate my ability to recite the actors from Doctor Who in chronological order, admire my collection of cosplay outfits (and preferably have their own), and who possess a modicum of common decency. Please tell me Jack is the exception to the rule.

Also, sigh. I'm just realizing, I must have terrible taste in men. Tell me I'm not the only one who's been so stupid. I don't know what to do with myself—or him. Any and all advice appreciated.

Brooke XX

He read it again. Then a third time, even though it probably meant he had a masochistic streak, because fuck, those words cut deep. He knew he'd hurt her, but this blog post spelled out exactly how much. He imagined her, with her cute lopsided topknot and over-sized glasses, hammering out these words with tears in her eyes, and he thought he might throw up.

Worse still were the dozens of suggestions beneath the post from her readers, who were apparently a creative and vindictive bunch. Peppered amongst the more inventive recommendations were a few that struck too close to home. One reader, TamsinG, had told Brooke to seduce him, then kick him out of her room before they got to the good stuff. Another, Amber, went a step further and said Brooke should date him and break up with him publicly in the most humiliating way she could imagine. A lot of others had jumped on board with that suggestion, but it was the response from Brooke herself that hurt the most.

Haha, great suggestion! Thanks for having my back. XX

Jack's throat burned, and it felt like a rubber band tightened around his chest. He could hardly breathe. His head spun, and his vision blurred. He couldn't read any more. Awful possibilities bombarded him from every direction.

Brooke had encouraged this hatefulness toward him.

Was she leading him on?

Was their entire relationship just some twisted revenge plot?

Did she care about him at all?

She'd exposed him to the world more assuredly than Claudia ever had, and the blow struck truer because he'd never seen it coming. His ex's betrayal had been embarrassing, and made him question his choices, but it had nothing on this, because while he'd cared for Claudia, he'd never loved her. And perhaps it made him a fool, but he'd tripped ass-over-heels in love with Brooke, only to discover she was playing some sick game. His fists clenched in his lap and he squeezed his eyes closed, shame and despair washing over him. He felt raw, vulnerable. Like she'd ripped off a Band-Aid and showed the oozing scabby part of him to everyone she knew.

How could she have done that? He'd wounded her pride, but she was a better person than him. God, he desperately wanted to believe she was. Unfortunately, the evidence to the contrary was right in front of him.

"*Fuck*," he swore. He couldn't go back to Te Awa Tui now, could he? Couldn't kiss her on the cheek and wish her luck while inside, his emotions boiled. But on the other hand, however conflicted he may be, she'd worked hard for this run, and he couldn't bring himself to ruin it.

He stood, kicked the chair back, and grabbed the GoPro. He locked the door behind him and ran up the hall, through the foyer and down the stairs. Reaching his four-wheel drive, he jumped in, then tore away from Sanctuary, ugly words still flying through his mind. He arrived at the mud run, just in the nick of time. The runners hadn't left yet, but he didn't think he could handle seeing Brooke. Either he'd yell, or cry, and neither option appealed. Spotting Bex's car idling nearby, her daughter Izzy in the passenger seat and Kat beside one of the rear doors, he called her name.

"Hey," he puffed when he reached her side. "Can you take this to Brooke?" He handed her the GoPro, hoping like hell that all of his painful emotions weren't painted on his face. "Something has come up. I'll be here to cheer, I just need to take care of it first."

"Sure thing," she said, eyes flickering over him with concern. "Are you okay?"

He shook his head. "Just tell her good luck for me, will you?"

"Okay. No problem, Jack."

Before she had the chance to ask more questions, he strode away, heading for the crowd, hoping to find a place where he could watch unobtrusively and mull over the situation.

23

Brooke jogged on the spot to warm her muscles. She'd registered, stretched, and chatted with a couple of participants who were dressed in matching pink outfits with angel wings and subsequently looked less intimidating than some of the other athletes present. With every passing minute, she grew more anxious. Her race would begin soon and Jack hadn't returned.

Someone yelled Brooke's name, and she turned, spotting a girl who was perhaps twelve or so and who'd joined her small group of supporters. Three of the other supporters held a banner with her name on it. She waved at them, although she wasn't sure they could see much of her from here. When other runners glanced her way, she ducked to avoid their attention. She wasn't a celebrity, or a true competitor here. She was just a girl who'd spent a lot of time in a hospital bed, had a boatload of determination, and a friend she needed to honor.

Raising a hand to shield her face from the sun, she scanned as much of their route as she could see. The circuit was five miles, and the first few hundred yards were a simple race over a grass field, then the track narrowed and entered a cluster of trees. Past those trees, she knew there would be a rope climb, a muddy army crawl, a river crossing, and whatever other inventive challenges the organizer had dreamed up.

Adrenaline spiked in her blood and sweat beaded on her eyebrows and upper lip even though the temperature was mild.

Where was Jack? If he didn't hurry up, she'd let down everyone who'd signed up to watch the livestream.

"Brooke!"

She turned, but her smile fell off her lips when she caught sight of Bex and Kat hurrying toward her, Kat clutching a GoPro.

Taking the camera, Brooke connected it to herself. "Where's Jack?"

Kat pursed her lips. "He said something had come up. I think he needed to make a phone call, but he's here, I promise."

Brooke's stomach plummeted. She'd wanted to see him before she started. He was the one responsible for her being here.

"He said to tell you good luck," Kat added.

"Thanks," Brooke replied, her mind turning over scenarios. "Do you think something is wrong?" She couldn't imagine any other reason he'd rank a phone call above being here for her. He'd made it clear how proud he was.

Kat shrugged. "Hard to tell. He's not an open book. But I wouldn't worry yourself, sweetie. You just focus on kicking some ass."

A voice crackled over the loudspeaker, instructing the contestants to report to the starting line. Brooke took a last sip from her water bottle and handed it to Bex, who kissed her cheek. "Go make me proud, girlfriend."

"I'll do my best."

Bex winked. "Then I already am proud. We'll be waiting over there with your fans."

"They're not my…" The protest died on her lips. Maybe they were her fans. Because Bex was right. She was a kickass woman, and she was doing this for people like them. For people like Olivia, who'd never had a chance to do it herself.

Nerves tightened her muscles and her stomach felt hollow. She strode toward the starting line, her pulse pounding in her ears, and everything else sounding as though it was being filtered through water. She held her shoulders straight and put all her energy into believing she could do this. She'd worked hard, been persistent, not given up.

She *could* do this.

She *would* do this.

And then all the little girls and boys out there with helicopter parents and doctors who told them they'd never be normal would know they had a chance.

This is for Olivia.

The race marshal counted down from three, then a gunshot cracked the air and Brooke lurched into motion. Everyone moved faster than she'd expected and she quickly fell to the back of the pack, her arms and legs pumping as she struggled to keep up. Her calves burned, and her breath came in short gasps. But then, miraculously, the group slowed to form a single line as they entered the trees, and she settled into a rhythm behind a woman with the number 159 pinned to her back and the logo for a local parenting group beneath it.

Not far into the trees, they came across their first challenge, a rope net that hung almost vertically, blocking the path. She wiped her palms on her leggings and hauled herself up without much trouble. But at the top, she straddled the wooden beam, afraid to swing herself over in case she screwed up and fell eight feet to the ground. She'd twist an ankle, at the very least.

"Get a move on," the man behind her urged. "Get over, or get off."

Resisting the urge to flip him off, she took a breath and slid over the top, exhaling in relief when she caught herself and managed to shimmy to the ground. She resumed running, her legs wobblier than before.

A short distance later, they exited the trees into a farmer's paddock, which was slushy and muddy with a number of pipes crossing it, each wide enough for a man to slide through on his belly. Brooke didn't hesitate to throw herself into the nearest one and slither through it like a snake, using her hands, knees, and elbows to drag herself toward the light at the end. She was smaller than many of the participants and gained ground.

When she emerged, she staggered back to her feet and ran across the uneven terrain, then up the ramp of a truck that had its trailer lowered, leaping off the other end onto a padded mat. Next, she navigated over a mountain of tires, and arrived at a stream. Three wooden rafts bobbed on the water, a couple of feet separating them. The stream looked shallow, but her sense of balance wasn't the best and her heart was in her throat as she jumped onto the first one. It wobbled, and she used her arms to steady herself, then jumped to the second, amazed when her legs didn't give out beneath her. On to the third, and then she thudded onto solid ground.

Stumbling up the stream bank, she tried to catch her breath, wondering what awaited her. As she crested the bank, relief flooded her. People were strung out across the next two paddocks, with no obstacles in sight. Some were jogging, some walking. The über-fit competitors were out of her range of vision, but enough people were behind her that she felt a rush of pride. She forced herself forward, jogging at a steady pace that wouldn't win her any awards but which she could maintain for twenty minutes.

At the end of the first paddock, she clambered over a fence and paused to huff on her inhaler to ease the tightness in her chest, then carried on. When she arrived at the end of the next paddock, the track turned onto a road, and in the distance, she could see a net laid over the ground, people on their bellies beneath it, crawling military-style. Past the net, a wooden wall rose up, with no footholds or grips visible. She gulped. How was she supposed to scale that freaking wall?

Her damp shoes pounded on the seal, and she wondered how far she'd come. Was she halfway yet? Must be. With how badly her legs were shaking, she couldn't fathom it being any less. At least, not if she were hoping to finish. She reached the netting and dropped to her knees, wincing when a stone dug into her flesh. Thank God she'd worn yoga pants, or it would have cut her. Disregarding the sharp twinge of pain, she worked her thighs hard, propelling herself over the muddy grass, keeping her head low to avoid becoming entangled. Then she was at the end, and the wall loomed high a hundred yards from her.

"Go Brooke, go!" A chant caught her attention and she looked around, spying a car full of young women parked on the far side of the road. One had her head out the window, yelling, "You got this, Brooke! Go hard!"

Tears filled her eyes, and her throat clogged. She faced the wall with renewed determination. She *could* do this. To show others like her that they could achieve their goals, no matter how far-fetched they may seem. She ran at the wall, praying the momentum would carry her over the top before she fell. It was eighty yards away. Fifty. Ten. She leapt into the air, scrabbling on the smooth surface, one arm swinging over the top, the rest of her body hanging like a dead weight. Her shoulder and bicep screamed. She struggled to find purchase with her feet, but there was nothing to support her. Just as she was ready to drop, a hand fastened around her forearm and yanked her up. The air whooshed from her lungs as she was slung over the top. Glancing across, she made eye contact with the man who'd hurried her on earlier.

He shrugged. "Looked like you needed a hand."

"Thanks." Then he was gone, landing nimbly and running off. She followed, hardly able to believe the wall hadn't defeated her.

"Two miles to go," one of the women in the car called, pulling alongside her. "You're nearly there. We're all with you. There are more than eight hundred people on the livestream, cheering you on."

Eight hundred people? Watching *her*?

Well damn, now she was going to cry.

"Keep going," the girl shouted, and Brooke realized she'd slowed.

"Thank you," she gasped. "What's your name?"

"Tammy," she replied. "And I have Cam and Aubrey with me."

"TimTam95," Brooke said, recalling the girl's username.

She beamed. "I can't believe you remember me."

"I can't believe you're here," she panted.

Tammy rolled her eyes. "Of course we are. Now run your inspirational butt off. We'll see you at the finish line."

The car pulled away, multiple pairs of hands waving at her through the windows. Brooke carried on, turning onto a narrow trail beside the golf course, the last stretch of the run. She counted her steps because otherwise she couldn't ignore the wheezing in her chest and the weariness of her feet, which were almost dragging on the ground.

One-hundred-seventy-five, one-hundred-seventy-six.

A series of logs appeared in front of her, the first as high as her groin. She rolled over it, then over the eight that followed, finally flopping to her hands and knees, out of breath. She hung her head. Her palms and knees were scratched, her shins bruised, her ribs aching, and her throat was so raw she suspected a doctor would hospitalize her if they saw it. She rested her forehead on the ground. She couldn't go any further.

People passed by, some of them hesitant, as though wondering whether they should check on her.

"Hey, are you okay?"

Brooke looked up. It was one of the women she'd met earlier, wearing pink with angel wings. She shook her head. "I can't do it."

"Yes, you can," the woman told her. "You've come this far. It's only another half mile, and I can't see any more obstacles." She offered a hand. "Come on, get up. I'll run with you."

"I'll hold you back." Just like she did with everyone.

The woman snorted. "That's crazy talk. I rolled my ankle getting off that wall. I'm not running so much as limping."

Brooke contemplated curling into a ball and calling Kat to pick her up after all the people she'd disappointed had departed. But then she remembered the livestream audience. The eight hundred people who had a great view of the ground, waiting for her to get up and show them what she was made of.

She got to her feet. "Okay, let's do this shit."

Side by side, the two women jogged around the golf course and into the open. The finish line appeared in the distance, with a group of people holding her banner not far behind. Off to the side was Jack. Her heart lifted. Seeing him, and the people there to support her, gave her the boost she needed to keep going and plaster a smile on her face. They were nearly there. So close she could taste success. Then she and her new friend passed over the line and fell to their knees, embracing each other.

"Thank you," Brooke puffed. "I couldn't have done that without you."

The woman laughed and shifted to a cross-legged position. "That was all you. I was ready to throw in the towel when I saw you."

Brooke stared at her. "You were?"

"Yeah, but knowing I needed to make sure you got to the end motivated me to keep going."

"That's so sweet."

A hand landed on Brooke's back and she looked up. One of the girls from the car stood above her, with Tammy at her side. Only now Brooke could see what she hadn't before: Tammy was in a wheelchair.

"You did it!" Tammy shrieked.

"I did?" The truth hadn't sunk in yet. She glanced at the white line painted on the grass and confirmed that she had, indeed, completed the course.

Finally, background noise began to filter into her consciousness. She heard clapping and hollering. The sound of celebration. They were celebrating *her*. These people were here for her, and that took her breath away. For the first time, she could see them all in person. Some were younger than Brooke, some older. Amongst them, a man in a sports jacket had his arm around a red-headed girl. Sarah and her dad?

"You guys..." Tears welled in Brooke's eyes and she raised her voice so they could all hear her. "You're the best.

Like, actually, the *best*. Thank you so much for coming. You kept me going out there."

"Thank *you*," Tammy amended. "For repping us all. You have no idea how much it means to those of us who've followed you from the beginning, to see you making life your bitch."

Brooke reddened. It wasn't the terminology she'd use, but it was flattering, nonetheless. She scanned the crowd, searching for a crooked grin on a handsome face. Where had Jack gone?

<hr>

WHEN BROOKE'S adoring fans surrounded her, Jack backed away. They were cheering for her, clapping her on the back, complimenting her. Their love for her was a tangible thing. But then, he shouldn't be surprised, should he? Not when he'd seen how they'd leapt to her defense after she'd blogged about him. Hadn't it been one of them who was responsible for their fraudulent relationship?

A bitter taste filled his mouth. She'd been stringing him along, and all of these people were in on the joke. A few of her supporters glanced his way, and he wondered if they knew who he was. Were they laughing at him behind his back? Had she shared the details of their relationship, doling out salacious stories and making a mockery of his feelings for her?

Hell, he loved her, and he wasn't even sure he knew who she was. Because the woman he'd believed her to be would never have done something so awful. But he'd never been a good judge of character when it came to his romantic life, had he? Maybe he had her all wrong.

He'd give her one thing though—she was a damned good liar.

Brooke looked up, searching the crowd, and he stepped further back, out of sight. He'd been here for her. He'd done the right thing. But he couldn't handle talking to her now, or pretending everything was okay. Not when she'd ripped his heart from his chest and fucking shredded it.

He turned and walked away.

24

———

"WHERE HAVE YOU BEEN?" Brooke demanded, glaring at Jack across the sparsely occupied pub. The patrons either stared at her, or became fascinated by their drinks. She was causing a scene, but she didn't care. After weeks of training together and dating, he hadn't bothered hanging around to congratulate her. And what had been so urgent that he'd had to leave? The need to drink beer and glower? She'd been frantic, worried for him, and he'd been here all along.

"Please tell me there was a legitimate reason why you ditched me." She'd meant the words to sound snarky, but they were leaning toward the pathetic end of the spectrum. She pulled herself together. She wasn't the one in the wrong here, and it wasn't unreasonable to have expected him to be there for her. They were a team now. Partners. Only she didn't have a clue what was going through his head.

Jack didn't reply, just sipped his drink in sullen silence.

"Brooke," Logan said, from behind the bar. "Think you could take this outside?"

"I'd be happy to, but he doesn't look like he's planning to move anytime soon."

"Mate." Logan turned to him. "I think you've had

enough." He gestured to the wall. "Sign says I can't serve you if you're inebriated."

"I'm not fucking drunk," Jack snapped, "and I don't want to air my dirty laundry in front of half the town. Mind if we use your apartment?"

Logan rubbed his temples and sighed. "Fine." He tossed him the key. "But no kinky make-up sex on the sofa."

Jack shoved his stool back and stalked to the private living area without waiting to see if Brooke would follow. Out of sheer stubbornness, she didn't want to go after him, but she needed to know what she'd done to make him so angry he'd desert her on their big day. If something important had come up, he could have called. Texted. Sent her an email, so she'd know not to worry. Instead, she'd come up with all kinds of awful scenarios to justify his absence.

One of his parents had died.

He'd been in an accident.

A terrible illness had struck him down.

The last possibility had tormented her most. How typical would it have been if she were in the best shape of her life and the man she was falling in love with became ill.

But no. Instead, he seemed to have decided to go to the pub, for no good reason that she could see. She climbed the stairs, her legs protesting. The door at the top was ajar and she let herself in, looking around. She'd never been in Logan's apartment before, but she didn't get much chance to appreciate the décor because Jack shut the door behind her and folded his arms over his chest, his brows lowered in a scowl.

"What's your problem?" she demanded, mimicking his stance. "I was worried sick about you. I thought something was wrong. But you're here, having a drink. Please tell me there's more to the story. Something I'm not seeing. Because at the moment, it looks like you're a bastard."

The lines around his mouth deepened and his gaze became flinty. "All of your *adoring* fans were there." He said "adoring" as if it were a synonym for slimy and disgusting. "Why would you need me?"

She flinched. Did he actually believe he was superfluous? She turned over the possibility in her mind. Had she done anything to give him that impression? Taken him for granted, perhaps?

No, she didn't think so. She never took anything for granted.

Damn, this was unfair. Today should be a celebration. An evening of happiness. She'd passed the test, achieved something she'd never dreamed she could, and the future was falling into place. But she couldn't enjoy her success if he wasn't with her.

She gentled her tone. "I would never have gotten so far if it weren't for you. Of course I wanted to be with you after, and it hurt that you weren't there."

Jack scoffed. "You know what hurts? Finding out that the woman you care about has been manipulating you as some kind of revenge plot, and that hundreds of people are in on it."

He'd lost her. "What do you mean?"

"I read your blog," he said meaningfully. "Parts of it were very enlightening."

She winced, recalling the way she'd moped online about him not contacting her after their kiss, and then ranted when she'd realized he didn't remember who she was. Her face heated, but she resisted the urge to shrink into herself. Yeah, she'd vented, but she'd also never said anything untrue, and he had to know that. Besides, she'd been singing his praises lately. A number of her readers had asked about their relationship, wanting to meet him at the race. She'd had to tell them he was unwell.

"Did you read all of it?" she asked.

"I read enough. I saw you agree with some girl who said you should string me along, humiliate me and break my heart. What were you planning to do? Dump me as soon as I got you to Everest? Were you going to crush me and blog all about it?" He laughed bitterly. "That'd teach me for forgetting you, huh."

She stared, mouth agape. How could he think so little of her? They knew each other. Or, at least, she'd thought they did. And while she recalled the comment he was referring to, she'd never agreed, just thanked the girl for being supportive. If he'd read the very next post, surely he'd know that.

"I would never do the things you're saying," she told him. "Didn't you see—"

"Don't try to explain yourself away," he interrupted. "Whatever you're about to say, it won't change the fact you put the private details of our relationship on the goddamned internet and made me public enemy number one with your doting fans."

Her self-righteous anger fled and she deflated, her arms falling to her sides. He was right. She had done that, without even thinking. Who cared if it had been a mistake, or if she'd tried to smooth it over as soon as possible? She couldn't go back in time and erase her actions. She'd behaved childishly, and he was calling her on it.

"I'm so sorry."

"Sorry doesn't cut it." Sighing, he scraped a hand through his hair. The grooves etched between his brows had lessened, but he looked weary. "It all comes down to one simple truth. You're exactly like my ex."

She flinched, as the words struck with the precision of a slap.

"Did I ever tell you why we broke up?" he asked. When she shook her head, her lips wobbling dangerously, he continued. "She was—is—an Instagram model. Quite a successful one. We met at a photo shoot at the outdoor equipment shop where I worked. They'd made an endorsement deal with her. It was instant attraction between us. We were different people—she was all about high society and art gallery exhibitions whereas I preferred the outdoors and my own company—but I thought we loved each other anyway." He laughed bitterly. "More fool me. I found out I was one of her projects. She was trying to turn me into the perfect boyfriend to hang off her arm at fucking brunches and shit, and chronicling it all for her Instagram audience." God, he'd been furious when he found out none of it had been real, and that he'd been reduced to entertainment for a bunch of wannabe socialites. "The worst part is, it was working. I'd actually cancelled an annual hiking trip with an old buddy of mine to go to some stupid gala with her. It was there I overheard her talking about it."

Brooke looked stricken, her face pale, splotches of red across her cheeks. "Did you ask her about it?"

"I did. I asked her to explain, and I asked if she thought I wasn't good enough for her. She said..." His fists clenched. "That I could stand to change a few things."

Fuck, that had ruined him. He'd left before he could say something he'd regret and gone straight to their apartment, where he pored over her Instagram feed and agonized over every single derogatory comment she'd made about him. As soon as she arrived home, he broke up with her, and he left the city the next day.

"Oh, Jack." Brooke took a step closer. "I'm sorry she was such a bitch. You must know that isn't a reflection on you."

"Isn't it?" he asked. "Once is a coincidence, but twice? It seems like I have a type."

He saw the moment his barb struck true.

Great job, Farrelly. You finally got through to her.

He suppressed a twinge of guilt—it wasn't his fault the truth hurt—and embraced cold satisfaction because her feelings finally mirrored his own.

"If you want somebody who'll carry you to the camp when you can't hack it, you can hire someone for the job. I'm not interested."

She stumbled back, a hand to her mouth, tears filling her eyes. "You were never just a guide to me," she whispered. "And I haven't been using you, I swear. I'm not like her, Jack. I know you're only saying that because you're upset, and you don't mean it, otherwise I'd be out of here, but I can't stand for you to think I'd do that to you. That's not how it is, I promise."

Her voice was strangled, and he wished he could believe her, but he'd seen the damning evidence with his own eyes.

"Yeah, right."

Her arms encircled her waist and she cradled herself. He hated seeing her so small and huddled, but she'd brought all of this on herself.

"I'm sorry," she said. "I shouldn't have been so open on my blog. That's just how I've always been and I didn't think to tone it back. I can see how it would bother you, especially given what happened, but I had no way of knowing that, and I really am sorry."

"Bother me?" he demanded. "You think this is me being fucking bothered? I'm angry as hell." Disappointed, too. Not that he'd admit it. "You violated my trust. You shared intimate details of my life with hundreds, maybe thousands, of people. How do I know everyone at that event today wasn't laughing at me? That they're not all in on some joke, where I'm the punch line?"

"They're n—"

"Don't." His hands fisted again and he willed them to relax. Mad as he was, he would not physically intimidate her. "I knew you were like Claudia from the beginning, but I talked myself into believing you were different. I should have listened to my instincts and stayed away."

Brooke's back straightened and her hands went to her hips. She reminded him of a cat with its fur standing on end. "Don't compare me to another woman. Because you know what? I'm sick of always being judged against someone else's scale. I'm not your ex, and I don't appreciate you saying I am, and making assumptions about me. You don't know the full story."

He opened his mouth to say he knew enough, and to enumerate the ways in which she was exactly like Claudia, but she stormed past him, threw the door open, and slammed it behind her. Just as Claudia would have done.

He waited for his breathing to even out, then returned downstairs and drained his beer, feeling empty on the inside. All of the alcohol in the world couldn't fill the Brooke-shaped hole in his heart.

25

"THANKS FOR COMING WITH ME," Brooke said to Kyle as she touched up her concealer. Unfortunately, there was only so much makeup could do to hide her puffy eyelids, and there was no masking the bloodshot whites of her eyes.

"No problem at all," he replied from where he was sitting on the edge of her bed. "I'll always be here when you need it. I'd offer to beat him up for you, except he's a rugged outdoors type, and I'm a librarian." He grinned at her reflection in the mirror. "I doubt it would end well. Tione would probably be up for the job though."

She couldn't laugh, though she knew he'd intended her to. "I don't want to think about Jack right now. Besides, it was as much my fault as his." She pivoted to face him. "What do you think? Do I wear a dress, or go casual?"

"Casual. You don't want the daughter to be too starstruck."

At that, she did laugh. As if anyone would be starstruck by her. Gathering jeans and a blouse, she carried them to the bathroom to change. Every part of her body ached, but it was the ache of a job well done. Once she'd dressed, she returned to the bedroom and tugged on a pair of black boots with a little heel, then put a necklace on.

"What do you think?"

Kyle nodded his approval. "I think Jack Farrelly is an idiot for letting you go."

Brooke sniffled. "Shush. It's too soon for that."

He mimed zipping his lips. "Sorry. You look nice. Ready to go?"

She drew her shoulders back and nodded. "Let's go impress my sponsor."

He stood, slung an arm around her shoulder and squeezed. "You're gonna rock this."

She leaned into him, absorbing his strength. "I hope so."

"Come on." He urged her forward. "You can mope later."

She didn't argue, knowing very well that she would mope later. And probably curse both herself and Jack. In the foyer, she waved goodbye to Kat, then strode to Kyle's old Ford and slid into the passenger seat.

"I'm glad you brought this and not the motorbike." Her makeup wouldn't have survived a brief ride on the back of his Yamaha. They drove to Sailor's Retreat, the only restaurant in town, and parked opposite the beach pavilion. When they entered, Brooke scanned the circular tables until she found one with the red-headed girl, Sarah, and headed over.

"Hi, Sarah. Great to see you again." They'd spoken briefly earlier.

"Hey, Brooke." Sarah grinned, revealing slightly crooked teeth. She was small for her age, a byproduct of her heart condition, but she had a warm, cheerful personality. "How are you feeling?"

Brooke tested her limbs. "Sore, but in a really good way. No regrets."

Sarah bounced in her seat. "I can't believe you actually did it."

"Me neither." Brooke tucked her hair behind her ear. "It's so weird to think that this time last year I was only out of bed for a couple of hours each day." She glanced at the older couple seated with Sarah. "Why don't you introduce me to your parents?"

"Oh yeah." Her cheeks went pink. "This is my dad, Andrew, and my mum, Adrienne."

Brooke shook Andrew's hand. "Nice to meet you in person. Thank you so much for sponsoring me, it means a lot."

He glanced fondly at his daughter. "It's my pleasure."

"Nice to meet you, Adrienne." Brooke nodded to Sarah's mother, an attractive woman with hair the same shade as her daughter's.

"Likewise, Brooke." She smiled. "I feel like I know you already. Sarah talks about you all the time."

Sarah's blush deepened. "*Mum.*"

"Well, you do."

Brooke suppressed a giggle, and stepped aside so the others could see Kyle. "This is my friend, Kyle. I hope you don't mind him coming along."

A groove formed between Sarah's ginger brows. "Where's Jack?"

"He's still not well," Brooke lied, guilt pricking her conscience. She should come clean, but she didn't have enough control over her emotions to voice the truth yet. "He couldn't make it, sorry."

Kyle directed his most charming smile at Sarah, and Brooke could have sworn the girl melted in her seat. "I hope you're not too disappointed."

"Oh, n-no," she stammered, now the color of beets. "It's great you're here. I mean, Brooke's talked about you, but this is so not what I thought you'd look like. Um, I mean, you're a librarian, but you, uh..." She trailed off, flapping her hands, and met Brooke's eyes with a desperate entreaty.

Brooke knew what she meant. Kyle was undeniably hot. Not at all how a teenage girl thought of a male librarian with a penchant for gaming. She pulled out the chair beside Sarah and sat, forcing Kyle into the one on her other side, next to Andrew. She was afraid Sarah would combust if seated too closely to her attractive friend. The girl sent her a grateful look.

"Did you guys have a good trip over?" Brooke asked.

"We did," Andrew said. "We took our time. Stopped in a few places along the way."

Kyle turned to face him. "Are you staying in Haven Bay for long?"

Sarah answered for him. "Two nights. Tonight and tomorrow." She narrowed her eyes at her parents. "But I wish we could stay longer. It's so cool here, and the beach is amazing."

"Maybe next time," Adrienne replied evenly. "Your father and I need to be at work on Tuesday."

Sarah pouted. "It needs to be before Brooke goes to Everest."

"We can make that happen, sweetheart."

"While we're here," Andrew began, "we'd love to meet the people responsible for getting you into shape for the event today."

Brooke stiffened. "I can introduce you to Bex, my personal trainer, but you won't be able to meet Jack." She tried to swallow past the boulder lodged in her throat. It was time to be a big girl. "In fact, you should probably know that he won't be coming with me overseas anymore."

"That's a shame."

Brooke nodded, and Adrienne caught her eye. Something must have given her away because she saw pity and understanding in the other woman's expression.

"Is there anything we can do to help recruit a replacement? Having the right company can make such a difference."

Brooke sighed. Adrienne couldn't possibly understand exactly how much it had meant to her to have Jack's unwavering support, but she appreciated the sentiment anyway. "Perhaps. I'll give it some thought."

Adrienne smiled at Kyle. "I don't suppose you're the adventuring type?"

He laughed. "Only in my mind. Brooke's the more outgoing of the two of us."

A half-sob half-laugh caught in Brooke's throat. She'd never been considered the more outgoing part of any friendship before. She loved it, but it also made her unaccountably sad. If Jack were here, he'd have held that role, and acknowledging his loss really sucked.

"Tell us a bit more about yourself," Adrienne said, and Brooke latched onto the life raft of a question, casting Jack to the back of her mind.

"It all started when I was born with a heart defect."

***

Darkness had descended, and the town square was illuminated only by streetlights. A few tourists lingered by the fountain while Jack nursed his third—fourth?—glass of beer and glared at them through the pub window. They all looked so damned happy. Couples with their arms around each other, kissing and laughing as though his world hadn't imploded.

"Just rub it in, why don't you?" he muttered, wondering if he ought to go home, where he didn't have to watch every other person in the world smile with their loved ones.

"Are you still scaring off my customers?" Logan asked.

Jack glanced up, and the world tilted precariously. The tables, walls, and his friend blurred and merged into each other. "No. Just asking myself why everyone chose today to be so damned cheerful."

Logan sighed. "I think you've had enough. You're being maudlin."

"I'm not maudlin," he said. "Not drunk, either. I've had exactly the right amount."

"To what? Forget there's a woman who tolerated your ungrateful self, but you pushed her away?"

"Wasn't my fault." Bleak despair boiled beneath his surface, threatening to break through. He couldn't bear the thought of Brooke. Not when the wound in his heart was so fresh. His tongue became thick and clumsy in his mouth, and he couldn't find the will to articulate this to Logan, or to explain why she was responsible for his current predicament.

"Whatever you say, man. You're done for the night, and I mean it this time. That's your last drink."

Logan left him, and Jack gazed into the amber liquid remaining in his glass, as though he'd find the answers to everything in that cold, foamy brew. When he raised his eyes and looked out the window again, his heartbeat seemed to slow. Like he'd conjured her from his thoughts, Brooke appeared in the square, her blonde hair flowing over her shoulders like a beacon designed to lead him home on a stormy night. He lurched to his feet, and his equilibrium shifted. Planting his hands on the wall to steady himself, he sought her out again, this time noticing what he hadn't before. Kyle had his arm around her shoulder, his head dipped close to hers.

Blood pounded in Jack's ears. His vision tunneled in on Kyle's hand curved around Brooke's upper arm, and a savage growl tore from his throat. He shoved away from the wall and stomped toward the door.

"Whoa!" Big hands closed around his shoulders, restraining him. Jack tried to shake them off, but they stayed firm. It was Logan, holding him back, keeping him from Brooke.

"Let go," he exclaimed. "I need to…" He trailed off, because he didn't know what he planned to do once he got outside, except for separate her from Kyle. Then what? It wasn't as though anything had changed.

"No can do, buddy. You're in no shape to see her. You'll do more damage than good. And I see that look in your eye. I'm not letting you anywhere near my brother right now."

Jack slumped with defeat, knowing that Logan spoke the truth. Anything he did or said now, while he was fueled by raw emotion, he'd regret soon after. Righting himself, he brushed Logan off and yanked a hand through his hair, then huffed in frustration.

"Sorry, you're right. I just… Fuck, my head isn't in a good place, man."

Logan nodded, his expression softening with sympathy. "Come on. You can sleep it off upstairs. Maybe you'll see things more clearly in the morning."

"Thanks," Jack replied, then took the key Logan offered and trudged up to the apartment. Inside, he used his friend's mouthwash, stripped off and climbed onto the spare bed, then he lay down and closed his eyes. His pulse was racing, his head throbbing, and he squeezed his eyes more tightly shut, wishing he'd wake up tomorrow and discover this whole nightmare of a day had never happened.

26

FOR THE NEXT FEW WEEKS, Brooke studied. She trained, ate, and slept. She wrote entries in her blog full of faux enthusiasm that miraculously passed muster with her readers. The only thing that brought her any joy was seeing the changes exercise rendered on her body. Her legs became toned, a groove formed down the center of her abdomen, and slender muscles encased her shoulders and upper arms. Every morning, she woke and reminded herself how far she'd come and why it was so important for her not to give up on her and Olivia's dream. But every evening, when she curled up alone in her bed, her mind flitted over the time she'd spent with Jack, conjuring hundreds of "what ifs."

What if they'd never kissed at that cursed party?

What if she'd never mentioned him in her blog?

What if she'd been up front with him at the beginning?

What if he was right about her?

Sleep was a long time coming.

Jack stared at the offending piece of material. A Star Wars t-shirt with a pun he didn't understand, hanging over the back of a chair, exactly where Brooke had left it weeks ago. He hadn't returned the shirt, thrown it out, or even moved it from sight because he couldn't seem to find the heart. It was a part of her. A reminder of their time together. As was her toothbrush in the bathroom and her moisturizer on the bedroom dresser. He hated seeing them, but couldn't bring himself to let them go.

Turning away from the t-shirt, he padded into the kitchen to make coffee. Birds chirped in the trees outside but otherwise, the house was silent. There was no feminine voice calling from another room. None of the background noises he'd grown accustomed to while Brooke had been around. He should be happy. He'd always appreciated his solitude, but instead it seemed too quiet.

"Pull yourself together." God, he was even talking to himself.

He drank the coffee, leaning on the kitchen counter and gazing out the window, over the rows of houses toward the beach. When he finished, he rinsed the mug and laced up his hiking boots. If he didn't get out of the house, he was going to go as crazy as Jack Nicholson in *The Shining,* and start cutting people down all over the place.

He drove to the beginning of one of his favorite tracks. One that was steep enough to keep his mind off Brooke—or so he'd thought. When a robin hopped along a branch in front of him, all he could think of was how excited she would have been to see it. He couldn't resist snapping a photo, although he didn't understand why, and when he heard a tui singing in the trees, he pictured the expression of wonder that would've spread across her face if she were here with him.

In short, everything reminded him of her, and it was fucking miserable. Was this how it felt to be lovesick? He'd never suffered this way when he and Claudia broke up. Yeah, he'd been lonely and angry at the world, but nothing like this. Stomping to the end of the track, he stared straight ahead, afraid to let his gaze deviate lest he find something else to bring Brooke to the forefront of his mind. He circled back and drove home, passing by his storefront to make sure Erica had everything under control.

While he was in the town square, movement through the library window caught his eye. Kyle was leaving, and locking up behind him. Jack's hands fisted, but he forced them to relax. Every time he saw the younger man—which was often, given they worked opposite each other and attended the same poker night—he itched to grab him by the lapels and demand answers as to whether he'd made any moves on Brooke.

What a shithead.

Him, not Kyle. Although he wasn't opposed to calling them both shitheads if the opportunity arose. Tione had certainly made it clear that he believed Jack to be a complete shithead at the first poker night after the mud run. He'd stopped short of violence, although Jack wasn't sure he was in the clear yet.

Sighing, he took his phone from his pocket and dialed Shane's number. He'd had enough of this lone wolf stuff. He needed to spend time around people. The type who wouldn't give him any space for introspection.

"Hi, Jack," Shane answered, sounding distracted as usual. Being a single father of two seemed to have that effect.

"Hey, man. Look, I, uh..." He struggled for words, not accustomed to asking for help. "I gotta get out of my own head. You mind if I bunk down at your place for a couple of nights? Help you keep an eye on the boys?"

Shane chuckled. "Seriously? You're asking if I mind?" A muffled noise came through the line, and he heard Shane say, "Hunter, get off the cat. You can't ride her." Then he was back. "I'll buy you a six-pack and a chocolate cake if you can get me an hour of alone time so I can finally shower and shave."

Jack grinned. Exactly what he'd wanted to hear. "Done. I'll be there soon. Tell the boys to get their fishing rods and camouflage gear out."

Shane released a long, weary sigh. "I appreciate it. You're a lifesaver."

27

Jack survived a week with Shane's unruly sons before he retreated to his fortress of solitude. On his first morning back home, where he woke—blessedly—without a miniature face above him, he rose early and went to the marina, where his boat was docked and ready for a dolphin spotting cruise.

A lone man waited nearby, his designer jacket zipped to his chin to ward off the chill. He was leaning against a post, jean-clad legs crossed at the ankles, and when the breeze ruffled his perfectly coiffed hair, his hand shot up to flatten it. Light flashed off the gold ring on his left hand.

"Mornin'," Jack grunted.

"Lovely day, isn't it?" the man enthused, coming toward him. "Jack, I presume?"

"Yeah."

He extended a hand. "I'm Warren Pinkly." He looked at Jack meaningfully. "I'm coming on the cruise with you this morning."

"Good to meet you, Warren." He checked his watch. "You're a bit early. You'll have to excuse me, but I have a few things to sort out, and there are another five people due to arrive before we begin."

Warren clasped his hands together in front of his crotch, as though shielding his balls. Weird guy. "One of those other people is my wife. She'll be here any minute. She just went to fix her lipstick."

Jack fought the urge to roll his eyes. Of course she had. That was in keeping with Pinkly's persona.

Don't judge, he warned himself. It wasn't his place to criticize others' priorities.

"Right. Well, I'll get a move on, and be back soon." He nodded to Warren and headed for his boat.

Twenty minutes later, he'd readied everything for the cruise and returned to the marina, where another four people had joined his strange passenger. They turned to face him, and he stiffened, suddenly feeling like a pane of glass that had fractured down the center.

Warren's wife had dyed-blonde hair, streaked in a way that was intended to appear natural.

Hair he'd buried his hands in.

She also had painted pink lips, which he'd kissed a thousand times before.

"Claudia."

"Hi, Jack." Her voice was as soft as he remembered. Her eyelashes—or rather, her eyelash extensions—fluttered. "How are you?"

He stared at her, scarcely able to believe she was here. "You're married?"

She seemed taken aback by the question, but those pink lips curved in a smile. "Yes, for two months now."

Two months. Jesus. The two of them had only broken up a couple of years ago, and she hadn't mentioned being engaged when he'd seen her a few months back.

"Congratulations." The word tasted bitter. "No wonder I didn't recognize your name on the manifest."

"Oh, you didn't know," Warren said, drawing his attention. The man was nodding like everything made sense now, but nothing made sense to Jack.

"Why would I?" He shrugged and turned his back, masking his turmoil. "We don't talk."

That was the way he preferred it. Why would he have anything to say to the woman who'd effectively told more than a hundred thousand people that he wasn't up to her standards, and broken his heart in the process? He pretended to check something on his phone while he struggled for composure, then pocketed it and glanced from one member of his group to another, skimming over Claudia.

"Hi, all. Great to see you here. Are you ready to spot some dolphins?"

The response was a resounding yes, despite the curious glances between Jack, Claudia, and Warren. The sixth member of the expedition joined them, and Jack began his usual spiel about water safety, followed by a disclaimer with regards to whether they would actually see dolphins. He said all the right things because he'd said them hundreds of times before, but inside he was a seething mass of emotions.

Why was Claudia here? It couldn't be a coincidence. Had she tracked him down on purpose? Was she flaunting her ring to show him what he'd missed out on? What he could have had if only he'd swallowed his pride and changed an integral part of himself? Peering over at her, he didn't think she looked like a woman with vindictive plans. She looked happy, hanging on her fashion-conscious husband's arm, and murmuring in his ear.

She looked like a woman in love.

Jack led the group to his boat and helped them aboard

one by one, holding onto Claudia's arm as briefly as possible then releasing her as though she'd singed him. Hurt flickered in her mint green eyes, and he pretended not to see. Where did she get off giving him that wounded puppy look anyway?

When they were all aboard, he explained how the morning would go, and invited questions. There were none, so he left the group to outfit themselves with life jackets, disconnected the boat from the dock, checked everyone had geared up correctly, and started the engine. For the next half hour, he steered the boat through the bay, to the spot where the school of dolphins could usually be found at this time of day. His guests leaned over the sides, scanning the water to check for sleek gray fins or snouts.

Claudia rose and came over to him, perching in the empty co-captain's seat. "Hey," she said, her tone gentle. "It's good to see you again."

He grunted something unintelligible.

Undaunted, she continued, "I'm pleased everything has worked out for you. I know you always wanted to be out and about doing something like this, rather than stuck in the shop all day." She tucked a blonde lock behind her ear and laughed self-consciously. "I should never have tried to turn you into a city man. Even a fool could see you weren't cut out for it."

He shrugged, simultaneously annoyed by her tone and disarmed by her candor. They'd never been particularly open with each other, and perhaps that had contributed to the horrible way their relationship had ended. She'd wanted him to change and tried to prod him along rather than coming out and saying it, and he'd resented every subtle dig she made and viewed her veiled comments as emotional manipulation. Their relationship had been a series of silences interspersed with moments of passion and screaming fights.

"We should have talked more," he said.

"Yeah." Her gaze darted over to her husband. "We should have."

"Does he make you happy?" He wasn't sure why he asked, but he didn't take the question back. Perhaps it would be nice to know that it was possible for someone who had failed in a relationship as spectacularly as she had to be part of a healthy one now.

She smiled. Possibly the most genuine one he'd ever seen from her. "We are. I just..." She trailed off.

"What?" he prompted.

She turned to look out over the water, her cheeks pink despite the cool wind. "Sometimes I can't believe he really wants me. I wake up and think 'how can this amazing guy really have chosen me, out of all the women he could have had?'"

Jack flinched. While she hadn't meant it as an insult, it flat-out sucked to hear how much more she thought of Warren than she had of him. But besides injuring his pride, it didn't hurt the way he would have expected. Maybe that was because he no longer loved her. In fact, except for the lingering resentment, he didn't care about her one way or the other. Claudia had found what she'd been searching for, and that didn't bother him in the least.

Someone called out, and he turned in time to see the dorsal fin of a dolphin break the surface. Another followed. And another. They circled around the boat, curious.

"Wow," Claudia breathed. "They're beautiful." She glanced up at him. "I can see why you love it out here."

He didn't say anything. He didn't need to.

The dolphins frolicked beneath the water, surfacing occasionally to investigate their audience, or perform for them. Cameras snapped, and Jack sat back and enjoyed their excitement. This was why he loved what he did.

Claudia hurried over to Warren, who handed her a camera. She leaned over the edge of the boat and snapped photographs of the dolphins while her husband held onto her waist, anchoring her. They worked as a team. A unit. When she finished, he took the camera and photographed her against the backdrop of the ocean, pausing while she changed positions as smoothly as a model at a photo shoot. Then he tucked the camera away and together they posed for a selfie with the dolphins behind them, using a cell phone on a selfie stick. They looked ridiculous, but in all the time he'd known her, Claudia had never smiled like she was now.

But then, this was what she'd always wanted, wasn't it? A man who was content to escort her around, humor her obsessive need to photograph everything, and be a suitably stylish companion to brag about to her followers. She had it all now, and it looked good on her. The tension that used to stiffen her shoulders wasn't there, nor was the sharp edge in her voice. He couldn't help but wonder, had he caused those things? Had he made her as miserable as she'd made him? It had never occurred to him before that perhaps he wasn't the only one who'd suffered in their relationship.

The truth struck him like an anvil: Claudia may not have been a good fit for him, but he hadn't been good for her, either. Yes, she'd screwed up and that had been the final nail in the coffin, but at the heart of the matter, they simply hadn't been suited to each other. One of them would have called a halt to things sooner or later.

With Warren, she was a better person. For some reason, seeing them gave him hope that one day, he'd be able to open his mind and heart to a new partner the same way she had. Someone who was more compatible with him. Strange how he'd never realized quite how badly he wanted that until now. Seeing them together, it really hit home how alone he'd allowed himself to become because of his fear and bitterness.

He processed this new perspective while his clients watched the dolphins. When the pod moved on, he steered them back to the marina, remaining silent during the trip and allowing them to converse amongst themselves. He kept an eye on Claudia and Warren, who had their heads ducked together over their camera screen, talking in low voices. They worked well together. Kind of like he and Brooke had.

Brooke.

Even thinking of her brought a pang. He shook his head, trying to forget the way her eyes had flashed with anger when last they'd spoken. Then how they'd become shiny with unshed tears.

Don't think about her.

After what felt like an eternity—too long to spend in introspection—he docked and helped the group off. Claudia was the last to disembark.

"Thank you, that was wonderful," she said, and then paused, as though weighing her next words carefully. "I read an article online about your new girlfriend." He must have frowned because she clarified, "The one you're going to Mount Everest with. It seems like you found someone just as crazy about the outdoors as you. I'm happy for you." Then she patted his hand and walked away.

Just like that, the cogs slipped into place. Jack's grip slipped from the boat and the world tilted until he managed to right himself. All this time, he'd been thinking of himself and Brooke as opposites because that's how it appeared from the outside. But on the inside, where it counted, they were the same. They both wanted the same things. They were both adventurers. Sure, she'd had a tougher run of it than he had, but that didn't make the core of her personality any different, or lessen her wild spirit. She sure as shit was as stubborn as him.

Forget opposites. He and Brooke were two of a kind. And suddenly, he wanted to see her with a desperate, aching longing. He'd acted like an idiot, yet again. Yeah, she'd been too open with the world about their relationship and revealed things he'd rather people didn't know, but he'd made a lot of assumptions without much in the way of evidence. He'd judged her harshly without giving her a chance to explain. On top of that, he couldn't help but wonder if he'd deliberately pushed her away because he was afraid of being hurt. He hadn't been willing to risk his heart, and she'd given him the excuse he needed to bow out.

Had he destroyed her feelings for him? God, he hoped not.

JACK KNOCKED on Brooke's bedroom door. No one answered. He tried again. "Hey, are you in there?"

Still nothing. He wiggled the handle. Locked.

"She's not here."

Spinning on his heel, he spotted Kat at the end of the hall. "She's not just ignoring me?"

Her mouth tightened into a line. "Nope. But fair warning, while I'm trying to stay neutral, I'll have to choose a side if you start harassing her. Why are you here, Jack?"

He paused. Why *was* he here? He hadn't really thought it through. He'd just finished his cruise and driven straight over, compelled to see her. "I want to talk."

"Talk, as in a two-sided conversation where you each speak and listen? As opposed to you telling her what she did wrong and refusing to let her defend herself?"

Ouch. Guess he needn't wonder whether Kat knew how everything had gone down.

"Yeah, that's right." He stuffed his hands in his pockets. "Do you know when she'll be back?"

She took pity on him. "Not until tomorrow. She's visiting her parents in Tauranga."

"Oh." That took the wind out of his sails. "Guess I'll be back tomorrow then."

He drove home, and the blue of the sky seemed a bit dimmer. He helped himself to a can of beer, then sprawled on one of the deck chairs outside, soaking up the sun and pondering his relationship with Brooke. Halfway into the beer, he remembered the question she'd asked when he confronted her.

Did you read all of it?

The truth was, he hadn't. Even if he'd wanted to, he wouldn't have had time. Getting to his feet, he strode to his office and switched on his laptop. He drained the beer while the computer awakened, then entered her blog's URL and waited. The first items to appear were two photographs side by side. One was of a teenage girl in a hospital bed, tubes sticking out of her body, her eyes sunken and limbs spindly. His breath caught in his chest. He hardly recognized her as the woman he knew. The adjacent photo showed his Brooke, covered in mud and grinning, her arms around Kat and Bex. He swallowed, and a lump burned its way down his throat. Tearing his gaze from the photographs, he selected the oldest post, dated seven years ago, and began to read.

Three hours later, he'd caught up on everything prior to the New Year's Eve party, and his insides were wrung out. He was emotionally wrecked. Brooke had told him she'd always been ill, but he'd never realized the extent to which it had affected her. Reading her blog was like poring through her private diary. She shared every setback, every doubt, and he understood now why her readers had turned up to support her at the mud run. She'd come so far, and she was an inspiration to them all.

With trepidation, he read her first post after the fateful New Year's Eve party. She'd been positively giddy. Raving about how much she admired him, and how wonderful their kisses had been. Flash forward a few days, and she'd been confused. A little hurt. Another week and hurt had escalated to anger. He swallowed. His eyes wanted to shut so he didn't have to read about how he'd upset her, when that was the last thing he'd ever intended. Shame clawed at his gut. He'd been a massive prick, even if it had been unintentional. No wonder she'd lashed out online.

When he reached the post he'd already read, he scanned over them again, making sure he didn't miss anything. Then he carried on, coming to a post the following day.

Thanks to everyone for the comments and suggestions. I'm a bit embarrassed about venting to you all. I appreciate your thoughts and well wishes, and I'm going to do my best to take the high road. I'll try to forget what happened and focus on the important thing. I need Jack to help me get in shape and tackle some big challenges on the horizon. I'm excited for them, and I'm sure you will be too when you hear what I've got planned.

And that was the last time she mentioned him in a negative context. He continued reading until after the mud run, and she only ever extolled his virtues or referred to him in the context of training. There had been no grand scheme to humiliate him or crush him, heart and soul. He'd been completely and utterly wrong.

Slashing a hand through his hair, he swore. He'd made baseless accusations. Not once had she said anything about breaking up with him, or manipulating him for the sake of revenge. She'd wanted to make use of his skills to help her in her mission, but he'd known that from the beginning. And yeah, he'd rather his private life stayed private, but she hadn't lied or tried to get back at him. What's more, it seemed she actually cared for him.

In short, he'd overreacted and been a real fucking jerk. He exhaled, long and shaky, then scrolled to some of the more recent posts. She'd done a big write-up about the mud run, including all the people she'd met, how some kind strangers had encouraged her to get to the end, and the dinner she'd shared with her new sponsor. He gobbled up the information, aware that he should have been there with her. Should have met the people she did and shaken hands with the guy, Andrew Walters, who was making her dream a reality. Instead, she'd had Kyle by her side. Kyle, who hadn't let her down. Hot, painful emotion simmered within him, but he tamped it down and tried to be grateful that she'd had someone with her while he'd been pickling his liver.

After that came a handful of short, bubbly posts discussing her plans to go hiking with Kat, and the travel preparations she'd made for herself and a woman named Holly McDaniel, who would be her support person and guide. His replacement. At least she'd chosen a woman. He wasn't sure he could have handled the thought of her lodging with another man.

Perhaps it meant he was a bad person, but part of him hoped she was faking her excitement. He wanted her to miss him as much as he'd missed her. He searched the text for anything that might clue him in as to her mental state, but came up empty. She was a pro at putting on a good face for her audience. He supposed that's what came of learning at a young age how to set those around her at ease.

He closed his laptop and went for a long walk along the beach. As far as he was concerned, the night couldn't pass quickly enough. All he wanted was to see Brooke and find out whether he'd burned his bridges.

28

———

S*HE'S BACK.*

The minute he read the message from Kat, Jack jogged to his four-wheel drive, jumped into the driver's seat, and threw it into gear. He'd been waiting all morning, in his best jeans and a blue button-down shirt, ready to go at a moment's notice. A gift-wrapped box occupied the front seat because he hadn't wanted to turn up empty-handed. When he arrived at Sanctuary, he parked, smoothed his shirt, grabbed the box, and headed straight to Brooke's bedroom.

"Come in," she called when he knocked.

He eased the door open and stepped inside. She was sitting cross-legged on the bed, her hair in a messy bun with a pencil sticking out of it, and her glasses askew on her nose. Her laptop was on her knee and when she straightened, he noticed her t-shirt had a picture of Darth Vader printed across the front, with the words *Who's Your Daddy?* beneath. His heart pitter-pattered and a smile broke out over his face. She was completely adorable, completely perfect, and—if he could persuade her—completely *his*.

"Hi, Brooke."

"What are you doing here?" Her eyes narrowed, but

246

rather than the anger he'd expected, her tone was icy and oddly hesitant. Her expression faded to something neutral, like she was shielding herself from him until she knew whether he could be trusted not to snuff out her vibrancy.

He yearned to touch her. To reawaken her natural zing. Not just because he found her attractive and likable or any other foolish lie he might once have told himself, but because he loved her. He *adored* her. If she decided she wouldn't be satisfied until she'd sat atop the peak of Everest, he'd carry her there on his shoulders.

He hoped he wasn't too late. "Can we talk?"

Her gaze flicked to her laptop, then she set it aside and slid off the edge of the bed, coming to her feet a few yards from him. He longed to gather her into his arms and kiss the ever-loving hell out of her.

"Let's get coffee and sit outside," she suggested.

His stomach sank to his shoes. She didn't want to be alone with him, and it stung. "I'd rather we speak privately, if you're comfortable with that."

She cast around, looking for a way to avoid him, but he didn't offer up any solutions. He couldn't afford to. Finally, her shoulders slumped and she jerked her head up. "Fine. But only for a few minutes. I've got a lot of work to do."

Relief weakened his knees, and they tried to knock together but he ignored them. He'd take what he could get. Before he launched into what was bound to be a difficult conversation, he stuck out his hands and offered her the box.

"This is for you."

WAS THIS SERIOUSLY HAPPENING?

Big, craggy Jack Farrelly was in her room, looking sexy as

all get-out despite the weariness dragging down the corners of his eyes, while she was sloppy and unkempt, wearing clothes from the bottom of the drawer because she hadn't made it as far as the shower yet. As if that weren't enough, he was trying to foist the ugliest gift box she'd ever seen onto her. Swear to God, whoever wrapped it had used a whole roll of tape, scrunched the edges, and tried to hide that fact by covering the outside with ribbon. All the ribbon in the world couldn't hide the words "Merry Christmas" in repeating green script across the paper.

"What's this?" she asked, accepting it with the same caution she'd reserve for a hand grenade. She studied his face, trying again to deduce why he'd come. Did he want to yell at her some more? Because she wasn't in the mood.

Shoulders hunched, he shoved his hands into his pockets, and shifted from one foot to the other. "A gift."

She made no move to open it. "Why?"

He shrugged, staring at her from beneath his lashes, strangely shy. "I think it's customary to bring a present at times like this."

"Times like what?" she growled, frustrated by his pussyfooting around.

Holding her gaze, he sank onto the end of her bed, his weight causing her pens to slide toward him. "Why don't you just open it?"

"Fine." Rolling her eyes, she yanked out the desk chair and lowered herself onto it. She grabbed scissors and slit the paper open because she didn't think she'd be able to bust through the tape, then she drew the paper back to reveal something soft within a layer of tissue. Peeling off the tissue, she shook out something fabric, and held up a pair of merino wool tights.

Jack cleared his throat. "They're icebreakers. The very best."

She tossed the empty wrapping aside, and something else fell from it. Bending, she scooped up a small flashlight. The kind that could be strapped onto a person's forehead.

"It has a long-life battery, and once the battery dies, there's a solar component so you never run out of light."

"Unless you're in Antarctica in the middle of winter," she replied absently, flicking it on and rearing back when a brilliant white beam shot into her eyes. She switched the light off and blinked to clear the spots from her vision, then looked from the headlight to the tights and back again, too scared to ask why he was giving them to her out of the blue.

"Thank you, this is very sweet. I—uh—" She tried to modulate the pitch of her voice, which had risen precariously. "I don't know what to say."

He clasped his hands together, and she studied them, not meeting his gaze—afraid that if she did, she'd be captured and drawn back into his magnetic field. "They're for when you go to Everest. I wanted to give you something useful, rather than something you'd enjoy for a few days and throw away." His voice was husky. It slid over her like velvet on skin, and she shivered. "I hope you like them."

"I do." She forced herself to look up. His eyes were a deep, unfathomable brown, drilling directly to the core of her. "Thank you. But—"

"Why?" he finished, one side of his mouth tugging up in a smirk so familiar it had her heart thumping double-time. She'd missed it, missed *him*, but she'd thought he was done with her. He'd made his feelings painfully clear. "Be patient, I'm getting there."

"Okay, okay." Patience wasn't her strong suit, but she pressed her lips together and chewed on her tongue, determined to let him say his piece even if he intended to berate her again. Although given the circumstances, she was beginning to doubt that.

"I read your blog," he told her. "All of it."

She closed her eyes and sighed. Back to that old chestnut. "Can I say again how sorry I am for sharing too many details about our private life online? Would you like me to go back and remove every post that mentions you? Because I can. But if you want to tell me I'm like your awful ex again, forget about it. You can just leave."

"No, I don't want that, and that's not why I'm here. I'm a private guy but I've accepted that the blog is part of who you are. I can see now how important it is to you, and a lot of other people too." He smiled at her. "They really love you."

Just like I love you. She wouldn't say it. Not yet. Maybe not ever.

"Plus, taking out those posts would disrupt the narrative. You've created something powerful, and I don't want you to diminish it for my sake. That's also not why I came."

She swallowed, and wiped her moist palms on her leggings. "Are you getting to that part yet?"

He nodded, his grin widening. "Don't hurry a good thing."

A good thing?

She didn't move a muscle. Her breath bottled up in her chest, and a jolt passed through her, adrenaline flooding her veins, making her aware of every beat of her heart and every dizzying moment that passed. She'd been afraid to hope, but with one phrase he'd decimated her defenses. Clenching handfuls of her leggings, she waited for him to go on. After a millennium passed, he reached for her hand. She released her death grip on her leggings and took it, loving the roughness of his palm on hers as he pulled her, and the chair, closer.

"I'm sorry I didn't wait to talk to you after the mud run, Brooke. I'm especially sorry that I accused you of using me for revenge, and I'm sorry for misjudging you because of my ex. That was a really crappy thing to do."

Were her ears deceiving her? Was he actually apologizing? Jack Farrelly—*apologizing*?

She squeezed his hand to check she wasn't dreaming. It was warm and solid in her grip. She opened her mouth and no sound came out. She closed it. Swallowed. Used her free hand to grab her water bottle and choked back a mouthful of lukewarm water.

"I understand why you felt the way you did," she said, in hardly more than a whisper. "I can see how it would have looked from your point of view. You were trying to keep your heart safe. That's the most understandable thing ever."

He leaned toward her until less than a foot of air separated them and a furrow formed between his brows. "How did you know that? I didn't even realize myself until yesterday."

"I guess it's easier to see from the outside."

"Even so, it wasn't fair of me. I was a dick to you, and I'm sorry. I ran into someone yesterday who made me look at things from a different perspective."

She nodded encouragingly, wanting him to get to the part where they talked about their future and more specifically, whether or not they had one. The way his thumb stroked the back of her hand suggested they did, but she couldn't allow herself to relax or get too comfortable until everything was out in the open. Their feelings, insecurities, and fears—warts and all.

"I realized I was focusing on the differences between us. The things I thought would ruin whatever we had. But those differences are only superficial, and I got so caught up in them that I couldn't see how similar we are on a deeper level." Raising a hand, he skimmed his fingers along the line of her jaw. Her eyelids fluttered, wanting to droop closed, but she held them open and nuzzled his palm. "You and me. Inside, we're the same."

Her gaze dropped. His lips were still moving, but she heard no sound from them. She scooted forward, obliterating the last of the space between them, and kissed him. Her lips clung to his. She yearned to drink in the taste of him, re-familiarize herself with the way he parted his lips and let her in, but she drew back before it went that far. Everything inside of her hummed with pleasure. Whether he knew it or not, Jack had just validated everything she'd long believed. Whatever external struggles she faced, at her heart, she was an adventurer. Like him. His equal.

"I'm really pleased you said that," she murmured, and kissed him again.

His mocha eyes gleamed, alight with desire and another undefinable emotion. He looked at her like the wolf had looked at Little Red Riding Hood. As if he wanted to eat her up. She wouldn't mind one bit if he did. But first, they had more to discuss. He must have read her thoughts because he hauled in a deep breath, preparing to say something. She tried to beat him to the punch, but he put a finger to her lips.

"I love you, Brooke. I want another chance with you. Please tell me it's not too late."

She did a double take, her hand flying to her throat. "You what? I mean, you do?" She forced herself to breathe, and the pressure in her chest ebbed. "That's not what I was expecting you to say."

Though God only knew what she had expected. Her mind was still trying to catch up with the fact that he was in her bedroom, holding one of her hands. She studied his rugged face, so dear to her, and the hope in his eyes broke her heart. He really *did* love her, and he feared she didn't feel the same way.

She wet her lips. "Next time I do something that upsets you, will you talk to me before leaping to conclusions?"

He nodded firmly. "Yes."

She raised a brow. "I expect there to be open and honest communication between us at all times. If I do anything you don't like, you should tell me right then and there." She paused, then amended, "Or as soon as reasonably possible."

"Done."

"Just like that?"

"Just like that."

"Good. And if you ever compare me to your ex again, or talk to me the way you did that day, don't expect to get a third chance."

He nodded. "I won't."

She eyed him. "You'd better not. From now on, I'll run each of my blog posts past you before I publish them. Sound fair?"

"That's not necessary." He raised her chin with his fingers and searched her eyes. "I trust you. I'm sorry I didn't before. Does all of this mean you forgive me?"

Standing, she released his hand, then kicked the chair out of the way and straddled his lap. His pupils dilated, and they both sighed with pleasure at the sudden closeness. She settled onto him, one knee on either side of his thighs.

"I do." She framed his face with her hands and wriggled impossibly closer. "I'm glad you love me, Jack, because I love you, too." He tried to kiss her but she shifted a hand to his mouth. "Nuh-uh. It's my turn to talk." She grinned, heat flickering through her when he parted his lips and licked the tips of her fingers. "I've had a crush on you for ages, from a distance. I admired your attitude, and how you made the world your backyard. But I didn't know you."

His hands went to her hips and held her tightly to him.

A puff of air escaped her, but she didn't let him stop her. She needed to get this out, and he needed to hear it.

"I had a crush on you for who I thought you were, but I love you for who you are. Every part of you." She punctuated the declaration with kisses.

The world spun, pens scattered, and then Jack's face hovered above hers. He'd flipped her, and his hard body was pressing her into the bed.

"I'm the only one who's going to Everest with you," he said. "From now on, it's you and me going on adventures together. You up for it?"

She dragged his head down to hers, feeling weightless and grounded all at once, scarcely able to believe this strong, wonderful man was hers. She was more than up for a life exploring uncharted territory—both emotional and physical—with him.

"I was born ready."

EPILOGUE – NOVEMBER OF THAT YEAR

The sun beamed down on Brooke's back from a cloudless Nepalese sky. Cold and weary, she stumbled the last hundred yards to the lodge where she and Jack would be staying in the settlement of Gorak Shep. Snow sprinkled the ground, and her feet dragged as she passed through the entry and then dumped her pack on the floor.

Throwing back her head, she gasped for breath. An inhaler appeared in front of her and she clicked and huffed. Climbing over boulders and crossing glacial streams, all while the air thinned, had really taken it out of her. But she was nearly there. Another hour and a half and they'd arrive at Mount Everest Base Camp. She handed the inhaler back to Jack, who tucked it into his pocket.

He smiled, his eyes hidden behind sporty sunglasses. "Not far to go now, babe."

"I know! I can hardly believe it." Excitement fizzed within her. Impulsively, she looped her arms around his neck and kissed him. Someone cleared their throat and she let him go, laughing. Their guide touched her arm and gestured for them to follow him. Reluctantly, she lifted her pack again and carried it the short distance to their room for the night. There were two single beds on opposite sides of a tiny space. It was simple, but to Brooke, the mattress may as well have been a castle of clouds. She flopped onto it, groaning as her muscles relaxed.

"One hour," the guide said. "Have lunch, and then we'll head for Base Camp."

"We'll be there," she assured him, and patted the spot beside her as he left. "Join me?"

Jack laughed. "I'll stick to my own bed, thanks. I won't fit on yours."

She waggled her eyebrows. "I could make room."

He laughed, then removed his sunglasses and tucked them into a pocket. She couldn't put her finger on it, but something was different about him today. Perhaps the altitude was getting to him, but he seemed on edge. Not in a bad way, but more than the circumstances warranted.

"Come on," he said. "Let's eat. If you lie down too long, you'll never get up again."

Accepting the hand he offered, she stood. He was completely right about seizing up if she rested for more than a few minutes. They made their way to the communal dining area, lined up to purchase lunch, which was some kind of cheesy potato dish, then sat opposite each other at a wooden table.

"Just the fuel we need to get us up the hill," she said, digging in.

Jack's eyes tracked her movements in a way that was more intense than usual, but just when she was about to mention it, he dropped his gaze and started eating. They'd taken their gloves off, but the temperature was low even though they were sheltered from the weather. Her fingers fumbled as she scraped up the last of her potato and stuffed it into her mouth. She shoved her gloves back on and swigged a mouthful of hot chocolate. It could be her weariness talking, but the drink was the best damn thing she'd ever tasted.

"Don't forget your electrolytes," Jack cautioned. This high up, it wasn't uncommon for people to display mild symptoms of altitude sickness in addition to being short of breath.

She rolled her eyes. "I won't." Ripping open a packet, she emptied it into a glass of water and drank the lot. "There. I'll have another when we get back, and I'll be better than new. Have you had yours?"

He shook his head. "Will soon."

Before they left the lodge, she made sure he did.

The hike to Base Camp was a series of short ups and downs over loose rocks. Despite the electrolytes, a thumping had begun behind one of Brooke's eyes, and the length of time between each step seemed to grow exponentially. Fortunately, she wasn't the only one in their group with this problem. Together, they made slow progress. Even Jack seemed to have difficulty. But as they ascended the final ridge and Everest Base Camp came into view, her spirit soared.

They'd made it. She and Jack, as a team. A slow smile spread across her face and she managed to pick up the pace as they neared a sign that proclaimed they'd arrived. She was here. She'd done what she and Olivia had dreamed of since they'd been little girls. Reaching out, she ran a gloved finger down the sign, feeling its solidness. Its realness.

"I did it, Livvy. I did it for us." And for Sarah and Tammy and all of her readers. She turned to Jack, ready to kiss him like crazy, and found him on one knee. All the air in her lungs vacated. "W-what are you doing?"

Unzipping his jacket pocket, he reached inside and drew out a small black box.

Oh, my God. Oh. My. God. Is this actually happening?

Her hand flew to her chest. "Jack?"

He lifted his sunglasses, squinting against the glare, and she did the same so they could look into each other's eyes. His were dark in his tanned face, and the depth of emotion in them floored her.

"I love you, Brooke," he said, still on one knee. The ice had to have soaked through the leg of his pants, no matter how waterproof they were supposed to be, but he didn't react at all. "I've had the time of my life on this trip with you. You're so strong and determined, but fun, too. You make me laugh at myself, and you know that isn't easy."

She giggled nervously, but didn't say anything, afraid he'd stop if she did. With his gorgeous, crinkled eyes, cheeks flushed with cold, and the dab of pink on the end of his nose, he was the most breathtaking sight she'd ever seen. Better, even, than the panoramic views over the Himalayas.

"You're truly my partner in everything, and I want you by my side for every adventure from here on out." He sucked in a deep breath, looking a little faint. "Will you marry me?"

"Yes!" she cried, jumping on the spot. "Yes, yes, yes!"

She slipped on ice, and he caught her, sliding an arm around her waist and drawing her close. Around them, people applauded. Apparently they had an audience. She didn't care. She pressed her chilled lips to his and gave them something to whistle about.

When they broke apart, Jack offered her the box. She peeked inside. The ring was gorgeous. Simple, with a gold band and three diamonds glinting in the center.

"They represent our past, present, and future," he explained. "Because that's what you are to me."

Her heart melted as he eased off her glove and slid the ring onto her finger. "I love you so much, Jack Farrelly. I could never have imagined we'd end up here. You make me so happy." To her embarrassment, her eyes teared up. She blinked rapidly, before the water froze to her lashes. "I'd be honored to marry you and go on adventures with you until our legs can't carry us anymore."

They kissed, and she could have sworn their hearts beat in tandem through all the layers between them. She was on top of the world. It didn't get better than this.

THE END

SAFE IN HIS ARMS EXCERPT

Tione Kingi bolted upright at the warning bark. Laying his book on the pillow, he extended a tattooed arm to scratch his Chihuahua, Pixie, behind the ear.

"What is it, girl?"

Pixie yapped again, her tiny body vibrating with nerves. She scrambled to her feet and jumped to the floor, landing on light paws. Trevor, a bull mastiff, lifted his massive head to watch her dart toward the cabin door. Bella, the border collie, perked her ears up, and Zee the rescue pup stretched and circled before settling back onto her bed. It seemed that Trevor, Bella, and Zee hadn't heard anything, but that didn't mean much. Pixie was the most sensitive, and she reckoned something was out there. Tione sighed, scratched his bearded chin, and slipped from the bed. Chances were that all she'd heard was a possum in the trees but it was worth checking. As Tione yanked his sneakers on, Pixie started to growl.

"Yeah, yeah. Be patient, will you?" he muttered. Maybe she needed to do her business. Wouldn't be the first time one of them had disturbed him under false pretenses.

Switching on the security light, he opened the door.

Pixie shot through the gap like the proverbial rocket and raced down the slope toward the lodge—his place of employment. She vanished from the illuminated patch of garden and into the shadows, barking and snarling like the *mata kai kutu*—warrior—she believed she was. Something had really set fire to her tail. A flurry of yaps ensued. The kind she made when she'd locked sight on her prey. With a reluctant glance back at his bed, Tione closed the door to keep the warmth inside and then followed her into the dark.

A moment later, he heard something that gave him pause. The squeak of a rusty hinge. There was no way a possum had made that noise.

Someone is out here.

In his backyard. Trying to get into the lodge.

Whoever it was, they had a prime view of him silhouetted against the forest by the security light. The barking continued, and his shoulders stiffened with tension. Moving out of the light, he padded along the strip of lawn between the flower beds. Slowly, his vision adjusted and he could make out a figure at the lodge's back entrance. The person tried the handle, then paced over to a window and pried at it.

Seriously? Who would want to break into the lodge at Sanctuary? And why?

It didn't matter. Fact was, they were.

"Oy!" he shouted, hoping to catch them off guard. "What the hell do you think you're doing?"

The figure jerked around, their face hidden beneath a deep hood. They froze for all of two seconds and then broke into a run. He gave chase, closing the distance quickly. The would-be thief was slower than he'd expected, and moved awkwardly. He reached out and grabbed a fistful of the thief's jacket. The guy was smaller than he'd seemed from a distance. Perhaps a teenager out for a thrill.

And then the thief took him by surprise. He'd assumed that once caught, he'd see he was outgunned and stop. Maybe cuss for a while. Instead, the kid fought like a fucking hellcat. Small and slight, but no less fierce for it. Arms flew, limbs twisted, and a kick landed solidly in his nuts, but within a matter of seconds, Tione had him pinned to the ground, struggling to break free.

"Let me go," a voice hissed. "I won't let you hurt me. I *won't.*"

Tione went rigid. That voice. The soft, petite body beneath his. Not a teenage boy.

A woman.

"Bloody hell, I'm not going to hurt you," he growled, his guilt over manhandling her growing by the second. "Why were you trying to break into the lodge?"

She whimpered. "Break in? I just wanted—" He shifted his weight, and she cried out. Shit, he couldn't have hurt her that badly. They'd tussled for only a few moments. Was she playing him?

She sniffled. Damn, she was convincing. Real sobs wracked her body as she whispered on repeat, "Please don't hurt me, please don't hurt me, please don't hurt me."

Disgusted with himself, and with her, he reared up and yanked off her hood before she could retreat. Then his stomach hardened and his mouth dropped open.

"*Motherfucker.*"

His gaze swept her face, inventorying injuries. Purple cheek, left eye swollen shut, split lip encrusted with blood, a deep wound at her temple that was weeping fluid. Dark smudges ringed her neck and looked an awful lot like impressions from someone's fingers. Big, male fingers. Like his. But he hadn't grabbed her by the neck. None of this was his doing. Someone had worked this woman over with as much finesse as a bulldozer.

Her eyes squeezed shut, and even though they weren't touching, he could feel waves of fear emanating from her. She was terrified. Completely and utterly scared shitless. Jesus, who was she, and what the fuck had happened to her?

He didn't recognize her. Although to be fair, with her face how it was, he couldn't be sure. He guessed she might be blonde, but in the dim light, with blood set into her hairline, it was impossible to tell for certain. She scuttled back, drew her knees to her chest and winced, her mouth contorting in pain. His chest constricted. Her injuries must extend beyond her face. Who knew how battered the poor thing was beneath that oversized jacket?

Taking a mental step back, he tried to remain calm. Yeah, she'd been searching for a way into Sanctuary, but he didn't know it was for a nefarious reason. Fact was, she looked like a woman who desperately needed help. Exactly the type of woman that Kat, his employer, was notorious for taking in.

"Why are you here?" he asked.

ALSO BY ALEXA RIVERS

Haven Bay

Then There Was You

Two of a Kind

Safe in his Arms

If Only You Knew

Pretend to Be Yours

Begin Again With You

Let Me Love You

Little Sky Romance

Accidentally Yours

From Now Until Forever

It Was Always You

Dreaming of You

Little Sky Romance Novellas

Midnight Kisses

Second Chance Christmas

Destiny Falls

Stay With You

Come Back to You

Always Been Yours

Blue Collar Romance

A Place to Belong

ACKNOWLEDGMENTS

From the bottom of my heart, I give the world's most massive thank you to my advanced reader team. You guys are the absolute best, and I love you so much. You're what encourages me to keep going and to make each book better than the last.

To my husband, you are the most uplifting and supportive person. Thank you for being patient with me and reminding me over and over again of what I'm capable of. I'm so grateful to have you in my life. Thank you to my family, for their ongoing support, and to Shannon for reading this first and giving me early feedback.

Thank you to Kate, for your enthusiasm and helping me bring the best out of this story, and to Serena, for smoothing out the rough edges. Deranged Doctor Design, I love my cover and thank you for being so easy to work with.

Last but not least, thank you to everyone who has read this. I couldn't be an author without you.

ABOUT THE AUTHOR

Alexa Rivers writes about genuine characters living messy, imperfect lives and earning hard-won happily ever afters. Most of her books are set in small towns, and she lives in one of these herself. She shares a house with a neurotic dog and a husband who thinks he's hilarious.

When she's not writing, she enjoys traveling, baking, eating too much chocolate, cuddling fluffy animals, drinking excessive amounts of tea, and absorbing herself in fictional worlds.

www.ingramcontent.com/pod-product-compliance
Lightning Source LLC
Chambersburg PA
CBHW021246060726
47590CB00005B/1912